PRETTY LITTLE THING

A RICH BITCHES NOVEL

TABATHA KISS

ONE

NORA

"*Watch where you're going, asshole!*"

The truck zooms by, swerving around my sedan to make it through the intersection before the light changes. It doesn't, obviously, and he nearly slams into another car as he flies through the very red light. No cops to catch it. Typical.

I grit my teeth, still fuming long after it nearly crushed my damn bumper.

Sunday morning Chicago traffic is the fucking worst. I'd rather walk but it's starting to get cold. If there's anything I hate more than asshole drivers, it's being cold. I'm five-foot-nothing in heels. I get cold fast.

Then again, maybe a little more physical activity will help with my stress.

Screw that.

I hit the gas, rushing toward the one thing in my life I know won't stress me out.

I reach the cafe shortly after noon, technically late, but

my friends don't give a shit about that. We don't get together for brunch once a week to nag at each other. We do it to forget our problems and support one another. No matter what.

I ride into the parking lot and slam the brakes in front of the valet booth. A man rushes out the open my door and I pass my keys off to him with a quick nod.

"Good morning, Ms. Payne," he says.

"Good morning," I say, trying to be polite as I shuffle my shivering ass toward the entrance.

As soon as I step into the cafe, the hostess greets me with a smile. She doesn't say a word to me but she doesn't have to. She gestures behind her at the table in the back. *Our* table.

I slide my jacket off, shaking the stress from my shoulders along with it. I make it halfway across the restaurant before I hear Trix's voice. She's not speaking English, meaning she's talking to her grandmother. I can only make out a few of the Italian words falling from her lips — mainly just the slurs or dirty words.

I arrive at our table-for-three and Trix looks up at me. Her big, painted eyes roll back and she raises an apologetic, red-tinted fingernail as I settle into the chair to her right.

As soon as I sit down, a server lays a menu down in front of me, along with a nice, tall mimosa. I offer him a wink. He winks back and quickly cowers away from the table as Trix's Italian tirade ups the volume a little.

"Ma. Ma. *Ma!*" Trix exhales. "I gotta go. Nora's here."

Oh, thank god. Trix always whips out English when she wants to signal to her grandmother to wrap it up.

"Yes, she still has that blonde hair you like," she says

into the phone, looking at me. "No, she's not married. No, I won't tell her—" She heaves and lowers the phone an inch. "She wants you to get married."

"Tell her I'll try," I say with a laugh.

"She says she'll try, Ma." Trix pauses to listen. "I'm not telling her that. ... Because it'd set feminism back fifty years."

I chuckle and reach for my glass. The fresh orange juice tickles my nose as I take a long sip and the champagne bubbles twitch all the way down. I wait all week for this. Judging by the two empty glasses sitting in front of Trix already, she needed it, too.

"Okay, Ma, bye. Bye. I said bye. *Addio. Ti amo.*"

She ends the call and drops her phone onto the tablecloth with a dull clink. *"Aughhh,"* she groans, letting all her breath out.

"So, how's Ma?" I ask her.

"Charming, as usual. Is it warm in here?"

"Not really."

She flares her jacket to brush air into her face. "Feels like Satan himself just gave me a facial."

I laugh. "Everything okay?"

"It will be. Ma's just freaking out about my dad's trial. This prosecutor is out for blood and has refused every plea our lawyers have thrown at him. Fuckin' shark."

I pout. "Poor Papa 'Gento."

Trix tosses her jacket over the back of her chair and continues fanning herself with a cloth napkin. "Like I said, it'll work out. It just might get worse before it gets better, that's all."

"Such is life."

We raise our flutes and clink them together before downing the rest of our drinks. As soon as I look up, the server is back again with a tray of fresh mimosas. Keep 'em coming, buddy. As always.

He gathers our empties, his eyes sneaking a peek at the sleeve tattoo up and down Trix's right arm. Not the usual sight you'd find in an upscale place like Moira's Cafe but we've been regulars here for years.

Also, no one on staff would dare kick out Angelo Argento's only daughter.

She's heiress to the fucking mob.

"Oh, my god, I hope you bleed to death."

"Ain't gonna happen, honey."

"Don't call me that. Never call me that."

"Yes, honey."

I look at Trix and we both grin at the voices carrying through the restaurant toward our table.

"Well, this should be good," Trix says.

We both sit back and watch for Melanie to come into sight around the corner. She beelines for the table and throws her purse over the back of the third chair before plopping down on it.

"Hey, guys," she says, slightly out of breath.

I open my mouth to ask what's wrong but I stop when I see Robbie following her path back here.

"Oh, hey, Robbie!" I greet him.

Trix beams at him. "Robbie! Hi!"

Melanie flexes her jaw. "Don't *hey, Robbie* him."

Robbie strolls up to the table in his usual leather jacket and jeans. He jerks his head to flop his hair to one side. It's getting a little long but Robbie's one of the only guys I've ever met that who can really pull off that look.

"Hey, ladies," he says at me and Trix, smiling back at us.

"And don't *hey, ladies* them either," Melanie spits.

I look down and gasp at the thick, white bandage wrapped around his right hand. "Robbie, what happened to you? Are you okay?"

He opens his mouth to answer but Melanie talks over him.

"Don't answer that," she says at him. "They don't actually care."

He reaches out and nudges her chin. "Aw, you seem tense, honey. Did you fall off your broomstick this morning?"

She recoils. "Why did you even follow me in here?"

"It's Sunday morning so I figured you'd be running over here to compare notes with the other *Powerpuff Shrews.* Thought I'd stop in and say hi."

"Hi," she says. "Bye, now."

"Actually, wait," Trix says. "Robbie, I could use your opinion on something."

Melanie glares at her. "Seriously?"

Robbie throws on a wide grin and steals a chair from the nearest empty table. He sets it down backward and lowers himself onto the seat with wide-open legs. "How can I be of service, milady?" he asks her.

Trix gestures at him. "Well, you're a guy."

Melanie scoffs. "Debatable."

"Yes," Robbie says, ignoring her. "Last I checked. Wait..." He reaches below and cups himself. "Okay, go ahead."

I bite my cheek to keep from laughing as Melanie's eyes roll.

Trix leans forward. "What would be the nicest way a woman can deny sex to you?"

I twitch. "The hell?"

She shrugs. *"Marcus."*

"Your dad's bodyguard?" Melanie asks. "You're still fucking him?"

"Since I was fourteen," Trix muses.

"Uh." Robbie laughs. *"Wow."*

"He was fifteen," she says, waving a hand. "It's not as squicky as it sounds. Long story short: We grew up together, he joined the Army, came back ripped, my dad hired him as a bodyguard, and we kept fucking on the side. Totally casual."

He nods. "Ah, I see. Continue."

"Anyway," she continues, "before my dad went to jail, it was all taboo and fun but now that it's so easy to get away with... kinda lost the shine."

"Makes sense."

"He's not a bad guy or anything, but lately, he's just kind of gotten a little clingy like he actually wants to start a *relationship* and that's just not my thing."

"So, you want to stop sleeping with him but you don't want to disturb the peace in the process?"

"Exactly!"

Robbie shrugs. "You could tell him you met another guy," he suggests.

"See, if I did that, then I'd have to provide info so he can be properly vetted because—"

"Bodyguard," he finishes with a nod.

"Right."

"That's quite the pickle, Trix." He scratches his nose.

"Have you tried saying no?" Melanie slaps his shoulder. *"What?* It's a serious question."

"You had a tone," she says.

He smirks in her direction. "Don't you have a litter of newborns to feast on?"

Melanie frowns at him.

Trix tilts her head. "Won't that piss him off?"

"Oh, it might," Robbie says, "but any man who gets pissy over a simple *no, thank you* isn't worth your time, Trix."

She smiles. "You're right. It was so simple. Thank you, Robbie."

"Hey. I believe in you," he adds, pointing his non-bandaged finger. "You got this."

Melanie stares at him. "Hmm," she hums.

Robbie's eyes flick in her direction. "What?"

"Nothing," she says. "I mean, I've *heard* of men speaking out of their asses before, but I'd never seen it so up close before."

"Well, you always were a little prude when it came to butt stuff, Mel."

I share a glance with Trix, both of us holding back our chuckles.

"That certainly was some top-tier counseling, Rob, but it's time for you to go," Melanie says, her teeth clenched together.

"Aw, honey," he says, making her nostrils flare out. "Don't you want me to stick around for a drink or two?"

"No, thank you," she says, stabbing every word.

He grins. "That's my cue, then."

"Yes, dear god, please piss off."

Robbie shakes his head, amused. "You sure are testy when you're ovulating."

Her jaw drops. "I am not ovulating!"

"What's the date today?" he asks the table.

"The fifteenth," I say.

"Ah, yep." He nods. "She is."

She scoffs. "How could you possibly know that? *I* don't even know that."

"I just know."

"Well, you can *just know* somewhere else. Go away, Robbie."

He stands up from his chair and slides it back under the next table with his good hand. "Ladies, it was a pleasure, as always," he says to us.

"And update your forms, please," Melanie adds.

"Oh, calm down, Mel," he says. "You were barely inconvenienced."

"No, you're totally right. You only wasted five hours of my life. I suppose my consolation prize is the fact that you're not going to be able to jerk off properly for weeks."

"You're more than welcome to come over and help me out," he quips. "As long as you wear a mask to conceal those bags under your eyes, of course. You're looking a little worn out, Mel. Books not selling?"

"Eat me, you limp-dick loser."

"Blow me, you frigid hag." He looks away from her and smiles at us instead. "See you around, ladies. Nora, Trix..." he glares at Melanie, *"Maleficent."*

I give a wave. "Bye, Robbie!"

"Good to see you," Trix says.

"We should do this again soon."

Trix blows a kiss. "We love you."

"Bye," he says, tossing another wink in our direction.

He wanders through the restaurant toward the exit, leaving Melanie fuming in her chair.

"Would you guys please stop being so nice to him?" she asks. "You're gonna give him self-esteem."

Trix cackles. "What the hell was that about? Did you two wake up together again?"

The server slides in, sets down another round of mimosas, and takes off just as quickly. He's working for that tip today. Good boy.

"Four months," Melanie says, yanking her jacket off. "It's been four months since our divorce was finalized and that bastard still lists me as his emergency contact."

I take a fresh drink. "What's up with his hand?"

"Well, I was up all night writing, as usual," she begins. "Got to a really great stopping point and passed out around five to get a good bit of sleep before brunch. Two hours later, I get a call from some nurse telling me that my husband was injured at work. Right away, there are red flags. One, *husband*. And two, *work*. Robbie's never held down a *job* before in his life. I never even heard him say the word unless it immediately followed *blow*. Obviously, there was some kind of mistake but she insisted on me coming in anyway. So, I dragged my ass down to the hospital and there's Robbie with a nail sticking through his hand."

We gasp. "Oh, my god!"

Melanie downs a gulp of her mimosa. "At that point, I realized *injured at work* was Robbie Code for *got wasted and did something stupid* so I just stood there while the nurse made flirty eyes at him until the doc patched him up and let him go."

Trix raises a brow. "Why do you care if the nurse was making flirty eyes at him?"

"I don't..." Melanie says, sitting up. "I just think it's inappropriate in that setting for a medical professional to come on to her patients, especially in front of his ex-wife who wants to watch him suffer a life of pain and anguish and die alone. It's a very complicated emotion. I don't expect you to understand."

Trix shrugs. "Good. Because I don't."

"And who works on a Sunday, anyway?" she asks. "His lie — much like his hand — was full of holes."

"I do," I say with a sigh. "Right after this, I have to go into the office. The new temp screwed up some paperwork *again* so I have to rush and fix it before tomorrow's budget meeting."

"Can't you just get a new temp?" Trix asks.

"And be forced to re-train another idiot all over again? No, thanks." I stretch my neck to the side, taking a deep, relaxing breath that doesn't do its job. "Honestly, I'm blowing it out of proportion. It's an easy fix. I just need to hold his hand for a little while longer until Ira gets back from paternity leave. He'll get it eventually."

Melanie flashes a knowing smile. "That sounds perfectly reasonable of you, Nora."

I nod. "Thank you."

"Patient. Wise."

I point my thumb at my face. "That's me."

She smirks. "He's *hot*, isn't he?"

"Fucking gorgeous." I fall forward, feeling a wave of heat in my cheeks. "It's like Gaston had a love child with Captain America. I can barely concentrate."

Trix chuckles. "Well, in that case, maybe *you* screwed up the paperwork."

"You bite your tongue. And..." I pause. "Yeah, maybe.

Hot temp aside, I've been so damn stressed out lately. I don't know what to do. Yoga doesn't work anymore. My massage therapist fired me."

Trix gasps. "Lenny fired you?!"

"Apparently, four AM house calls are outside of his job description," I explain.

Melanie creases her cheek. "Have you looked into meditation?" she asks.

"Oh, you mean the *sit quietly and reflect on everything I've ever done wrong* happy hour?" I joke. "Nope."

"You're supposed to *suppress* those thoughts, Nora," she says with a laugh.

"I don't want to *suppress*. My natural state is the exact opposite. I need to *project* and act out and I can't do that sitting behind a desk all damn day."

Trix nods. "Didn't you join a kick-boxing class?"

"Yeah, but they booted me out for being *too scary*."

"Yikes." She reaches for her glass. "Well, you're on your own."

"Not necessarily," Melanie says. "There's one very obvious omission from your list, Nor."

"Yeah? What's that?" I ask.

She clears her throat and nudges Trix's arm. "Back me up, cheerleader. Give me a B!"

Trix grins. "B!"

"Give me a D!"

"D!"

"Give me an S! M!"

"BDSM!" they cry in unison.

I glance into the wide, staring eyes of silent patrons around us. "Please don't ever do that again," I say. "I really like this place."

Melanie exhales. "I'm telling ya, girlfriend, it'll change your life."

"No," I say, recoiling. "I don't want to be that cliché boss who *demands control* or whatever. It's so stupid."

"That's a myth!" she says. "Statistically, CEOs and other authoritative figures act as subs. Not Doms."

I blink. "Really?"

"Yeah. They spend all day bossing other people around, barking orders, telling them what to do and where to go. That's *exhausting*. They need a few hours a week to let go and submit to *someone else's* demands. It's cathartic as fuck and it's exactly what you need."

I pause to think. "That does make a strange bit of sense..."

Melanie nods. "What are you doing for lunch tomorrow?" she asks.

"Shoving a cold turkey sub down my throat at my desk, probably."

"I'll pick you up and we'll go to Judy's."

"No," I say, shaking my head. "I don't think I can do that."

"You're the boss," she says with confusion. "You can take an hour lunch."

"No, I mean…" I lower my voice. *"Judy's."*

"Why not?" She turns up a hand. "You don't have to pay a membership or commit to anything. Just go there with me, take a look around, dip your toes into the seas of sinful things, and you'll go from there. They're not even open until dusk, so you'll get a chance to see the good stuff up close."

I furrow my brow. "You can just walk into a sex club and look around while it's closed?"

"It's not a *sex* club. It's a *kink* club," she argues. "There's a difference. And yes, you can, *with me*. Judy and I go way back. One call and we'll have the whole place to ourselves."

"What's the difference between a sex club and a kink club?" I ask.

"Go with me and I'll show you," she says, teasing. "I go all the time — for research, of course." She flashes a wink.

"And why are you divorced again?" I joke.

She sticks out her tongue.

"Beatrix Argento?"

We glance up at a suited man suddenly standing above our table.

"Yes, sir?" Trix answers with a smile and looks him up and down.

He reaches into his jacket and withdraws an envelope. "You've been served," he says, holding it out.

Trix snatches the papers from him. "And a *fuck you* to you, too, asshole," she spits as he turns around and takes wide strides back to the exit.

I rub Trix's shoulder. "Well, that sucks."

She shoves the envelope into her purse without opening it. "It's all right. It was expected for my dad's trial. Ma told me earlier."

Melanie frowns. "Want to come to Judy's with us tomorrow?" she asks. "Perk you right up."

"Nah, I need to meet with our lawyers to walk me through my deposition," she says. "Rain-check me, please."

"How's Papa 'Gento doing?"

"An aging, old mobster in the slammer?" she quips. "He practically owns the place. Doesn't mean he's eager to hang up curtains or anything, though. Of course, all of this is secondhand knowledge since they won't let me see him myself."

"That's for the best, Trix," I say.

"I know, I know. The more distance I keep, the less they'll shine lights on me. But... still. I miss my dad, you know?"

"But hey…" I tap her inked shoulder. "By the time he gets out, this should be done, right?"

She glances at her arm and nods. "Yep. Just a few more trips to the tat shop and my marque is complete. Then, I can secure my rightful place in Papa's inner circle."

"Look at you." Melanie sighs, smiling. "All growed up and joining the mob."

"Daddy's little *goombah*," Trix says, fluttering her lashes. "Of course, none of that will happen until I get him out of jail because the old fogies currently squatting in charge don't like the *females* making decisions, but fuck 'em. I'm Trix Argento. That's *my* family's crest up there."

"*Rawr.*" Melanie hisses and claws the air. "I love feisty Trix."

"Me, too," I say, raising my glass. "To Trix."

Trix grins. "And to Nora and Mel. May we always give 'em hell."

We all clink our glasses.

"So, Nor…" Melanie says, tapping the table between us. "You? Me? Judy's, tomorrow? Yes? Yes? Harder, baby? Harder?"

I let out a groan, though I am oddly curious. "Okay, fine. Meet me in my office at noon sharp. We'll go then."

She claps twice. "Yes! Trust me. You will find what you need to cure what ails you."

"Yeah, yeah," I say dismissively, hiding behind my glass.

"Okay..." Trix says, grabbing a menu. "I should probably eat something to soak up all this champagne."

I nod, feeling light-headed. "That's a smart idea."

The three of us go silent as we scan the menus.

I glance at Melanie and my lips twitch. "Are you really ovulating?" I ask.

She slams her fist on the table, shaking the glasses. "How does he do that?!"

TWO

NORA

The lobby is dead quiet as I walk inside. It is Sunday, after all, and most of the companies who work here are nine-to-five Monday through Friday jobs. Mine included but I'm a confessed workaholic, so it's not unusual for me to sneak in and do a little extra during the weekends.

The security officer up front doesn't even ask questions as I pass by the front desk on my way to the elevator. He glances up and nods, gently twitching his silver mustache into a kind, familiar smile.

You'd think the founder of a major dating website would have more going on in her personal life than this.

But you'd be wrong.

It all started when I was a teenager.

Hey, you two should go out.

You know who you should meet? My pal, Johnny.

You'd get along great.

My talents for tagging compatible partners grew more and more until friends of friends of friends all over Chicago were practically paying me to start setting them up on dates from my famous black book.

Yes, *the* Little Black Book. The number one dating app in the entire world.

That was all me and my picture-perfect love-matching algorithms.

Add in a little luck with early investments in cryptocurrency and I made my first million before the age of twenty-five. Five years later and I'm one of the Top 3 Wealthiest Women Under 30 in Chicago. The other two?

Beatrix Argento and Melanie Rose.

That was last year's list, of course. We all turned thirty this year but we'll still be just as influential without the benefit of our 20s. The fire beneath Little Black Book is far from burning out.

Unfortunately, my talents for love-matching don't work so well on yours truly, but you know what they say.

Those who can't do; teach.

I ride the elevator to the fifteenth floor. The lights are down as I step off but I could navigate this sea of desks with my eyes closed. My office is on the far side — in the corner, naturally — and I walk toward it on autopilot. The paperwork I need to fix is on my computer so it shouldn't take too long to take care of. Then, maybe I'll head home and actually take the rest of Sunday off.

Or not. We'll see.

I twist the knob and push open my office door. I instantly grind to a halt as I see someone sitting in my desk chair in the dark, the sharp features of their face illuminated by nothing more than the bright blue of my computer monitor.

My new temp. My hot, new temp.

"Excuse me." I flick on the lights. "What are you doing in here?"

"Whoa—" He jumps out of the chair and throws up his hand. "Hi, there. I was *not* expecting you to be here today."

I step up to the desk. "Why are you on my computer?" I ask him.

He lowers his hands. "Okay, I'm sorry. I was in bed last night and I suddenly realized that I made a really big mistake on the budget report—"

"Yes, you did." I cross my arms.

"Right. So, I rushed out here as soon as I could today to try and fix it before you came in tomorrow but then I remember that it gets locked at five on Fridays and the only way to access it was..." He waves at my computer. "So, I jimmied the lock and—"

"You *jimmied* my lock?" I repeat, my voice pitching as I inspect the door.

"It's not broken or anything, I swear. But I fixed the thing! And the numbers add up now and... I'm really sorry, Mrs. Payne."

I squint, letting my eyes hop from him to the computer and back again. "You fixed it?" I ask.

"I did." He gestures to the monitor. "See for yourself."

I set my purse down on the edge of the desk and walk around to take a look. He stays on the opposite side of me the entire time, rounding to stand in front looking nervous as all hell. I might as well have caught him with his pants down based on that white-faced reaction.

Still, he's no less stunningly gorgeous with broad, muscular shoulders and a thin layer of sweat on his brow *and those cheekbones—*

Focus, Nora.

I sit down in my chair and look at the monitor. My budget software is indeed open right to the mistake he made. Perfectly corrected.

"Again, I'm *really* sorry," he says above me.

"It's..." I scan the lines again, double-checking for accuracy. "It's okay. You did the right thing — though I am a little protective of my stuff, so next time, maybe just leave a note?"

"I did leave a note," he says, pointing down.

My eyes catch the bright pink post-it note stuck to the edge of the monitor. I peel it off to read it.

"*Sorry for the fuck up, Mrs. Payne. Clive.*" I chuckle at the casual tone. "That about covers it, then."

"And there won't be a next time," he says. "I promise. I know how much of an opportunity it is working here for you and I'll do better, starting right now."

I smile, trying hard not to fawn over him. I don't know what it is I find so attractive about a younger guy who just wants to *please* me, but...

Clive clears his throat and walks backward a few paces. "Well, anyway, I should get out of here. Last time: I'm sorry, Mrs. Payne. It won't happen again."

"Clive," I say.

He stops in the doorway. "Yes, Mrs. Payne?"

"It's *Ms.*"

He smiles, revealing a gorgeous set of bright, white teeth. "I apologize, *Ms.* Payne," he says slowly. "Won't happen again."

"Enjoy the rest of your weekend," I add.

"I will," he says. "You, too. I'll, uh... I'll see you tomorrow."

My eyes wander downward as he exits my office,

instantly clinging to the tight rear just begging to rip free of those pants. I sign hard once he's out of earshot.

Goddamn, that's a good tushy.

I kick my ankle off the floor and spin my chair around to look out the windows at the Chicago sky.

Maybe I should go over my notes again for the meeting tomorrow.

Or, I could go home and take Sunday off.

Notes, it is.

THREE

CLIVE

That was close. Too close.

The elevator begins its descent downward and I release the breath I've been holding since the second I left her office.

Now, what?

I hang my head, counting the floor indicator dings all the way down to the ground floor.

As the doors open, the old security guard looks up from his phone. I fake a smile and wave at him as I pass, trying very hard not to make it so obvious how much my heart is struggling to remain in my chest.

I step outside and zip up my jacket to block the windchill as I bolt down the street.

Alex isn't going to like this but how the hell was I supposed to know she'd show up today? It's fucking Sunday.

We made plans to meet at the coffee shop down the street after I got it. I'm not looking forward to that excited look he'll have as soon as I walk in, like a kid on Christmas morning.

Sorry, kiddo. Rough year. Enjoy the socks.

I linger outside with my fingers on the door handle, dreading the next few minutes of my life, but I've been through worse. We both have and we're still here. That counts for something, right?

I pull open the door, knocking the entry bell, and exactly one head in the whole place turns to look.

Alex's face instantly lights up from the corner table. I don't smile back. There's no reason to get his hopes up over nothing.

He studies the look on my face as I move closer to his table. By the time I sit down across from him, I've officially kicked his Christmas puppy in the face.

"Did you get it?" he asks, grasping at the last bit of hope he has.

I shake my head. "No, I did not."

His shoulders fall. "Why the hell not?"

"She walked in before I could get it," I answer, glancing around at the occupied tables on either side.

"She walked in?" he repeats, his voice growing.

"Yeah."

"But it's *Sunday.*"

"Well, she came into the office today."

"Who the hell works on a *Sunday?*"

A few heads turn in our direction.

"*Ms.* Nora Payne, apparently," I say, giving him a sour look.

Alex takes the signal and reels his shit back in. "Well… *fuck,*" he says under his breath. "Now, what? We were supposed to deliver the list *today.*"

"Call and tell them we hit a snag," I say. "No big deal. I'll just have to figure out a more creative way of getting alone with her computer. One that doesn't risk me getting fired. Still kind of need this job…"

His face turns white. "Whatever you think of, *think it fast,* Clive."

I furrow my brow. "What's the hurry? The thing will be worth just as much in a few days. Hell, it might actually be worth *more—*"

"I don't have a few days—" He stops, snapping his lips shut as he realizes he's raising his voice again.

I exhale hard. "Alex, what exactly are you not telling me?"

He waves a hand. "Don't worry about it."

Don't worry about it. The ultimate deflector. Alex's default setting.

Alex reads my concern. "Look, man, I have this under control."

"Yeah, you're looking real stable right now, Alex."

He ignores it. "I promised I'd handle the details and *I'll handle the details.* You just focus on getting the client list. Okay?"

"I am focused on getting it. I just don't think your buyer realizes how difficult it is to access a CEO's private computer software."

"I never said it'd be easy." He points at me. "In fact, I said it wouldn't be, but you still volunteered. Remember?"

"I remember. I also remember you telling me it'd all be worth it."

"It will all be worth it," he says, clearly not giving a shit about his volume again. "I gave you my word that I would make it all worth it. Do you trust me?"

I shift in my seat. "Yeah, Alex. I do. Calm the fuck down."

He takes a breath. "I'm sorry, I just…" He taps the table with his thumb. "I feel like I've let you down."

I shake my head. "You haven't let me down. No one's let anybody down."

"Your life isn't what it should be and that's my fault." He lets out a chuckle and glares into his empty coffee mug. "It's always been my fault. I'm gonna make it up to you."

I sigh, moving on. "Give me another few days," I tell him. "I'll get the client list. Just tell your guy I'll do my best. All right?"

"How long we talking here? Can you get it tomorrow night?" he asks, a glimmer of hope in his voice.

"No, I work tomorrow night."

"It's an office temp job, man. Why the fuck do you have to be there on a Monday night?"

"Not *that* job. My other job."

He grunts with amusement. "The gym or the sex dungeon?"

I snort. "It's not a dungeon."

"Oh, yeah? Well, what do you call it?"

"I call it work," I say. "Work is work."

"Hey." He taps the table, smiling wide. "We finish this job and you won't even *need* to work. The two of us will never have to work a day in our lives *ever again*. Eh? How's that sound?"

"Yeah." I nod. "It sounds pretty good."

FOUR

NORA

My eyes keep shifting toward my desk clock and each time I feel just a little more disappointed that only minutes have passed. Monday is usually a rough start day but ever since Melanie urged me to check out the sex club, I've felt a rush of excitement I haven't experienced in a good long while.

Excuse me. *Kink* club. Not *sex* club.

Of course, I should have known when I told Melanie to meet me at noon, she wouldn't actually make it *sharp*.

I squint at the clock. 12:15.

Bestselling romance author, Melanie Rose, lives in her own little world — which is fine. She's more than earned it. But for the rest of us that live in a world of alarm clocks and time sheets, a blatant disregard for punctuality can be quite annoying.

I grab my phone to prepare a biting text message just as someone knocks on my door frame.

"What's up, bitch?"

I sigh at Melanie's grin and reach for my purse. "You're late," I tell her.

"You're surprised?" she asks.

"No," I answer. "Just tell me you finished that chapter you were working on."

She hesitates. "Define *finished.*"

I throw my purse over my shoulder. "Let's get this over with."

"Nu-uh," she says, pointing at me. "Not with that attitude. No one walks into Judy's with cat-butt face."

"I do not have cat-butt face."

"I want bright, smiling faces and wide-open minds," she says. "You'll never find a good Dom if you look like you just bit into a rotten fish. Though, who am I kidding, there's probably a fetish for that out there somewhere."

"I'm not even—" I lower my voice, realizing my office door is still open. "I'm not even looking for a Dom. It's a little soon for that, isn't it?"

"Oh." She winces. "Probably shouldn't have put out that ad, then."

My face drops. "What ad?"

She breaks character and slaps my shoulder. "Just kidding. Let's go get our whips and chains on."

I heave a thick sigh to conceal my laugh as we make our way toward the elevator.

Judy's — despite what Melanie calls it — isn't actually called Judy's at all.

The club is called The Red Brick Road and it's nestled, of

all places, in plain sight a few blocks down from my own office building between a coffee shop and some hipster record store.

I blink from the sidewalk, staring up at the wooden sign above the red doorway. "The *Red* Brick Road?" I ask.

Melanie nods. "Yeah, you ever notice how when Dorothy and her friends skip down the yellow road, there's a red brick road heading in the opposite direction?"

"No," I answer.

"Well, now you won't be able to unsee it," she says with a smile. "Come on."

Melanie steps forward and holds the door open for me. I lower my head and force myself to walk in quickly just in case someone sees me. There's a deep throb growing in my gut. I don't know what makes me so nervous about all of it. I'm not committing to anything. I'm just taking a look around.

The Red Brick Road lives up to its name. The entryway is a closed off room with one very large red door and a reception desk that looks way too innocent, not unlike the counter at the DMV. A path made of red bricks curls from the door to the counter, branching in the middle to lead toward the red door.

Even the woman sitting behind the counter seems out of place for some sadistic sex dungeon. She's middle-aged and round as a blueberry with thin, wire-rimmed glasses hanging from a chain about her neck and tiny earbud head-phones in her ears. My gaze lingers on her neck and the large, leather collar just beneath her chin with a thick, silver padlock.

Melanie throws up her arms. "Yo, Judy!"

The woman flinches in her chair and pulls the earbuds out of her ears, quickly popping her hanging glasses up over her nose. She gasps, her wide, red-painted lips instantly cracking a grin.

"Mel Rose, is that you?" she asks.

"The one and only." Melanie leans into the counter on her elbow. "You're looking well. How's business?"

"As pleasurable as ever," she answers, glancing over Melanie's shoulder at me. "And this must be the friend you mentioned."

Melanie reaches back to grab my wrist and yanks me closer. "Yes. This is my BFF, Nora, and we're here to play."

"Well, not *play* play," I say, clearing my throat. "I mean... we don't... I mean, she and I don't play..." I shut my trap.

Judy smirks at Melanie. "A virgin, huh?"

Melanie snorts. "Might as well be."

"Well, go on in. Should be pretty quiet in there for you."

"Thank you, Judy."

Melanie grabs my hand and lays it flat on the counter. She picks up an ink stamp and presses into the back of my hand, leaving behind a curvy, womanly shape on my skin.

"What's this for?" I ask.

"Just giving you the full experience," she says with a wink at Judy. "Come on." Melanie hooks my arm and draws me to the door with her.

We pause outside until Judy taps a button and the lock flicks open with a dull thud. Melanie pushes it with her free arm and shoves me forward with the other. My breath catches but I force myself to keep my balance as I walk into the main room.

I glance around, once again surprised by the reality of

my situation. I'm not sure what I expected, to be honest. Something closer to a strip club with cages and flashing fluorescent lights with a pit for the pervs to throw out money.

Not Victorian furniture.

It's one large room with a staircase leading upward at its center. Hardwood floors with plenty of seating scattered around every wall from gorgeous loveseats to comfortable benches for multiple people. I can easily picture old ladies sitting around drinking tea — and I would if it weren't for the occasional leather leash left hanging from a hook along the walls.

It looks… nice.

"You're straight-up flabbergasted right now, aren't you?" Melanie asks, smiling at my face.

"Okay." I clear my throat. "You have my attention."

"Good." She hooks my arm. "Because the fun stuff is upstairs. This is just the quiet room."

"The quiet room?"

We move forward, the gentle clack of our heels echoing off the floor.

"Yeah, you come in, grab a bottle of water from upfront, and hang out," she says, waving a whimsical arm. "Casual, nonjudgmental atmosphere. Everyone is always so friendly and welcoming."

"Well, yeah, they want to get laid," I say with a laugh.

"Not necessarily. I mean, sure, some people use the space to pick people up, but others just like to talk. I haven't been here for a while, but I've gotten some great info on kinks and limits and all that. I should come back soon. Might help my writer's block."

"Limits?" I ask.

"Hard, soft," she says. "You know, the things you're not-so comfortable doing."

I nod, though I'm not really sure I understand. "Okay..."

"Clothing mandatory, no sexual contact allowed — so you know the seating is nice and clean, at least."

"Oh, good..."

Melanie twists us around and targets the stairs. "Anyway, the bottom floor is the welcome area but upstairs is where the magic happens."

I let her pull me along and I grasp the railing on the way up the unfamiliar staircase. As we ascend, the lighting dims and that comfortable, warm atmosphere disappears into something darker.

The walls are painted black. Gone are the beautiful Victorian couches. They're replaced with black, leather benches along the walls but this doesn't feel like a place for sitting for long periods of time.

There's a track along the ceiling with strategically-placed lights that barely illuminate much of anything. There are three open areas on each side of the staircase, each one with a piece of furniture at the center, some as simple as a table. Others...

An X-shaped cross with cuffs at the end of each arm. A bench that seems a little like a massage table but it's all out of whack, like it would force you to sit on all-fours like a...

Oh.

I swallow.

"Nora Payne," Melanie says beside me, "meet pleasure."

I roll my eyes. "How long have you been saving that one?"

"Shush."

She slaps my calf with a riding crop.

I flinch. "Where the hell did you get that thing?" I ask.

"Off the wall." She hits me again. "So, what do you think?"

I take a wide step out of her crop's reach. "This…" I chuckle. "This is a little closer to what I expected."

"Clothing *optional*," she says. "Still no sex allowed up here but play is highly encouraged."

"Play?"

She swipes at me again, which I easily dodge. *"Play."*

I look at the tables and crosses again, quickly realizing that there are no curtains or doors on the entire floor.

"They do it in front of *everybody?*" I ask.

"That's part of the fun!" she says. "Being watched is super hot."

I laugh. "Is it?"

She stares at me, unblinking. *"Yes."*

"Have *you* done this before?"

"Once or twice. Rob and I came here a little back in the day, but…" She shrugs, going quiet.

I throw on a sympathetic face. Melanie doesn't usually talk about the details surrounding the fall of her and Robbie too often. I can tell it bums her out more than she lets on. I won't push for details.

"Anyway…" She waves her crop around like a magic wand and points at the X-shaped cross in the opposite corner. "The St. Andrew's cross, a few cages, restraint tables, and — my personal favorite — the punishment bench."

I look at the wonky massage table again. "Punishment bench…" I murmur.

I feel the surprise tap of her crop on my rear.

"See anything you like?" she asks.

I twist away from her. "I have no idea. I mean… it *looks* fun?"

"That's step one," she says, waving upward. "Wide-open minds."

"Uh-huh." I glance at the stairwell, noticing that it leads up again. "And the third floor?"

Melanie smiles. "Anything goes."

"Anything?"

"Private rooms rented by the hour," she says. "If this floors a-rockin'…"

"*Wow.*"

"Leave your usual self at the door and don't forget to wrap it."

"Your usual self?"

"BDSM, in general, is…" She bites her cheek. "*Intense*, to say the least. I've interviewed a lot of people here and they've all told me the same thing: the headspace they get into when they're here is nothing like the person who wakes up at seven AM on a Monday morning to go to work." She points her crop at me. "And that should intrigue you, in particular."

"It should?" I chuckle.

"Nora, don't get me wrong, you're one of my favorite people on this planet, but…" Her head tilts. "You need an off-switch. When is the last time you slept through the night?"

"2015, maybe," I joke.

She nods. "This place isn't just about getting laid. If that's all you need, Trix and I can wing-lady you a keeper any night of the week. No, you need something deeper than a little random dick. Or *big* random dick, as it goes…"

"So, what do I do?" I ask. "Just hook up with some guy, he ties me up, calls me I'm a bad girl… and that's supposed to help my stress?"

She sighs. "The idea behind it is power-play. It might look like a bunch of kinky whips and chains to some, but deep down, at its core, it's about one person giving themselves over *completely*. Their actions, their words — all controlled by someone else — and *you can't tell me* that's not appealing to you in some way."

I glance around into the blackened rooms. Kinky whips and chains, that's definitely what it looks like on the outside but there's something else to this that I can't quite put my finger on.

I pause by one of the crosses and flick the soft, padded restraint near the top with my finger. The idea *is* appealing. Being tied up, held down, and pleasured until it hurts. Or hurt until it feels good. That might work, too…

I pause and lower my hand.

What the hell did I just think?

"In the end," Melanie says, breaking the silence, "can you think of anything else you *haven't* tried yet?"

"Acupuncture?" I quip.

She rolls her eyes. "This is way better than acupuncture. For starters, acupuncture can't potentially get you laid." She points her crop at me again. "Don't lie to me. I can tell you're in a dry spell."

I squint. "No comment."

Melanie sighs. "Come back tonight when they're open and watch a few scenes play out. I'll even come back here with you if you want."

"No, I think…" I bite my lip, my skin tingling with

embarrassment. "I think I'll give Lenny a call instead. Beg him to take me back."

"*Or...* you can come back here and beg Daddy to make you his dirty, little girl."

She flogs the wall beside her, making a loud slap echo throughout the room.

I cringe. *"Daddy?"*

"I know, it felt icky saying it." She slides the flogger back into its place on the wall. "Well, if you've seen enough, you wanna get some coffee? The place next door has a killer caramel frappe. My treat."

I nod. "Absolutely."

Melanie starts down the stairs. I linger in place, briefly taking one last quiet glance into the corners or the room. My wrists tingle, involuntarily reacting to the possible feel restraints digging in. I imagine a hard caress on my exposed rear end, all within sight of a dozen strangers.

I clear my throat and follow Melanie down.

"Did you girls have fun?" Judy asks us as we reach the entrance.

"Always will," Melanie says. "Thanks for having us. I'll be in again soon, I promise."

I nod. "Yes, thank you. You have *quite* the place here, Judy."

She flashes a sinister wink. "We'll be seeing you again," she says, staring at me.

I nod, feeling a warm chill radiate down my spine.

We step outside and Melanie nudges my ribs.

"She says that to everybody. She's not a psychic or anything. Just a dirty, old lady."

"Yeah, I figured," I say, playing it cool.

"I want to be her when I grow up."

I laugh. "Well, you're on your way."

We take a few quick strides toward the coffee shop next door. Melanie reaches for the handle but the door flies open and she slams right into the person leaving: a man with wide shoulders, a leather jacket, and shaggy, brown—

Of course.

"Slow down, lady! You leave your cauldron plugged in or something?"

I silently groan at Robbie's twisted smirk.

Melanie's face drops all patience. "Ugh, *move.*"

She shoves him back and bolts into the shop, leaving him grinning with a to-go cup clutched in his good hand and his bandaged palm hanging by his side.

I stop beside him with my crossed arms as he watches her go, patiently waiting while he takes a long, hard look at her ass.

Finally, he turns around and notices me. "Oh. Hi, Nora."

I shake my head. "Robbie, why do you say shit like that to her? You *adore* Melanie."

"I do. She's the love of my life," he says with a defiant nod.

"Then, *leave her alone.*"

"The thing is..." he takes a swig from his coffee, "dumping on Mel is like... well, it's like taking a dump. If I don't do it at least once a day then things start to feel weird. Go a whole week without and that's just unhealthy."

I frown. "I *do not* understand you two."

"Yeah. Me, neither."

"You were made for each other, you know that, right?"

He smirks. "I know."

I tap my foot. "Then, *be nice.*"

"Nor, it's *fine,*" he says. "If I know Mel like I *know* I do then she's pissed off right now. But when she goes home tonight, she'll get all curled up in her soft and warm bed, and before she drifts off to sleep, she'll reach under the covers for a little down-low tickle, and she'll think of *me.*"

"No, she won't." I scoff. "She hates your guts."

"Ask her yourself." He turns to leave but pauses. "And when you do, text me her answer. I need an ego boost."

"Yeah, I won't be doing that."

He shrugs, amused. "Okay but then you won't experience the elegant satisfaction of proving me wrong which means that you are in a perpetual state of *being wrong* and that's gonna eat away at you until... you... *pop.*"

I shift on my toes. "No, it won't."

His knowing grin curls along his cheeks. "Bye, Nora."

"Bye, Robbie."

He stops mid-stride, his eyes locking on my hand. "No way! Did she take you to Judy's?" he asks with excitement.

I shove my hand in my jacket to hide the stamp. "No."

"I thought you looked different!" He laughs. "Good for you."

"I don't look different!" I pause. "Do I?"

"Honestly, it's about time."

I furrow my brow. "What's that supposed to mean?"

"Oh, Nora, Nora, Nora." He sighs. "We both know exactly what that means. Did you try the cross?"

I swallow. "The what?"

"The St. Andrew's cross," he says. "Trust me. You'd *love* it."

"No," I answer. "I didn't try the cross. Melanie gave me a little tour, that's all. Just a bit of lunch break fun..."

"Go back and try the cross." He points at me with his bandaged hand. "The cross is your friend."

I clear my throat. "Okay, it was fun catching up, Robbie. I gotta go. Bye."

I take a wide step around him and pull open the door.

"Bye," he shouts after me. "But remember! *Try the cross!*"

I give the door a little nudge to close it faster, hoping no one heard or understood the tail-end of that conversation. Hell, I'm not even sure *I* understood that conversation.

I cut the line to join Melanie halfway up but everyone, herself included, is too stuck in their phones to notice.

"Hey," she mutters, smacking her thumbs against the screen with lightning speed. She rarely texts, so she must be jotting down an idea for one of her books. "Talking to Robbie?" she asks, her voice dripping with audible annoyance.

"A little bit," I say.

"Well, make sure you shower at the earliest convenience," she jokes. "You have no idea where he's been."

I chuckle. "Hey, Mel."

"Yeah?"

"Do you ever think about Robbie when you masturbate?"

"Oh, all the time," she says, giving a passive shrug.

My eyes roll back. "I *do not* understand you two."

"Yeah. Me, neither."

I pull my hand from my pocket and turn it up to check my stamp. It's a little faded from before but I can still easily make out the feminine hourglass shape still imprinted on my skin.

Do I really look different? I don't feel any different, unless you count the sharp stab of curiosity tingling my gut since the moment we left. That place seemed harmless enough in the daytime with lights shining overhead and empty couches but what happens after dark?

More importantly, what happens to me?

Only one way to find out.

FIVE

NORA

I can't believe I'm doing this.

I keep telling myself that it's not big deal. I'm just going to a club. I've gone to dozens of clubs before. They're all the same. You just walk in, grab a drink, listen to some music, do a little dancing, and go home — sometimes alone, sometimes not.

It's fun. It's exciting. It's...

Not at all the same thing.

I have no idea what will happen when I walk through this red door. I don't know what the kink club equivalent of dancing will be. Is it spanking? I've been spanked before. Sort of. I dated a guy that liked that. Didn't last, but that didn't have anything to do with the spanking thing.

"Are you lost, honey?"

I flinch, my attention instantly yanked away from the giant red door in the entryway. Was it this big earlier today?

"Huh?" I ask.

Judy sits behind the counter, smiling at me. "Just follow the red brick road," she says, waving a hand downward.

I glance at the winding brick beneath my feet. "That simple, huh?"

"Of course."

The entrance opens behind me and I jump out of the way as two men walk in. They each raise their hands to show her the stamp on the back. Judy waves them in, quickly tapping the button below the counter to unlock the red door.

They go through it so fast I don't get a chance to peek around them to see what this place is like after dark.

"Come here," she says to me, beckoning me closer.

I walk up to the counter and she stands up out of her chair. My eyes instantly fall to the tight, midnight blue corset around her waist but I raise them back up just as fast.

"Guest passes are twenty-dollars a night," she says, her voice deep and raspy. "Or you can purchase an annual membership."

I reach for my purse. "Guest pass, please. Might be a bit too early to think annually," I say, withdrawing my debit card.

"That's what they all say," she says with a wink. She takes my card and swipes it. "Do you have questions?" she asks. "That's why I'm here."

I inhale, prepping my tongue, but I quickly draw a blank. "Well..."

She grins. "You don't have to do anything here you don't want to do," she says.

I nod. "Right..." I pause, leaning in. "Do people really just let you watch?"

"Of course. However, do not interrupt, do not distract, do not get too close, and... do not touch yourself."

I blink. "Is that a thing that happens?"

"Not really, but it still needs to be said." She picks up a stamp and dabs it into a dark green ink blot. "Your right hand, please."

I lay my palm on the counter and she presses it into me. This stamp is different than the one Melanie used earlier. This one is shaped like a whip, all curly and snappy.

"If you have more questions, I'm here. Or you can speak to any of the uniformed staff on the floor. Look for the reflective armbands."

I nod. "Thank you."

"Enjoy your stay," she says, reaching below the counter.

The red door unlocks. I swallow hard. Point of no return, as they say. Then again, I already threw down twenty dollars to be here. Might as well get my money's worth.

I step forward and push the door open.

Soft music greets me, a deep and moody track that definitely sets the mood. The lights are dimmer than earlier but much brighter over the Victorian chairs along the wall. The seats are mostly occupied by a wider variety of people than I would have expected. Some sit back in cocktail dresses and ties while others mingle in corsets and... full body latex suits.

I glance at my little, black dress. At least I'm not over-dressed.

Or am I?

"Dom or sub?"

I flinch at the sudden voice next to me in the corridor. I look up into the shadowed eyes of a man in a gray suit with a bright, blond perm.

"Huh?" I ask.

"Are you a Dom?" he asks, enunciating. "Or are you a sub?"

I ease back from his hard, impatient stare. "Neither, currently..."

His eyes fall from my face, slowly gliding down my body to my strappy heels, and in that moment, he makes up his mind. He turns away and moves on to a tall woman in pink boots sitting in the nearest chair. He very audibly asks her the exact same question.

"Sub," she says.

Once again, he turns and walks off. She shrugs and starts chatting up the girl in the seat beside her again. Guess he didn't like her answer either.

"Well, aren't you a pretty, little thing?"

I spin around and gasp at the hidden face. It's a man — I think — obscured behind a skin-tight, black latex suit from head-to-toe. I squint, searching for eye holes. How the hell does he see out of that thing?

"Uh-huh," I say.

"I'm Roger. You look familiar but I don't think I've seen you around here before."

I shake his hand and he squeezes my fingers. Hard. "Yeah, I'm new," I say, hoping he doesn't actually recognize me from somewhere else. There have been plenty of articles published about me in the last few years. I should have thought about that before. I would be walking around here in one of these bodysuits, too.

"Sweet! I remember my first time here. It can be pretty traumatic for a newcomer." He laughs like a jolly child. "So, do you work around here?"

I shift awkwardly, double thinking this whole conversation thing. My eyes drop for a brief moment and I pause at the very obvious erection tenting his suit.

"Uhh... sorry..." I pause, forgetting his name.

"Roger," he says.

"Roger, would you excuse me? My friend just arrived."

"Oh, yeah. Sure! No problem!" He steps aside, his suit squeaking. "It was nice to meet you, mystery newbie. Give me a holler later if you're down to fuck."

He walks off, leaving me with a feeling I can only describe as whiplash.

I blink. "O-okay, I will..."

Maybe the quiet room isn't the best place for me. Too much talking going on...

I take a quick step toward the stairwell. According to Melanie, the second floor is where the magic happens. Open rooms. Spying eyes. Come and watch a few scenes play out, whatever the hell that means.

I climb the stairs with one hand hovering over the railing. Again, the higher I go the lower the lights dim around me. That low bass music follows me up. It must be piped through a speaker system in the walls.

I reach the top and swallow hard. It's more crowded up here but the air is still and quiet. Just a brief whisper here and there. A chuckle or two.

A loud snap breaks the silence, instantly followed by a deep, guttural moan. It's a woman hidden somewhere behind this wall of people. I slink in, my petite height allowing me to pass through without so much as an annoyed glance from the others.

I ease to the front and spot a woman bent over a punishment bench. Both hands and feet are restrained to it with thick bindings. Her dress is ripped in three places, exposing the side of her breasts.

There's a man standing over her wearing nothing but a pair of tight leather pants. I spot the long paddle in his hand. He holds it up to her face and her body reacts to it like an animal, cowering and shaking. I crane to see more and I spot the large, red markings on her ass.

I bite my cheek.

My first instinct is to *do something*. She's hurt, obviously. But no one seems to care. People aren't speaking in cautious whispers. They're humming words of encouragement. I look from the man to her and back again as my heart starts racing.

"This is all you are to me," the man says to her. *"Understand?"*

"Yes, Master."

My nails dig deep into my arm.

He circles the bench and I flinch as he reaches out to her. My thoughts spike, thinking he's about to strike her or worse, but he lays the back of his hand on her cheek.

She smiles.

He leans over to whisper in her ear, something soft and sweet enough to make her cheeks crease. She even laughs. It's warm and comforting but it only lasts a moment.

The man stands up again and turns the paddle multiple times in his palm. She braces herself, locking her body in anticipation as he lays the paddle along her ass.

I almost look away. I'm glad I don't.

As the paddle connects with her skin, she cries out with a sharp, quivering voice. I feel it so deep in me, it makes me dizzy. The submission, the pain. She's lost all control over herself but she still looks so happy.

I breathe in, biting my lip as goosebumps tread up my back.

I want to try it.

Just once. Just to be sure. It might be horrible and terrifying but Melanie has a point. I've tried just about everything else and this…

I release my grip on my arm. My fingers are shaking. I should go back downstairs and find a place to sit down for a minute.

I turn, easing slowly through the crowd. Those who notice me happily shift to make room as I look to the man in leather again.

Her Dom. She must trust him completely, or else why would she even let herself be tied down like that?

Where would I even begin to find a guy like—

I slam into a body on the edge of the crowd near the stairs.

"Shit!" I say, looking up. "I'm sorry, I…"

I freeze, locking eyes with him.

The man leans back. His eyes quickly grow wide and he recognizes me the same time I do him.

Clive. The hot temp.

My *fucking* employee.

We both inhale, preparing to speak, but neither of us gets further than that. We just stare, unwittingly blocking the stairwell as we wait for the other to fucking say something.

Finally, I hop back and scoot around him, clinging to the railing as I bolt down to the first floor. I'm not stopping to chat anymore. I push through the small crowd near the entrance, thinking of nothing but getting the hell out before I run into someone else who knows who I am.

I am so fucked.

SIX

CLIVE

Nora Payne hasn't looked at me in two days.

To be fair, she didn't do much looking at me around the office anyway but she's going out of her way to avoid me now.

Until yesterday, her daily routine was set in stone. She'd get here before nine, pluck around in her office for an hour checking emails and reviewing everyone's work from the day before. Then, she'd get up and make a slow clock-wise ring around the desks, starting with marketing directly left of her office. Then, she'd check in with the creative team. And human resources. She'd go all the way around until she'd hit accounting, where my temporary desk currently resides.

Now, all of a sudden, that routine is practically nonexistent. She'd hit all the other places, but she won't come near accounting. Not even once in two whole days. If she needs something numbers-related, she calls my supervisor, Ali, and Ali goes into Nora's office.

I shouldn't care. I'm not here to make friends with her, but…

I've never seen her at Red Brick before.

I didn't even think she'd be the type.

My type.

This puts quite the wrinkle in my side hustle. I want to know more about the mystery that is Ms. Nora Payne but I also have to get that client list.

It's Wednesday. Alex will be bugging me any time now for an update and I've got jack shit in the realm of progress.

I have to get into her office.

End of the day will probably be easiest. It's not unusual for Nora to be the first employee in and the last one out. I just to find the right moment to—

Where is she going?

I crane my neck to peek out of my cubicle. Ms. Nora Payne just waltzed out of her office with her briefcase, her purse, and her phone. She shut off the lights and closed the door. She never does that unless she's leaving for the day but it's not even five yet.

I watch her walk from her office toward the elevator. She purposefully takes the scenic route to avoid accounting. My guts twist. She's literally going out of her way to avoid me but she's got nothing to worry about. Nothing Red Brick-related, that is…

I want her to know that.

I bolt out of my chair and follow her to the elevator. She walks quickly with her head is down, clearly not in the mood to talk to anybody but she's going to talk to me.

Nora boards the empty elevator and I pick up my pace to catch up before the doors close and I lose my one chance at a private moment to clear the air.

I slide a hand between the doors, blocking them from closing and they pop back open again.

Nora raises her head, looks at me, and her breathing stops.

I step on, turning to stand beside her and tapping the button to close the doors. She shifts slightly to the left, putting a foot of space between us and I try not to take it personally.

The doors close and the elevator begins its slow trek down to the ground floor. That gives me about twenty seconds to say what I need to say but that's not nearly enough time.

I reach out, hit the stop button, and the elevator crawls to a halt.

"Ms. Payne," I say, turning to face her. "Relax."

She blinks, her wide eyes staring at me with a mix of nervous fear and shame. "What?"

"Relax," I say again. "It's all right. Your secret is safe with me."

"Secret?"

"The Red Brick Road. We saw each other there."

She adjusts her purse strap on her shoulder as her cheeks burn a bright pink. "Look, Clive, I don't think we should talk about this."

"Why not?" I shrug, smiling. "So, we're into BDSM? It's not a big deal."

"I'm not..." Her voice breaks.

"Nora, it's okay. Luckily for us, privacy is the most important rule in the community. It's tighter than *Fight Club* in there. Believe me. No one's ever gonna know unless you want them to. I sure as hell won't say a word."

Her shoulders release a bit of tension. "Okay," she breathes out.

I lean against the wall, trying to shift the space into something more casual to get her talking. "I never saw you there before," I say. "First time?"

"Uh..." She wets her lips. "Yeah, kinda."

"What'd you think?"

A quick laugh twitches her mouth. "A little overwhelming."

I nod. "It can be. Dom or sub?"

She raises her head a little higher. "Is that how you guys shake hands or something?" I laugh. "I swear, I was there for maybe twenty minutes and I heard *so many people* asking that question."

"It narrows the pool a little," I say. "Lots of folks are there to get down to business and go home."

"I could tell." She squints. "Is that why you were there?"

"In a way," I say, being vague.

"Well, Dom or sub?" she asks.

I smile. "Dom. You?"

Nora pauses, her eyes shifting as if we're being watched but it's just us in here. "Sub," she finally answers. "I think."

My brow rises. "You don't say?"

"Is it that surprising?"

"Kind of."

"Well, if it makes you feel any better, it surprises me, too. Honestly, I haven't... you know. Just sort of learning the rules right now."

"Well, it's a good place to learn."

"That's what I hear." Her throat clears. "Anyway, I should get going."

"Bit early, isn't it?"

"I have a... personal matter."

I nod. "All right." I extend my hand to enable the elevator again, but stop. "Can I give you a tip?" I ask her.

"… Okay."

I turn to her again. "Wear a choker or a scarf the next time you go to the club."

She tilts her head. "A choker? You mean, like a necklace?"

"Yeah."

"Why?"

I lean closer. "Because it signifies that you already belong to someone," I explain. "Trust me, it'll deter some of the more *intense* patrons."

She nods. "Oh. Okay. Thanks. That's... a good idea."

"Like this..." I pull my white handkerchief from my breast pocket, quickly unfolding it as she watches with interest. I grab two opposite corners and roll it into a long line. "May I?" I gesture to her neck.

She doesn't say no but she doesn't do anything to make me stop either. I take a short step behind her and lay the handkerchief around her neck, tying it off at the back. Her throat clenches with nerves and her pulse pounds in her artery, thumping the skin up and down.

"There," I say. "No one will touch you. Unless you want them to, that is."

Nora looks at herself in the reflective wall. "That's a good tip," she says.

"I see a lot of beginners get scared off too quickly," I say. "Don't want that to happen to you."

Her eyes flick over at me. "Why not?" she asks.

"Because you seem like you'd be a lot of fun."

She lets her face fall to the floor, possibly concealing

some embarrassment. It's a side of Ms. Nora Payne I never thought I'd see — let alone exist at all. Nervous and delightfully timid.

I like it.

I look down her cheek, following a line to her neck and along her sharp collarbone. All the way down to her professionally-hidden cleavage. I catch something sticking out of her purse from the corner of my eye — a small, black hard-drive with the initials *LBB* scrawled in permanent ink on a worn, white label.

Nora shifts on her toes and straightens up. "Well..." She extends her arm and slaps the button with the flesh of her fingertips. The elevator starts again, softly bouncing an inch before continuing its decent downward. "I'll have to remember that."

She reaches behind her neck to undo the knot but I lay a soft hand on her elbow.

"Don't," I say. "You can keep it."

"No, I shouldn't—"

"It looks good on you."

Her fingers curl away from it as her eyes twitch in hesitation, but she slowly lowers her arms again.

"Thank you," she says.

We both look forward at the elevator doors. Just another few seconds and we'll hit the ground floor.

"Hey, Clive."

"Yes, Ms. Payne?"

"What kind of guy carries around a handkerchief anymore?"

I smile as the doors slide open. "The kind who likes to keep his hands clean," I answer. "After you."

She turns her head to look at me one last time with

puffy, pink cheeks before stepping off. When I don't move, she pauses outside the elevator.

"Are you getting off?" she asks.

I smirk. "Not yet but I will."

Her eyes widen but the doors close again before she can say a word.

I let out a quick laugh and hit the button to head back up to the fifteenth floor. Sure, blatantly hitting on my boss probably wasn't the brightest move but hell — she looks way too damn cute with that collar on.

Nora Payne is a submissive. Who fucking knew?

I lean into the corner and grip the rail on either side of me as the car rides back up.

Not just any sub either. A newbie sub. One who can easily be bent and shaped. One who isn't totally aware of her limits yet. The kind who's open to *experimentation.*

My favorite kind.

I bite my cheek. Bad idea. Very bad ideas.

Have I forgotten what I'm really here for?

The elevator stops and the doors slide open, revealing that illuminated, neon logo on the wall.

Little Black Book.

It takes another hour for the rest of the staff to clear out. Desk lamps flick off one-by-one until it's just the receptionist left. She has to stay and answer phones until the last possible moment. Poor girl.

"Have a good night, Clive," she says as she passes by my desk.

"Goodnight," I say, forgetting her name.

I wait until ten seconds after I hear the elevator doors shut again. Total silence fills the floor, practically screaming in my ears.

Finally, I stand up and walk across the room to Nora's office to jimmy the door open again.

Hopefully, this *personal matter* keeps Nora at home for the rest of the night. I just need ten uninterrupted minutes here. The janitorial staff usually starts emptying trash bins at six. I should have just enough time.

I sit down at her desk and wiggle the mouse to wake up the computer. She definitely charged out of here in a hurry if she left all of this on. Either that personal matter is serious or she was really, really eager to get out of here and away from me. I won't take it personally.

I take a breath before diving in. Client files. That's all I need to swipe and I'll be out of here...

I double click the database software, hoping the security there is as lax as the building. It pops open and I smile at the stupidity of it, to be honest.

Millions of users access Little Black Book every day and I'm about to get the names, addresses, and credit card numbers of each and every one of them.

I blink. It's empty.

I refresh the database, giving it a quick close and open again. Must be a glitch. It has to be a glitch.

Again, it's empty.

There's no way this is accurate. Unless...

I close it down and run an administrator search for the database's application files. There should be a log in there that will tell me the last time the client list was accessed. That will point me in the right direction.

I open it and scroll down to the most recent auto-entry.

Today at 3:45 PM.

Last accessed by *NPayne*.

Full copy and... deletion?

From the looks of it, this same entry occurs once every day. Monday to Friday.

I sit back with wide eyes.

That harddrive in her bag. *LBB.*

She walked right out the door with it. Apparently, she does it every freaking night.

I knock my knuckles against the desk in frustration. "Fuck," I whisper.

I stand beneath the shower head for far longer than I should. My skin tingles and my fingertips are starting to prune but it's not like I get to experience a hot shower every day.

"Yo, Clive! You in here?"

I think to ignore him. I can just claim I didn't hear him when he inevitably shows up at my locker in ten minutes.

"Clive!"

I take a deep breath and hold it for three more seconds of toasty water before reaching out and turning the knobs off.

"Yeah," I answer, my voice echoing through the showers.

Shoes tap in my direction across the locker room. I grab my towel off the rack nearby and wrap it around my waist before Alex pokes his head in here.

Alex pauses in the entryway, fully-clothed in his gray jumpsuit. "Hey," he says. "Why didn't you answer?"

"Because I'm naked... in the shower," I say, passing around him toward my locker.

"Fair enough. I caught the end of your run before. You've really got your speed back up."

"Yeah," I mutter.

He takes wide strides to keep up with me. He's either about to keep complimenting me or he's going to spit out the words I've been dreading all day ever since I left Nora's office.

"So, did you get it yet?" he asks, fulfilling the prophecy.

I pop open my locker and look around, focusing for any prying ears but the room is mostly empty. Late evenings are usually pretty dead at the gym but I don't mind. I don't get as many funny looks that way.

I reach inside for my deodorant. "No," I answer him. "I can't get it."

Alex blinks. "What do you mean, you can't get it?"

"I mean," I give my armpits a quick swipe and push the cap back on, "I got on her computer today and it wasn't there. She takes it with her. There's nothing I can do."

"Takes it with her *where?*"

"I don't know. Home, I guess." I fish inside my gym back for a pair of underwear. "I can't get it outside of work hours and I haven't the slightest idea how I'm supposed to access *the CEO's computer* while the place is crawling with employees, so… I can't get it. Sorry."

Alex grits his teeth. "Figure it out, man."

"Figure it out?" I repeat.

"Yeah, figure it out."

"I can't just *figure it out,* Alex. This shit is officially out of my league and I'm not risking my job over this."

"Clive…" He flexes his jaw. "Do I need to remind you how much money that list is worth to us?"

"No—"

"*Two million dollars,*" he says anyway, his voice echoing through the lockers. "Half for me. Half for you. I have a buyer lined up and he's willing to *pay cash,* Clive. *Cash."* His eyes fall on my leg. "I told you I'd make it up to you and you agreed one million bucks more than makes up for what happened."

My foot twitches. "I know I did, but—"

"So, *risk the fucking job,* man." He points the name badge on his jumpsuit. "I'm not cleaning gym toilets for the rest of my life here."

I step into my jeans and grab my boots. "And what exactly is this buyer of yours planning to do with the list once he gets it?" I ask.

He throws up his hands. "I don't know nor do I care. It's not my problem that a bunch of lonely losers plugged their information into an app in the hopes of getting laid. And it's not your problem, either, so get your shit together and find out how to get that list so we can both get paid."

"Alex, I'm desperate for that money as much as you do but this isn't about me getting my shit together," I say. "This is about Nora Payne taking—"

Her work home with her.

I can't get the client list during work hours, not without the very real possibility of getting caught, so I'll have to get it *after…*

And I already know where she likes to hang out after work.

"Taking what?" Alex asks impatiently.

I grab a black shirt from my bag and throw it on. The reflective bands on the arms flip up so I smooth them down again before stuffing my bag inside and slamming the locker.

"Give me a few more days," I tell him as I grab my jacket. "I have to get to work."

"Clive—"

I ignore him as I walk out of the locker room, listening to the hum of my own thoughts as a plan forms in my head.

Ms. Nora Payne is learning the rules.

She needs an experienced Dom to teach her how to be a good submissive. Someone she'll be willing to put her complete trust in.

She'll find one.

SEVEN

NORA

I stare at myself in the rearview mirror. This entire night has been taken one step at a time. First, I was at home and all I needed to do was focus on getting dressed. Then, it was doing my hair and throwing on some make-up. Small, easy tasks I do every single day of my life. No big deal. Nothing to worry about...

Then, it was getting in the car and driving through town to The Red Brick Road — or more specifically, the parking garage down the street, where I've been sitting and staring at myself for the last ten — make that fifteen — minutes.

This is what I want, I keep telling myself.

So, why was it so difficult to walk in there?

Clive, obviously.

He could be in there now, a familiar face among a sea of strangers. And a handsome one at that.

But the thing is... I'm not sure if I want to run into him tonight. Or if I *don't* want to.

Well, I won't do either if I keep my ass in this car, so I should make a choice now.

Anytime now.

You seem like you'd be a lot of fun.

He said that to me. He said he wanted me to keep coming to the club.

I don't want to get scared off. I want to have some fun. For once in… well, forever, it feels like.

Okay, how about this? Just open the door.

That's easy. You do that every single day. Just lay your hand on the doorknob and push the car door open.

There. I did it.

Now, step out.

There we go…

Now, close the door…

I take it slowly, quickly tapping my key fob to lock it down behind me.

I pause and reach into my jacket pocket, feeling for the soft, white material of Clive's handkerchief stuffed inside. I pinch the corners and roll it up like he did to make it easy to wrap around my neck.

"Agh—"

I cough and loosen it.

Christ, I'm so nervous, I nearly choked myself.

Why does that turn me on?

I take a deep breath and lean over to get one last good look at myself in my car window before marching toward the parking garage stairwell.

It's a clear night in Chicago. A little warm, but that just might be my body heat spiking upward with each step I take down the street.

That flashing red sign comes into view and I bite my cheek. Excitement builds in my chest. My palms break into a sweat.

Relax, he told me. *Your secret is safe with me.*

Judy greets me at the counter as I walk inside again. She flashes a wide grin, recognizing my face.

"So…" She leans forward, presenting her sizable cleavage over the rim of her corset — this one a deep scarlet red. "Have we changed our mind about the annual membership yet?"

I snap open my clutch to find my debit card. "Not quite," I say, setting it down.

Her mouth pinches in disappointment but she snatches the card off the counter. "Well, next time we'll get ya! I have a good feeling about you."

I laugh, feeling a bit more at ease than the first night but my heart isn't pounding any slower.

"We'll see," I say.

I lay my right palm on the counter and she stamps me again before firing off one more wink at me.

"Enjoy your stay," she says, reaching over and unlocking the door.

A rising laughter greets me as I step inside. It stops me cold in my tracks but my heart resumes its drumline as I quickly realize that their chuckles have nothing to do with me. This isn't a high school gymnasium, after all.

I look across the main floor, spotting a face I recognize at the center of attention. And by face, I mean mask. Roger, I believe. He must be telling some story because he's has two entire couches of women enthralled. Lucky guy.

I'm mildly curious to know what story he's telling but there's a deep urge in me and it tugs me toward the stairwell.

I only saw a little bit a few nights ago.

I want to see more.

A man passes me on the stairs. For a moment, he looks like he's about to say something to me but then his eyes fall to my neck. His head instantly snaps forward and he continues on without saying a word.

I touch the handkerchief around my throat and feel a hidden smile brush my lips.

A familiar grunt touches my ears as I reach the top. A bolt of excitement chills me as I gravitate toward it. It's the same couple from that first night, only this time he's tied her to a St. Andrew's cross.

Heat ignites on my skin the moment I see the pink lashes on her bare back.

The crowd breaks apart as I move closer. The Dom slides her restraints free and her left arm drops to her side, almost completely limp. He wraps his arms around her, holding her up as he releases her other hand. Sweat tumbles from her brow, staining her cheeks. I pause. Maybe they're tears.

He whispers in her ear, bringing that same loving smile to her lips. She stands up on her own and rests against him with her head on his chest.

I stay off to the side, watching as they slowly walk away from the cross toward the stairwell. They retreat up to the third floor.

I swallow hard.

Another couple takes their place on the cross. I think to stay and watch them but my feet carry me through the areas. I feel like a kid in a theme park, rushing from one attraction to the next, living and breathing the adrenaline rush. Floggers and belts. Leashes and chains.

My heart pounds for it.

"Ms. Payne."

My stomach lurches. Panic takes me for a second but as I

spin around and look up, I see Clive Snow staring down at me.

"Hey," I say, holding my breath.

He bites his cheek. "I have watched you wander around this place for almost thirty minutes," he says.

"You've *watched* me?" I repeat.

"You go from room-to-room but you don't talk to anybody, you don't play, you just... *watch*. Are you a voyeur?"

I squint. "No, are you?"

He grips the edge of his jacket and pushes it aside, revealing the club's emblem on his shirt and the bold letters beneath it that read *SECURITY*.

"It's my job," he says.

"Wait." I laugh. "You *work* here?"

"Didn't I mention that?"

"Uh, *no*," I say. "You didn't."

"Oh. Well, I work here."

"How many jobs do you have?"

"Three," he answers.

"Wow."

"Yeah, we can't all be CEOs." He smiles and glances at my neck. "I'm glad to see that's coming in handy."

"Well, it was working like a charm until about fifteen seconds ago," I quip.

"Do you want me to piss off?" he asks with amused eyes.

"No. The familiar face is nice... even nicer now that I know you're literally the muscle around here."

"Well, good."

I glance behind me, drawn to the sudden sound of a flogger and a woman's grunt-like moan somewhere else on the floor but I can't see through the crowd. "So, this seems like a fun gig," I say.

"It certainly can be," he says, shaking his head at the next area over. "Mostly just a lot of staring and cleaning. And keeping a close eye on singles, such as yourself..."

"Why, are we *dangerous?*"

"No, just vulnerable."

"I thought this was supposed to be a safe place."

"It is." He nods. "Doesn't mean I don't worry."

"Do you worry about me?" I ask.

"Honestly, yes." He clears his throat. "You took off out of here like a bat out of hell last time. I hoped you made it home all right."

"I did. Obviously."

"Obviously," he repeats.

Again, I'm drawn to that woman's deep groan. There's a pleasure in it, one that entices and scares me all at once. I've never felt anything like that before.

The crowd shifts and for a brief second, I catch a glimpse of her face. Red and glistening with sweat. With pain and ecstasy, both at once.

"Pick one."

I twitch back to Clive. "Excuse me?"

His eyes scan over my head to the corners of the room. "Pick one," he says again.

"Pick one... *what?*"

He doesn't answer. He just stares at me with one edge of his smirk curling up.

My jaw drops. "You mean..." I point back. "The equipment? In the rooms? With the benches and the spanking?"

"Yes," he says.

"For... you and me?"

"Yes."

"No."

"Ms. Payne, how do you expect to learn if you *never* crack open a book?"

"I'm your boss," I stutter. "That wouldn't be appropriate."

"Not in here, you're not." He leans down. *"Pick one."*

I hold my breath, locked in place under his intense, yet friendly, eyes.

I make a quick gesture at the unoccupied St. Andrew's cross in the far corner. Clive looks over and smiles. I can't be sure if he's excited and amused. Maybe both.

Clive grabs my hand. "Come on," he says.

He clings to me with hard, strong fingers and leads me across the floor. My chest twinges with slight pain as my heart pounds harder with each step we take toward the cross.

Clive looks back at me. His lips move but the words and sounds I hear don't match up.

"What?" I ask, a bit too loudly.

He turns around. "What are your limits?" he repeats.

Right. Limits. Hard, soft. I try and recall the kinky shit Melanie told me but I can't even hear my thoughts over my pulse pounding blood in my ears.

"Everything," I joke.

Clive smirks and spins me around to face the cross. He guides my arms up and rests my open palms on it.

"Don't move," he says in my ear. "Keep your eyes forward. You look at nothing but the wall. Understand?"

I chuckle. "What?"

He tightens his grip on my wrists. *"Understand?"*

His voice travels down my spine. I swallow hard and look forward. "Yes," I say. "I understand."

Clive takes a step back, his hands dropping from mine. I almost look as he walks away but I stop myself. I'm not supposed to look away from the wall.

I stare straight ahead through the two wooden arms of the St. Andrews cross at the red brick wall behind it. Dozens of eyes stare at me, making the hairs on my neck stand straight up. I fight the urge to turn and look for myself. I fight the embarrassment bleeding out of my skin. I fight all of it in order to do as I'm told and—

Christ. This guy is one of my employees.

What the hell am I doing?

I drop my hands to my sides and turn around to leave.

"Where are you going?"

I gasp as I run right into Clive. His feet are planted on the floor and his arms are crossed over his chest.

How long was he standing there? How long was he watching me... waiting to see if I'd break?

I glance over his wide shoulders at the observers. "I don't know if I can do this," I say.

"Don't look at them," he says, calmly. "Look at me."

"Clive—"

"Look at me."

I force my eyes upward to connect with his.

"These people will not judge you," he says. "No one thinks less of you for being inexperienced. They're not here to make you think less of yourself... and neither am I." He slides a single finger along the edge of my cheek. "You can leave if you choose to, Ms. Payne, but if you want to learn, I'm here to teach. You can trust me."

My teeth chatter in my mouth, rocked by adrenaline, and I say the first thing that pops into my head.

"I want to stay."

Clive nods. "Then, turn around… and place your palms back on the cross."

I turn, slowly breathing as I do as he says. I raise my arms and put them back where they were before.

"May I touch you?" he asks behind me.

I nod, my neck jerking back. "Yes."

"I'm going to remove your jacket, is that okay?"

I bite my lip. "Yes."

"You can lower your hands," he says as he slides his fingers over my shoulders, "but put them right back as soon as your jacket is off."

I tremble as his hands glide down my arms, slowly drawing my jacket down to my wrists. I obey his words, instantly putting my hands back on the cross when I'm able to. My fingers touch the metal fasteners hanging down, meant for ropes and locks and other things, I imagine.

"I won't restrain you," he says, noticing everything. "Not this time."

"This time?" I ask, my lips twitching.

He doesn't answer or acknowledge the question. Instead, he lays a flogger down on the cross in front of me. "I'm going to use this on you," he says. "It's made for beginners. You can touch it."

I take my right hand and run my fingers through the long strings. They're thick and made of suede. Light, fluffy… nothing to be scared of.

"It won't hurt unless I want it to," he says, taking it from me. "But your body might react as if it does, at first."

Another giggle shakes my chest. "You gonna give me a safe word?"

"If you want one."

"I do."

"Okay." He dangles the flogger along my back, tickling me with a dozen tapping strings. "If I go too far, say *wait*. If you want to stop, say *stop*."

"Simple." I chuckle. *"And if I want more?"*

"Say my name."

I flinch, not expecting his mouth to be so close to my ear. He steps back and I take a sharp inhale to calm my racing pulse.

"Keep your hands up," he says a few feet behind me. "Don't move out of place and don't forget to breathe."

"People forget to—?" The flogger hits my back and I accidentally bite down. *"Ouch."*

"I barely tapped you," he says.

"I bit my tongue!"

He sighs. "Relax and stay quiet."

I force my lips together, stifling my laugh. He hits me again, this time just a little bit harder. It really is just barely a tap. More like a tickle than a—

It hits again, this one more forceful and quick. I exhale hard, tensing up as he gives me another hit. He's right. It doesn't hurt but my body isn't used to this. It keeps flinching and flexing, preparing for a pain that's not— *ouch!*

Okay.

That one actually hurt.

My mouth sags and I gasp loudly as a bolt of pain fires down my left side. It fades quickly, sending heat throughout my core and I relish in the sensation.

"You felt that." I hear Clive behind me, just mere inches from my neck. "Do you know why?"

I look back in confusion, prompting him to raise the flogger again. I spin forward in time for it to snap along my back. It hurts — but not as much as before.

"Did I say you could turn around?" he asks.

"No," I answer.

"Then, *don't turn around.*"

I fix my neck, holding still.

"Do you know why you felt that?" he asks me again.

I nod. "Because you wanted me to," I answer, recalling his words from before.

"Good girl." He taps me, light and fluffy, and it almost makes me smile. *"Bad girl."*

He swipes me harder, making my knees lurch and I yelp in response.

"Understand?" he growls.

My voice shakes. "Yes," I say.

"Say, *I understand, Mr. Snow.*"

A laugh rattles my ribs and I feel like a different person. His voice, his words. I can't remember the last time someone else told me to do something — and I *had* to obey. It feels so new and unnatural, but completely free at the same time. I let go of everything — work and stress. I'll let go of life itself if it means pleasing him.

"I understand," I say, "Mr. Snow."

Clive leaves several pleasant raps along my upper back. I close my eyes, lulled into a sense of security — even if it might be a false one. It's an odd feeling. One of trust and encouragement but I still find myself bracing for anything.

He whips me harder. *"Hands."*

I cringe, realizing far too late that my palms have slid down the cross. *"Shit—"* I murmur.

"What was that?" He leans over, his warm breath grazing my ear. "Did you just curse?"

I bite down, unsure whether or not I should speak. He hits me again and again, three times in rapid succession and my eyes sting with the threat of tears.

Dammit. What did he tell me?

Say *wait* if he goes too far.

Say *stop* to make him stop.

No, there was something else.

"Nora?"

Several bright bursts of light invade my vision and my knees give out beneath me.

Breathe.

He told me to breathe.

A strong arm wraps around my waist before I even touch the floor. Clive yanks me back up, hoisting me into the air and cradling me in both arms.

"Nora?"

His voice sounds faint and distant even though I can feel his lips moving on my cheek.

"Stop," I murmur.

My eyes focus on his chiseled face as his smile stretches to one side.

"Way ahead of you," he says with a laugh. "Are you okay?"

I glance around, squinting beneath the bright purple light. A larger crowd has gathered around to watch and I cringe in embarrassment. "Uh-huh…"

Clive looks up and nods at another man in a black shirt

nearby. The man immediately starts waving people away, insisting that they give us our space.

"Come on," Clive says, still carrying me. He walks us over to a bench against the nearest wall and he sits down beneath the dim, gray lights, keeping me close. "I didn't think Ms. Nora Payne would have such a low tolerance."

"I don't," I say, my cheeks burning. "I just… forgot to breathe."

"Ah, that explains it."

"Sorry."

"Don't be sorry," he says. "It's all part of the learning process. I'm just happy I caught you in time."

I look down, suddenly very aware of his hands on my body. He keeps one clenched beneath my knees with the other wrapped around my back, his fingers dangerously close to my breast.

And my hands — *Oh, god.* I'm touching his chest. It's thick and flexed like some kind of… sports… person…

Athlete! That's the word.

My mind starts to clear up and I look around the quiet corner of the room. We're all by ourselves over here. Everyone else found something more interesting to watch, I guess. Or that's just the kind of respect people treat you with around here. Either way, I'm happy they moved on.

I clear my throat. "Well, I can't say I've been cradled like this in… twenty-five years, or so," I joke.

"Didn't want you to hit your head," he says. He looks at the seat. "And I didn't want to lay you down because I'm not sure when this bench was last cleaned, so…"

"Right. Smart." I swallow hard, getting lost in those bright, blue eyes. How did I never notice before that they were blue? "I think I'm good now."

"You sure?"

I nod. "Yeah."

I slide off his lap onto the bench and he lets me go. My body instantly wants his hands back. I almost feel unhinged without them. Like a ship with no anchor.

"Bathroom?" I ask.

Clive points toward the stairs. "First floor. Left of the entrance."

"Thank you."

I stand up, fighting the instant dizzy rush that plagues my head. He stands up with me but he doesn't follow. I squeeze through the lump of people standing between me and the stairs. The only eyes I feel on me are his and the feeling stays in my skin even after I reach the bottom and throw open the ladies' room door.

I duck into the farthest stall and lock it behind me. I remain standing, planting my back against the door and staring at the walls painted to look like red bricks.

What the hell just happened to me?

I've never passed out before. Ever. I've never even had an anxiety attack or a panic attack or any other of those things you see women go through in romantic comedies. I've never tripped and fallen in public. Things like that just don't happen to me.

Until now, that is.

Strangely, though, the thing I'm more upset about is how much I'm not upset by all of this.

I don't give a shit about passing out in front of strangers. I don't care that I got flogged in front of them either.

No, the only thing I feel is a deep throbbing between my thighs begging me for more.

"Clive," I whisper, involuntarily.

His voice in my ear. His hands on my body. The way he forced my hands up and placed them exactly where he wanted them. He didn't even restrain me. I didn't need to be. I wanted to go where he told me to go. I wanted him to do whatever he wanted to do to me.

Oh, Christ.

I flick the button on my pants, loosening it enough to slide my hand inside. With closed eyes, I touch myself. I rub the edge of my sensitive clit, teasing it to life and it doesn't take long before I'm actively holding back moans.

The bathroom door opens and closes. I don't stop. I ignore the sounds of running water and ripping paper towels. My mind replaces those with my own gasps and the flogger's snap and Clive's deep growl...

I come hard, harder than I have in weeks. My entire body tingles from head-to-toe. My knees nearly give out but I keep my free hand on the bar along the edge of the stall to keep myself up.

"Fuck," I whisper, moaning through my teeth. I instantly regret saying it. I could be punished again for cursing.

I smile. "Fuck."

I lay my head back, purposefully slamming it against the door. Something about this feels so wrong — masturbating in a public restroom aside.

I'm his boss.

He's my employee.

This could end badly.

But only if I let it begin.

EIGHT

CLIVE

Well, that's never happened to me before.

I've seen sub drop before but they've never literally *dropped* to the ground in front of me. At least I know my reflexes are still good.

My chest is still pounding. Seeing her — Nora Payne herself — facing a St. Andrew's cross. Her hands raised above her head. They weren't even tied. She kept them there, willingly obeying me. She *wanted* to submit to me.

She felt amazing in my arms. Her little body is tighter than I thought it'd be. Soft, pale skin beneath her clothes just waiting to be turned pink.

The bathroom door opens and some redhead walks out. I grit my teeth, honestly starting to get a little worried. Three other women have gone in and come back out since Nora rushed in there. Maybe I should grab Judy and ask her to go check on her.

Finally, the door swings open and I push off the wall. Nora stops the second she sees me standing by and her eyes drop to her shoes.

"Are you all right?" I ask.

"Yeah," she says. "I just needed a minute."

Her eyes refuse to lock on mine. She's obviously not all right. Not yet.

"Hey—" I touch her shoulder, giving it a comforting squeeze. "Don't worry. Trust me, these people have seen far worse."

Her smile presses on, feigned as it may be. "Oh, no. I'm cool. I'm *fine*. Really."

I hold out her jacket. "You forgot this up there…"

"Oh!" She takes it from me. "Thank you very much."

We take a step back to keep from blocking the bathroom door. Nora nudges against me by accident and I catch the subtle scent of her perfume. It struck me earlier by the St. Andrew's cross and my nose has been begging for another hit of it ever since.

Nora backs off, quickly moving to a more open area to get out of the way. I follow her, still not entirely convinced that she's okay.

"So, what's next?" I ask. "Was there another scene you were curious about?"

"Scene?" she asks, furrowing her brow.

I grin. "You really are a beginner."

"Yeah."

"Well, a scene is basically a—"

"Actually, Clive," she interrupts, "I think I'm just gonna take off."

A protective surge stuns my gut. "You sure?"

"Yeah. Things just got a little too real on me for a Wednesday night, ya know?" She chuckles and awkwardly pushes her hair behind her ear. "I should go and try to get some sleep."

"Right." I check my watch. Still a bit of time left on my break. "Where are you parked?" I ask.

"In the garage down the block," she answers, throwing up a hand. "But you don't have to—"

"I'll walk you to your car," I say over her.

"Clive, I'm *fine*."

"Come on."

I'm not taking no for an answer here. Hell, part of me wants to drive her home myself. She passed out under *my* hand. I pushed her too hard and I don't want her out of my sight again for the rest of the night.

I lead her to the exit, pausing to give Judy a quick heads up on my way out. She takes one look at Nora and gives me a subtle wink. *No worries*, it means. *Thanks for looking out for the newbies.*

I hold the door open and Nora follows me outside. She instantly throws her jacket back on and wraps her arms around her chest to block out the late autumn chill. The weather doesn't hurt me much but I've got fifty pounds on her, at least. It's admirable, honestly; How a woman so tiny managed to become such a big deal.

I let her point the way and we set out toward the parking garage a few blocks east.

After a minute of silence, Nora clears her throat. "So, how long have you worked there?" she asks.

I count back. "Six months. Give or take."

"Do you like it? I mean, it's gotta be better than plugging numbers for me all day."

I chuckle. "Well, when you put it that way…"

She smiles. "I won't take it personally."

"It's *different*," I answer. "More stressful, in a way. I usually don't have to worry about Ali in accounting passing out mid-spanking." Nora's face screws up and I cringe. "Too soon?"

"Little bit…" She laughs.

"Sorry."

"It's all right. I'm sure I'll wake up one day and find it hilarious." Her face relaxes. "Has anything like that ever happened before?"

I nod. "Yes."

"Are you lying to make me feel better?"

"No."

"Pinky promise?"

I chuckle. "I swear. Things like that aren't uncommon. It can get intense in there."

Nora looks at me and nods, seemingly satisfied with the response.

We reach the parking garage a bit too quickly. I need more alone time with her if I'm ever going to figure out where she stashes her client list. And I honestly wouldn't mind a few minutes alone with her in other ways as well…

My fingers tingle with the memory of her body in my lap. Her chest softly rising and falling. Blood rushing to my groin and me silently praying she can't feel the bulge against her hip.

"Just over here," she says, pointing across the lot.

I spot the scarlet red sedan in the corner, parked behind a giant, black truck. Once again, I'm instantly happy with my decision to walk her back to her car. It's not the safest neighborhood and a dark corner like this is ample opportunity for someone to try and mug her. Or worse.

But also…

I glance around. There are only a few other cars parked in this area and with that truck blocking most angles…

Nora turns to face me next to the driver's side door. "Thanks for walking me back," she says, popping open her little purse to find her car keys.

"No problem," I say. "I'm happy to do it."

She pulls the handle, opening the door an inch. "I'll see you tomorrow—"

I rest my hand on the door, blocking it. "Wait."

She pauses, her eyes slowly rising to look at me. There's a flush of color on her face, like a jolt of electricity she can't deny.

I lick my lips and shift just a little closer, forcing her head to tilt up as I stand over her. "Kiss me," I say.

She blinks. "What?"

"You heard me."

"No." Her head shakes back and forth. "No, I can't do that."

"Why not?"

"Because…" She scoffs. "I shouldn't have come back here anyway. I'm your boss."

"Only from nine-to-five," I argue. "And it's the 21st century. No one cares about that kind of crap anymore."

"*I* care about that kind of crap anymore," she says. "I don't mix business and… whatever the hell that was back there."

"Did it feel good?"

She tries to open the door but I pin it closed.

"Did it feel good?" I ask again, inches away from her ear.

Her breath skips. "Yes," she says.

"Which part?" I ask, digging deeper. "The pinch of the flogger against you… or that it pleased me?"

Nora closes her eyes. "I don't know…" she whispers.

I lay a hand under her chin and guide her up to look at

me. "I can make you feel like that again, Nora. You just have to submit to me."

She shivers.

"That's what you came out here for, isn't it?" I ask. "To find someone who will make you forget who you are for just a little while. Someone who can dominate you… and fuck you the way you were always meant to be fucked." She doesn't say a word. "Nora, I'll back off if that's what you really want. You can start coming to the club again and find some other guy who *might* know a thing or two." I caress her cheek. "Or you can stick with me, someone familiar but not *too familiar*, who can give you what you need."

"And what do I need?" she asks.

"You know what." I take a deep breath of her scent and it fires all the way down to my knees. "Let me give it to you."

She's breaking. I can feel it. I just have to push her a little bit further…

"*Say yes*," I urge as I glide my hand down over her breasts. "Say yes and I'll show you what I can do right now."

Her head rolls back, exposing her neck as she rests it against the car roof. My cock twitches in my jeans at the sight of that white handkerchief fastened to her throat.

My white handkerchief.

I reach her pants and I pop the button free as tires skid around the corner from us. Her breath catches in her throat and her hesitant eyes open wider with every inch I slide her zipper down but she doesn't stop me. The car continues on, disappearing up the echoing tower.

I kiss her, firmly enveloping her lips. It feels like a firecracker exploding against my face. Can't say that's ever happened before. I want to feel it again.

I kiss her a second time and her lips move to kiss me back.

She tilts slightly away from me. "We shouldn't…" she says, her vocal elongated by desire.

"You know what to say," I whisper. *"Wait. Stop. Or…"*

I slide my finger along the tip of her clit, making her gasp as she clenches my biceps. She's so sensitive. I can feel the wetness up to my knuckles already. I want to touch her and taste her and hear her say my name.

"Wait. Stop." I repeat it, prompting more from her. *"Or…"*

Nora reacts to the pressure I give her, her mouth sagging and her tongue just barely passing her lips. *"Clive,"* she finally says.

I part my lips to massage my tongue with hers. She fully kisses me back this time. A light moan vibrates the back of her throat, heating the blood in my veins. Her head falls again and I attack her neck, nibbling and sucking along the upper rim of the handkerchief.

"Outside the office…" I whisper, "you're to call me *Mr. Snow.*"

She nods, unable to speak.

"You're going to open yourself to me now."

She moans in my ear, my hips gently bucking against my fingers still pressed along her clit, using my hand for her own undeniable pleasures.

"I'm going to eat you out until you come on my face," I say.

She shivers in response and touches her lips to mine

with a deep, longing kiss. I feel it all the way down in my groin as my cock throbs with need.

"And then..." I lay my free hand on the back of her neck, curling my fingers around her dirt-blonde hair. I pull it back, making her look at me. "You're going to suck my cock. You're going to make me come with that pretty, little mouth. Do you understand?"

A wave of pleasure strikes her and I watch as it rolls over her eyes. "Yes, Mr. Snow," she says. "I understand."

I release her hair. "Backseat. Now."

NINE

CLIVE

Nora moves immediately, turning away to open the car door. I lay a hand on her shoulder to guide her inside and take one last glance around the parking garage before following her.

The seat is clean and barely used from the looks of it. It's also wide enough to comfortably seat three grown men. I feel a twinge of envy over it but it doesn't last. A beige garment bag hangs from a bar above the door beside her and my lips twitch with inspiration.

"Take your pants off," I tell her.

Nora bobs off the seat to push them down her ass.

"*Slowly,*" I add as I reach for my belt.

She does as she's told, inching them down to rest by her ankles.

"Lay on your back."

I pull my belt free but I keep it in hand. Nora shifts on the seat, pointing her feet at me as she eases down to rest her head by the opposite door.

"Give me your hands."

She hesitates, her eyes bouncing from me to the belt.

"Do you trust me, Ms. Payne?" I ask.

She twitches slightly, giving it a moment's thought before raising both of her hands.

I take hold of them, performing a simple knot to bind them together at the wrist. She sits forward, letting me pull them up over her head. I chuck the beige garment back to the floor and fasten her wrists to the bar.

Nora stares up at me, quivering with need and nervous fear and everything in-between.

I settle on the seat with my hands on her thighs. "How does that feel?" I ask her.

She exhales a shaking breath. "Good."

"Do you like it?"

Her smile spreads, even if she doesn't know it. "Yes," she answers.

I hook my fingers into her panties. "Then, you're gonna love this," I say, sliding them to her ankles.

I move down the seat, positioning my face between her thighs. Her essence touches my nose and my mouth instantly waters for her. It takes all my self-control not to bury my face in her right now. I focus on her skin instead, brushing my lips along her inner thighs and teasing the sensitivity there.

Nora reacts as expected with labored breaths and quiet moans just for me. "Mr. Snow..." she says, requesting more.

I reach up her body to grasp her neck. "Shh," I say. "You'll come when I want you to."

She squirms, raising her hips, and I tighten my grip to calm her.

"You want it that badly?" I ask. "Say it."

"I want it," she repeats.

"Beg me for it, then."

"Please, Mr. Snow," she says, speaking through the opening beneath her restrained hands. "I need it."

I kiss her mound, taking a deep breath of her. "You need *what?*" I ask. "Be specific… and I'll give you what you want."

Nora bites her lip. "I need you to eat my pussy," she says.

"Yes?"

"Fuck me with your tongue," she adds. "Make me come for you."

I reward her with a quick lap, just barely touching her clit. A moan falls free and her hips buck beneath me, wanting oh-so-much more. "You're a very dirty girl, aren't you, Ms. Payne?" I ask.

"Yes," she answers.

"You're going to come the second I touch this clit again, aren't you?"

She nods. "Yes."

I kiss her inner thigh, coming close to her slit but just barely. Her moisture covers the outer lips, enticing me enough to take just a little taste of her.

"Mmm," I groan. I lick her again, coating the tip of my tongue. "You are so," I steal one more taste, *"delicious."*

"Mr…" she begs, her voice falling fast.

I plunge my tongue between, separating her folds to find her dripping, wet entrance waiting for me. Her flavor takes me over, bewitching every thought I have. I start fucking her pussy with my tongue, reaching in as far as I can but it's not nearly as deep as I want to be.

Her knees twitch around my shoulders. She struggles to lie still, so I shift both hands to cup her breasts. They're perky but not small. Just large enough for me to get a good handful of her. I feel her nipples poking my palms and I adjust my touch to pinch them through the fabric of her blouse, bringing sharp winces to her face.

I keep fucking her sweet pussy. I can't stop fucking it. Every quick stroke brings more pleasure to her eyes and it's my mission to see her explode. Her body pulses and throbs, just begging me to let it all end. I massage her tits and lap at her until the windows fog over and she can barely speak English.

"Beg me," I growl.

Nora's lips tremble. "Please," she squeaks. "Let me come."

I seal my lips around her clit and Nora screams. I watch her climax for me, experiencing the most beautiful side of her. I slide my tongue inside once more to feel her inner muscles squeeze it right back out again. Her orgasm is swift but painfully pleasant. I want to make her do it again.

"Mr. Snow," she groans, her voice ruined with desire.

"Yes," I say, lapping her up. "Good girl."

I rise up, staying between her widespread legs. She relaxes a bit but I won't let her rest for too long. I reach up to slide the belt free of the bar, leaving her wrists bound together.

Her hands fall to her stomach, weak and shaking. I touch her wrists, sliding a finger between her skin and the belt to make sure it didn't get too tight for her.

"Take three breaths," I tell her. "Then, sit up on your knees."

Nora nods and closes her eyes while I inspect her wrists a little closer. I find a few red markings but nothing that will stand out to anyone not looking for them. She dug her nails into the belt and left behind tiny notches in the old leather. I smile, not mourning the future reminders of this scene one bit.

"Do these hurt?" I ask, running a finger along her pink wrists.

Her eyes flutter open and she exhales. "No," she answers, taking in her second breath.

I release her hands, giving her control to rest them again. She stares at the ceiling above her and I admire the new flush in her cheeks and the glow on her skin. She needs this. She needs this *badly*.

"Nora," I say, drawing her gaze. "What brought you out here? To Red Brick."

She sits up slowly and leans on the door behind her. "A friend," she says. "She told me it would help relieve my stress."

I smile. "Is it working?"

A giggle falls from her lips as she breathes in again. "I'll tell you tomorrow," she says.

"That's three," I count. I raise a hand and prompt her forward with a finger twitch. "Come here."

She shifts onto her knees like I told her to before. I sit down on the seat, motioning her over me and she moves into position above my groin. I'm tented already, eager and hard with anticipation and by the look in her eyes, so is she. She reaches for my zipper with bound hands without a word from me and I shift closer to give her a better angle. I push off the seat, letting her pull my pants down to my knees, but I stop her from taking them down any farther than that.

Nora stares at my cock and her eyes widen. It's not the first time I've seen that reaction cross a woman's face but it sure never gets old either. I lay a hand on the back of her head and comb through her bright hair. She wets her pink lips, preparing them to be stretched.

"Take your time," I tell her, caressing her neck. "I want you to enjoy it."

Her eyes flicker with desire and a little mischief. I may have underestimated how much fun Ms. Nora Payne can be.

She bends down, moving past my shaft to kiss near the base instead. I smile at each deep peck she leaves with her plump, wet lips and I rest back on the headrest.

Her tongue swipes my balls, forcing a soft laugh out of me, before she moves her tongue halfway up my cock. That warm breath and her wet touch make me clench. She's toying with me the same way I toyed with her. I might explode the second I enter her fucking mouth.

"Good girl," I tell her, grunting for more.

She moans, softly vibrating my glans, and I dig my nails into her scalp. Fuck, she feels so good. If her mouth feels this fucking good, I can only imagine what her tight cunt will do to me.

Her tongue touches my tip and I groan. Warmth throbs throughout my loins and my balls rise for release. I hold it all back, wanting so much more from her. I want to feel the back of her fucking throat. I want her to come while she's sucking me off.

I move my hand down her back and rest it on her ass. She doesn't seem to mind, as another moan slides from her lips as I squeeze her little cheeks.

"Keep going," I say. "Don't stop, no matter what I do. Understand?"

Nora makes eye contact and I look at her with the same mischievous glint she gave me. Her mouth opens and she lowers down to take my whole tip in her mouth. I flex my jaw, rocked with a pleasure I want to share with her.

I slide a finger inside her slick pussy. Her back tenses and her suction on me increases as she reacts.

"Keep going," I remind her.

She grips the base of my shaft between her palms, holding it steady as she bobs her head. I sync my movements to hers, thrusting my finger in at the same speed she moves on me.

"Good girl..."

I give her a second finger and she moans again, vibrating her cheeks.

"That's right..." I chuckle.

I press in, massaging her inner walls until I feel the spot that makes her moan even louder. She takes me deeper into her mouth, practically ravenous for it. My hips buck out of uncontrollable instinct but I hold back the urge to fuck her little face. I take it out on her pussy instead, twitching my fingers inside of her until she clenches with need.

I pull them out, keeping her on the edge. "Keep going," I warn as her mouth slips off my dick.

She takes a breath and obeys me, still just as hungry for it as before. Any second now, I'll coat the back of her throat.

"Where do you want it?" I ask her.

I'm giving her an option. I know where I want to finish but she's been a very good girl so far tonight. I'll let her choose.

Nora doesn't answer with words. She takes me in deeper, pushing my tip as far into the back of her throat as she can.

My lips twitch. That's where I wanted it, too.

I slide my fingers back into her perfect pussy. She picks

up her pace, pumping my dick over and over again to make me fuck her just as fast.

I tense up, feeling release take over as her cunt tightens around my knuckles. I come with a groan, filling her vibrating throat as she comes on my hand. She slows down but continues bobbing on me until I'm done, catching every drop of cum along her tongue.

Holy shit.

She's perfect.

Nora rises, gently pushing off my thighs with her bound wrists, and collapses onto the seat beside me. Her throat bounces as she swallows and she licks her lips.

Fucking perfection.

She silently wipes her cheek, breathing hard. She doesn't look at me. Her face rests straight ahead but I can see that same glow on her cheeks.

I reach over to unwrap my belt from her wrists. "Will you make it home okay?" I ask.

Nora laughs, her head rolling over as she looks in my direction. "I'm sure I will," she says. "Will you make it back to the club okay?"

"I'm sure I will," I say. "As soon as I remember how to walk."

We both laugh a little harder as we bend to find our pants. I zip mine up as she raises her toned legs to slide back into hers. I reach over to massage the back of her neck just behind her jaw, instantly feeling the muscles of her face and throat relax.

"Come back tomorrow night," I urge.

She presses her lips together. "Maybe."

"Do it."

"Is that an order, Mr. Snow?" she asks with a smirk dancing at the edge of her mouth.

"Would it make a difference if I said yes?"

"No."

I smile. "I want this, Ms. Payne. I think you do, too."

"What exactly is *this?*" she asks.

"You want to learn, right?" I raise a brow. "Become my sub and I'll teach you everything I know."

She breathes a laugh. "This is so strange."

"What about it is strange to you?"

Her fingertips swipe along her raw lips. "I barely know you," she says. "But you want me to trust you."

"I do."

"How?"

"Come back tomorrow night and we'll talk about it," I say, adding a smile. "I think you'll want to."

"Why?" she asks.

"Look yourself in the eye in the mirror tomorrow morning and you'll know why."

Nora pauses, thinking to herself as she studies my face. "Okay," she finally says. "I'll think about it."

I lean over, gently pulling her closer to me. I plant a soft kiss on her forehead and brush the blonde strands away from her eyes. Again, she looks at me with subtle confusion but excitement overwhelms it.

I push open the door and step out, doing a quick scan for others before turning back and extending my hand to her. Nora takes it and slides out, slightly wavering on her tired legs but she stands upright.

"Drive safe, Ms. Payne," I say.

"You, too."

I think to leave but I stand still, not ready to go yet. She doesn't move either. Her eyes fall to my lips, whether she means them to or not, and I can't resist just one more taste of them.

We kiss again, leaning our bodies against each other. She feels so good, digging her claws into me; mentally and physically. I don't want to let her go.

But I wouldn't say I'm compromised.

I pull back, breaking our kiss. "Goodnight," I whisper.

Nora's lips twitch. "Goodnight."

Slow and steady, I tell myself.

I'll get the client list. Alex doesn't have to worry about that.

But I'm going to have a little fun first.

TEN

NORA

*L*ook yourself in the eye in the mirror tomorrow morning and you'll know why.

The girl stares back at me and for a second... I don't recognize her.

She's thirty with blonde hair. That adds up, I suppose. Brown eyes, a little button nose, and a chicken pock scar on her chin. It's me. Definitely *me*, but...

I lean over the sink and wipe a bit more condensation off the bathroom mirror. My towel loosens around my chest, so I give it a quick adjustment to keep it from slipping off. My hair is damp but I haven't managed to gather enough morning energy to dry it just yet. Maybe after a few sips of coffee.

I stick out my tongue and crinkle my nose and furrow my brow but I still can't put my finger on it.

I look myself in the eye, just like Clive told me to do.

Something's changed.

I slept like a damn baby. I usually wrestle with my pillow

for several hours before drifting off but last night... I closed my eyes the second I hit the sheets and I don't remember opening them again until I woke up mere seconds ahead of my alarm. I felt refreshed and so deeply satisfied.

He's the first thing I thought of. His voice in my head was the first thing I heard. Memories of his lips and his tongue and — *oh, boy* — his dick. Definitely his dick.

I reach for my toothbrush and pause as I spot the light, red markings on my wrist. It felt so good and safe and he was so *dominating* — but not too much. I never once felt out of my element or in any danger.

I want to try it again.

"Goddamn," I say with a sigh, still staring at myself.

Who the hell is this girl?

Well, whoever she is...

I like her.

When people ask me what I do for a living, I'm never quite sure what to say.

The job title is Chief Executive Officer but my day-to-day is different than other CEOs I've met. A lot of them act as overseers. They did the work, built their empire, then hired people to run it for them while they make the occasional office appearance between trips to the golf course. Nothing wrong with that, per se, but I've spent most of my adult life with my little, black book and I'm not nearly ready enough to pass the golden pen off to other hands just yet.

I'm more of a racket-ball kind of girl, anyway...

I'm not the traditional boss. I wouldn't call myself a

matchmaker, either, as most of that has been fine-tuned by algorithms at this point. You say "app developer" and ninety-percent zone out immediately, so...

I guess I'm just Nora Payne, the girl with the Little Black Book.

Today, I have to finalize the holiday logos with my marketing department, setup a call with the local food drive director, and get through this meeting with my creative team but—

"Nora, are you all right?"

Fuck it. I can't do shit today.

I'm stuck in a Clive-filled trance. Part of me is still tied up in my backseat with my legs spread eagle and his face buried in my—

"Ms. Payne?"

"Yes, I'm here." I clear my throat and force my head up to look at Percy and Rachel sitting in front of my desk.

Rachel tilts her head. "Rough night last night?"

"No," I answer. "Well— *maybe*. But I'm fine. I'm here, I'm fine, and we're talking... about..." I pause, my mind suddenly very blank.

"The customer survey," Percy says.

I pick up my reading glasses and look at the tablet in front of me. "Right. Yes. Go on, please."

"We saw a growing trend in the number of users who want *additional* options for narrowing down prospective partners," he says.

"What kind of options?" I ask.

"They're interested in more *personal* methods of compatibility," he says slowly, his cheeks blushing slightly. "Sexual kinks, specifically."

I pique with interest. "Sexual kinks?"

"A significant percentage of users requested the ability to list kinks and fetishes right there on their profiles as a means of quickly finding a suitable match for their... lifestyles."

Dom or sub?

My lips twitch. "Yeah, I can see how that'd be a time-saver."

"*But...*" Rachel raises her pen. "We sent out a follow-up survey and the *same* percentage of users *like* the sleek simplicity of the app as it is and think sexual additions would be wildly unnecessary."

"But it doesn't have to be a dramatic change," Percy argues. "We can design profile badges to signify certain *things* they like to do."

She chuckles. "Okay, you clearly don't know much about sexual fetishism if you think one little profile badge is going to signify every possible kink someone could be into."

"And," I say, "some users might not be comfortable with the idea of listing them publicly. Black Book is more than just a hook-up app."

Percy turns up his hands. "Okay. Scrap the badges. We could open a new tab on the profile. People can take or leave it."

"Profiles are pretty stretched space-wise already," Rachel says.

I bite my cheek. "How significant is this percentage?"

"Uh..." He swipes his tablet screen. "Forty-three percent," he reads.

"That's high," I note.

"And of our user base, only thirty percent filled out the survey."

I nod. "Which means there's potentially half of our users that want this change."

"And half who *don't,*" Rachel says. "Can't forget about them."

"What if…" I squint in thought. "What if we create and launch a sister app? Leave Black Book as it is while giving that significant kinky percentage what they want from a proven resource they can trust."

They look at each other, both in silent thought.

"That…" Percy nods, "might work."

"Not a bad idea," Rachel agrees.

I follow the trip of sparks in my head. "We'll grandfather in the current user base at a heavy discount to get it up and running, partner with local fetish and kink clubs to promote and reach new users, then go from there. If we start this *now,* I can see us entering a beta by New Year's."

Rachel smiles. "I do, too."

"Then, let's do it," I say. "Ping the design team, have them put one or two people on the new app. Make it just as sleek but with more color. I'm thinking *pink.* You two start surveying the forty-three percent; find out what kind of specific options they're looking for."

Rachel rises from her chair but Percy raises his hand.

"Okay, but…"

"What?" I ask him.

"Do you…" He hesitates. "Excuse me, but you created Little Black Book based on a relationship compatibility algorithm from personal experience. Do you have enough experience in…" His hands twitch. "You know, *this stuff* to create an algo based on sexual fetishism compatibility?"

Rachel's face turns a deep red but she looks just as interested in knowing the answer as he does.

I throw on a smile. "Maybe purple. Have the design team try a purple option, too. Royal; not lavender."

Percy looks down. "Okay, then. We'll get started."

He spins around and bolts from the office. Rachel offers me a nod before following behind him with her lips clamped together between flushed, pink cheeks.

Do I have personal experience in sexual fetishism compatibility?

Nope. I do not.

But there's sure to be an expert out there somewhere I can hire to fill in the gaps.

"Ms. Payne?"

I look up over the rims of my reading glasses to find Clive standing in my doorway. He holds up a few sheets of stapled papers but my eyes barely even give a shit. They travel downward instantly, admiring his tight, tucked dress shirt and black pants — a rather different look than the t-shirt and jeans he wears to work at the club.

Maybe we should do casual Fridays…

"Ms. Payne?" he asks again.

"Uh, Y-yep! Mr. Sss… *Clive.*" I lean back in my chair, trying to act normal. "What's up, my temp?"

I close my eyes, rolling them up in shame.

"Ali needs a signature," he says, flicking the papers.

"Right." I reach for my cup of pens but I knock it over instead. My coordination has apparently taken the morning off. "Ah, hell…"

Clive strides in, his face twisting with hidden amusement. He bends down to pick up a pen off the floor and holds it out to me. "Nora…" he says, his voice low.

"Uh-huh?"

"Relax," he says. "We're just working here."

He lays the papers down in front of me, along with the pen on top.

"Just workin'," I repeat, letting my muscle memory take care of the signature. "Ali, right?"

He nods.

"Can you tell her to update me on her vacation dates? I know she was still waiting to hear back from her mother-in-law…"

"I'd be happy to, Ms. Payne," he says, taking the papers back.

I clear my throat. "Thanks, Clive."

"I had fun last night."

My lips twitch. "Just working, huh?" I ask, keeping my voice down.

"Couldn't help it." He smiles, matching my volume. "Had to say it."

"Yeah." My cheeks light up. "It was fun for me, too."

"Was I right?"

I tilt my head. "About what?"

His eyes fall to my chest and right back up again. "The mirror."

I feel a deep urge awaken beneath me. I shift slightly in my chair, attempting to smother it. "Uh…" I exhale a quiet chuckle. "You weren't *wrong.*"

I try not to make eye contact just in case the sheer force of it lights my panties on fire but the temptation is far too great.

Fuck it.

I let my gaze slowly climb upward, trekking past his groin and abs.

"Have you considered my offer?" he asks me.

I tap my pen against a stack of post-its to distract from the deep throbbing between my thighs. I could do it right now. I could tell him to drop to his knees, crawl under my desk, and make me come right here.

"I have…" I say slowly.

He waits for an answer, tilting his head.

"And…" I bite my lip. "I'm leaning toward a… yes."

"Leaning?" he asks.

"*Leaning,*" I repeat.

"Anything I can say to tip you over?"

I chuckle through the flashes of fantasy in my head. Me yanking on his hair with his head between my thighs. The swift flick of his tongue inside of me. Coming so hard on his face, I scream his name.

"Oh, I'm sure a quick gust of wind at the right time could do that just fine," I say.

He smirks. "Is eight tonight the right time?"

"It could be."

"Eight o'clock," he says, taking a step back. "Wear something comfortable."

"Comfortable?" I ask. "You mean *sexy* comfortable, like a little skirt? Or *home* comfortable, like my yoga pants with that weird stain I can't explain?"

He laughs. "Just say you'll be there by eight."

"Eight." I nod. "I can do eight."

"All right, then." He reaches the door and pauses, turning back. "The first option, by the way."

I wink. "Yeah, I figured. Oh, Clive—"

He stops again and I brace myself before he says my name that way again.

"Yes, Ms. Payne?" he asks, tingling my bones.

"Could you… close the door behind you, please?"

"Yes, ma'am," he says with a slight growl only I can hear.

The door latches and I let myself crumble to pieces.

"Oh, I'm a bad boss." I fall forward, pounding my head on the desk repeatedly. *"A very, very bad boss."*

ELEVEN

CLIVE

I close her office door, trying hard to suppress the smile begging to rise on my face. The last thing I need is someone getting suspicious and reporting us to human resources. Nothing to see here, folks. Just a low-level employee dropping off some paperwork to the boss' office. That erection he has is just business as usual...

She couldn't be more adorable today. Blushing and beautiful Nora Payne. It's a new side of her; one she rarely lets out but I don't blame her one bit. A woman like that would be walked all over if she showed signs of weakness at the wrong moment in the business world. Busting balls is how she survives.

So, that fact that she blushes for me is not insignificant.

But this deal isn't sealed yet. I just have my foot in the door.

I lay the newly-signed forms on Ali's desk as I pass it on the way toward my own. She's not there, so I pause to jot down a quick note to her, remembering Nora's request about her vacation days.

My desk phone starts ringing as I sit down and I clear my throat before picking it up.

"Accounting," I answer.

"Hey, Clive. What's up?"

I gaze around for eavesdroppers. "I told you not to call me here," I tell him.

He scoffs. "And I wouldn't need to if you had a cell phone like everyone else, man."

"What do you want, Alex?"

"An update would be nice," he says. "You ran off yesterday with a light bulb burning up your ass. Figured you might have some good news this morning."

I give the room another cautionary glance, sensing movement a few desks over. My eyes flick toward Nora's office. "Not yet," I say. "I told you I need a few days."

"For what?"

I drop my head. "If I can't get it here, then I have to get it *there.*"

"Where's there? Her house?"

"Yes."

"How are you gonna do that?"

I sigh. "Okay, genius. How exactly would *you* secure an invite to an attractive, single woman's private residence?"

He pauses for several seconds. Then, I hear a quick inhale. *"Ohhh—"*

"Fucking moron," I mutter with rolling eyes.

"Taking one for the team." He laughs. "I like it."

"Other way around, actually," I say. "It might take some convincing, hence the few days. So, don't call me here again. I'll call you."

"Tick-tock, buddy. Our buyers aren't exactly patient."

Nora steps out of her office carrying an empty coffee

mug, something I've seen dozens of times before but I can't pry my attention away from it this time. She rushes off toward the break room for a refill. Her hips swish in the most perfect way as she walks with her head high and back straight. Strong and confident Nora Payne.

I want to ruin her.

I want to see her with bruises on her nipples and rug-burn on her knees.

I want to watch her plead for release while I have my way with her.

"You still there, man?"

I swallow. "Yeah. I'll call you soon."

I hang up the phone, happy to focus my attention on Nora again. She leaves the break room with a fresh cup of steaming coffee. That dick from creative has intercepted her. He waves his tablet in her face, making her pick and choose between holiday logo designs but Nora obviously just wants to sit down and enjoy that coffee for five fucking minutes.

Then, for a brief second, she looks at me instead.

Her eyes draw to me, locking with mine. I feel a deep, stabbing pang in my chest but it doesn't hurt. It just tickles, like a silent secret between friends.

She doesn't linger for very long. She shifts forward again and she continues on back to her office out of my eye-line.

Eight o'clock.

That time yesterday, I had her in my arms. Limp and breathless Nora Payne.

That time tonight, I'll have her begging for it. Eager and submissive Nora Payne...

I like the sound of that.

TWELVE

NORA

"Hey there, newbie!"

I run into Roger the second I walk through the entrance of The Red Brick Road. He stares down at me, still obscured from head-to-toe in that black latex, but I find the concept a little less menacing the more I see him.

"Hey, Roger." I pause. "Can I ask you a question?"

He shrugs his wide shoulders. "Sure."

"How do you breathe in that thing?" I ask.

He leans down. "I don't." I raise a concerned brow and he laughs. "Well, not *well,* anyway. But that's part of the fun."

I squint. "You're one kinky dude, Roger."

"Yeah, look who's talking, newbie." He raises a finger and flicks the white handkerchief around my neck. "One day here and you're already owned. So, who's the lucky Dom?" His head rises. "Oh, I see."

"Keep moving, Roger."

I flinch at the deep voice behind me. I turn to find Clive

lingering over my shoulder with his arms crossed over his chest. Shadows fall beneath his brow, obscuring his eyes so only the slightest blue shines through at me and Roger.

Roger laughs and raises his hands in surrender. "My sincerest apologies, Mr. Snow," he says with amusement. "I didn't realize she was *yours.*"

"She's not," Clive says. "She's just not your type."

Roger's head turns down to look at me again. "Yeah, you're probably right."

I frown at the rejection. "Why not?"

Clive takes my arm. "You don't want to know."

"No, he's right," Roger says. "I would wreck you and your tight, little—"

"Roger."

His gloved arms rise again. "I'm going. I'm going." He salutes me. "See you around, newbie."

I blink with confusion as Roger disappears into the small crowd near the couches. *"My tight, little what?"* I ask Clive.

His lips twitch. "Honestly... it could go either way."

I wince. *"Yeesh."*

He extends his hand to me. "Shall we?"

I take it without hesitation and his strong fingers lock around mine. It feels safe, but several hairs on the back of my neck stand up as he leads me to the stairs. I make eye contact with a few as we ascend, some of which look from me to Clive and back again, flashing me a quick nod of approval. Thanks, I guess.

We reach the top and I grow a little more nervous with the number of people up here. My heart pounds as I recreate that embarrassing moment from the other night in my head. Is Clive taking me to a cross again? I'm not sure I'm ready for that just yet. I wouldn't be surprised if I never am again.

Clive and I continue, only we don't head toward one of the unoccupied crosses or punishment benches...

He's leading me to the third floor.

Anything goes, Melanie said. *If this floor's a-rockin'...*

I must have slowed down because Clive looks back at me over his shoulder. His grip never ceases on my hand and he draws me forward, holding me close as he guides me up.

We reach the landing and I stop. I haven't been up here before. It's dark, nearly pitch black save the hot pink fluorescent bulbs above each door, except for the one on the far right. It's also silent. Dead silent, unlike the constantly moving world downstairs.

Goosebumps curl up my spine, holding me in place.

"There," Clive says. He points to the room with no light and I start walking that way, dragging my feet a little as he gives my hand a light tug.

I stop at the door and Clive pushes it open, casually stepping to the side to let me in first. When I don't move, he releases my hand and walks in alone.

I could leave now. He's giving me that choice but I feel a presence in my gut, a nervous sway I haven't felt since I was a teenager. It's pushing me to go in and embrace a new experience.

I step forward, driven by an urge I can't say no to.

"Close the door."

I do as he says, taking one task at a time. Closing a door. That's easy.

"Lock it."

Yes! I can do that, too...

I turn the lock and the pink light above the door flickers on. I guess that means occupied.

I take a look around. It's a small space. One room with a

kitchenette and an attached bathroom. A closet in the corner. A few armchairs sit around but the main furniture is the large table set up in the center of the room.

"Was this an apartment?" I ask.

"Once upon a time," he says. "This whole place was an apartment building before. You couldn't tell?"

I picture the layout downstairs and nod. "It's very obvious now," I say, chuckling.

"All the walls were knocked out on the ground floor," he explains. "The second floor kept the rooms but no doors. And these..."

"Rented by the hour," I recall.

"I figured you'd want somewhere more private after what happened downstairs before," he says, his eyes soft on me.

"That's..." I nod, "a safe assumption. Thank you."

"Safe, sane, and consensual. That's the law around here."

"Good law."

He extends his hand. "Jacket?"

"Thank you." I push my jacket back over my shoulders, letting it fall to my hands. When I look up again, I catch him checking out my short, red dress but he looks away quickly. "You said a nice skirt, but..."

"It's perfect," he says, taking my jacket toward the closet in the corner.

Clive slides his own jacket off and my gaze locks on his arms. His shirt sits tightly around his large biceps. I recall the feel of his strong, toned chest beneath my fingers. He held me up in the air as if I weighed nothing at all.

I swallow hard.

He opens the closet in the corner and reaches in for a hanger. My eyes widen at the array of leashes, floggers, and chains hanging on the back of the door. He abandons his jacket inside but keeps the door wide-open, almost as if to tempt me.

"Clive, what are we doing here?" I ask.

He doesn't answer. Not right away.

"Whatever you want," he finally says, passively shrugging.

"Isn't that my line?" I quip.

"There's a lot of misconceptions about this lifestyle," he says. "One is that the Dom is always in control. They make the rules. They force their sub to do what *they* want. That's not true."

My brow furrows. "It's not?"

"The sub makes the rules," he says. "The sub puts boundaries on what their Dom can or can't do. One word from their mouth ends it in an instant. In that way, the sub is actually the one in control the whole time."

I flinch in disappointment. *Control.* Isn't that the one thing I wanted to give up for an hour? The main reason why I'm so damn stressed out all the time?

"Oh," I mutter.

"*But…*" he steps forward and tilts his head, "you have to trust that your Dom will follow your directives. Once you're restrained, you have to entrust yourself to them. Your pleasure, your pain, *your life* will be in their hands. Do you think you can do that?"

I lean back. Something about that just stops me cold. But in a really good way.

"Might take some time," I say.

"As it should. Who do you trust the most in the whole world?"

"My friends."

He nods. "And how long have you known them?"

"Ten years, at least."

"Now compare that to Clive the bubbling temp who fucks up your paperwork," he jokes.

I laugh. "I see what you mean."

"Trust is earned. It's *consensual*. No one trusts by demand. You ever do that thing where you fall backward and another person catches you?"

I look down. "Quite recently, actually."

He smiles and gestures around. "Then, you and I are already on our way. That's what this whole place is. Just one big trust fall. The more you do it, the stronger the bond. Is this making sense?"

"I think so..." I bite my cheek. "So, what did Roger mean before?"

"Oh, you'll have to be more specific," he jokes. "That guy says some weird shit."

I laugh. "I mean, he said I was *owned*. What does that mean?"

He gestures to the handkerchief. "That's what this is supposed to be," he says. "When you're *owned* that means you have a Dom... and they don't like to share."

I run a finger around the lip of the cloth. "So, you own me?" I ask.

He shakes his head. "It's just a hanky. I gave you that to help you feel more comfortable around here and keep guys like Roger from getting too handsy. Not to possess you. But..." He looks me in the eye, bewitching me with those soft, blue eyes. "Down the line. Who knows? We're just learning the basics here."

I take a breath. "Right."

"I want to try an experiment," he says, his lips curling. "Something that should *ease you in* without being too overwhelming."

"So, *not* strapping me to a St. Andrew's cross and flogging me in front of strangers until I pass out, then?"

Clive shakes his head. "No. It's just the two of us up here."

"And it's supposed to make me trust you?"

He smiles. "I hope so."

I inhale slowly, forcing my breath to fill my lungs to the top. "All right," I say, letting it back out. "Let's experiment."

His eyes fall from my face to my breasts, quickly bouncing away as he turns toward the closet. "Lay your palms on the table," he says.

Clive moves toward the open closet as a quick shiver rides up my back. I look at the table in the center of the room, suddenly noticing the gold metal rings hanging down from the corners, and wonder what I signed up for. He said it himself, though. One word from me and it all ends.

Assuming I can trust him.

I step forward and place my palms down on the cold surface.

Clive slides a black riding crop from its place on the closet door. "Don't move your hands," he says, walking back over and standing at on opposite side to face me. He curls his hand around the crop's handle with a tight, white-knuckle grip. "If you move your hands, you will be punished. Sound easy enough?"

"Punished?" I ask.

"Punished," he simply says.

I shift slightly into a more comfortable stance. "Okay—"

He slaps the back of my left hand with the crop, sending fire up my wrist.

I wince. "Ow!"

"I said don't move your hands."

"I didn't move my hands."

"You lifted the end of your pinky."

I laugh. "Oh, come on—"

He hits me again, this time on the right wrist. "You twitched your thumb," he says.

"Not on purpose!" I gasp.

"Control yourself, Ms. Payne."

I take a breath, my eyes bouncing from him to my hands and back to that damn crop. His own eyes move constantly, staring hard at my hands with sharp precision to make sure I obey.

Punished. Makes perfect sense now.

After a minute, he takes a step to the left and begins rounding the table, each step creaking the old floor beneath him. I isolate my focus into my hands to keep them still, even as I crane my neck to watch him move.

"Eyes forward," he tells me as he wanders behind my back.

I look ahead, using my sense of hearing to keep a fix on him. The crop's tip eases around me and he gently caresses my arm from the elbow down. I keep still, fighting the ticklish feeling beneath my skin.

"Good girl," he says, slightly growling.

"Thank you, Mr. Snow."

"Hm," he hums, the quickest laugh.

He reverses his path, moving the crop up my arm toward

my armpit. The closer it gets, the more my skin responds and I fight to stop from twitching.

"That's cheating," I say with a chuckle.

"No, *that's* the experiment," he says. He rests his free hand on my right hip. "You try to stay still... and I make that impossible."

THIRTEEN

NORA

The crop grazes my armpit, causing an involuntary spasm in my elbow, and my left hand lurches off the table.

Clive immediately slaps the back of my hand, this time harder than before. I cringe, biting my lip at the sharp, stinging pain. I rest my hand back down but it trembles on the table's surface.

He moves his touch up my waist, slowly crawling around my body to rest just beneath my breasts. Warm pleasure tingles me from the places he touches, completely neutralizing any pain my brain thinks I felt. I can hardly even remember it.

I look at my hands. Steady as rocks.

Clive slides his boot between my feet on the floor and nudges them apart. I put my weight in my hands and shift my legs wider.

"More," he demands.

I take another step out, putting tension on my skirt.

"If I go too far, say *wait*," he says, reminding me. "If you want to stop, say *stop*."

My teeth chatter. "What are you going to do?"

His hand falls from my belly and slips down my leg to hook the hem of my dress.

The riding crop touches my ankle and I flinch, quickly remembering that it's still there. He slides it up my calf to my knee, tapping between them twice as it inches underneath.

"Clive?"

The crop slaps on the table next to my hand. *"Mr. Snow,"* he corrects me.

"What are you going to do, Mr. Snow?" I ask again.

He pinches my chin and draws my head back. "I'm going make you move your hands," he whispers.

"Yeah, but how—"

His lips envelope mine and I drop the question. The heat of his kiss makes my ankles sway and I lose all sense of what I was doing. I kiss him back, reaching upward to touch him on the back of his neck.

He snatches my wrist in mid-air and slams it back down to the table before I even realize my mistake.

I brace myself for the quick sting of his crop. With pinched eyes, I wait, counting the seconds until it's all over with but... it doesn't happen.

I crack one eye open as the crop's tip grazes the back of my guilty hand.

"That's how," Clive whispers in my ear. "I'm going to touch you, Ms. Payne. I'm going to touch every inch of your body just so I can say I have."

I take a gasping breath. "Are you going to..."

The question falls but he figures out the rest of it. "Would you try to stop me if I did?" he asks.

I quiver, feeling his front pressed against my back and the hard bulge digging into my ass.

"I want you to *think*," he says. "Think of all the things that could happen right now, every single possibility. I want you to tell me what you *wouldn't* allow. These are your hard limits."

I furrow my brow. My mind is running a mile a second. I can hardly keep up with my pulse. "Can I have an example?" I ask.

"Can I put a knife to your skin and draw blood?"

"No!" I cringe. "God, no!"

"Well, that's a hard limit. No blood play."

"Obviously." I pause. "Do people really do that?"

"Yes."

I peek back. "Do *you* like to do that?"

He shakes his head and I sigh with relief. "Not my thing," he adds. "Can I smack you? Let's say the face?"

"No, I don't want to stir up questions," I answer. "Nothing on the face."

He lays an open palm on my rear. "How about here?"

I tilt my head as my skin tingles. "That should be okay, I think..."

His hand falls away. "Keep thinking as I touch you. Let your mind wander, find your limits. If you think of something you're unsure about and might want to try, that's a soft limit."

I nod. "All right."

He slaps the back of my hand with the crop. "That was for earlier."

I chuckle, feeling the pleasant pain in my wrist. "I was hoping you forgot..."

"Nope."

"Damn."

He goes quiet and guides my face forward again. I stand firm, planting my palms and fingers against the table, and wait for further instruction.

Clive takes a short step back and I feel his eyes wander from my head to my toes. He taps the crop lightly against the left side of my neck and my mind flashes with possibility. His lips there, kissing me. Biting me. The crop glides up to my ear and travels along my hairline. He takes his other hand and lays it at the base of my neck, fanning out his fingers before combing them along my scalp. He gathers my hair in his fingers, gently pulling until the taut strands hurt.

He waits here, studying me for a reaction.

Say *wait* for too much. *Stop* to stop...

But I want more.

"Mr. Snow," I say.

He gives me a quick, hard tug, yanking my head back.

I yelp in surprise, fighting the urge to twist and bring my hands up. My right wrist slips anyway and I grow tense, hoping he didn't notice.

The crop smacks my fingertips. Guess not.

The pain fades as his lips caress my neck. His wild and warm breath fires up along my ear, sending goosebumps in all directions and I have to practically turn to stone to keep my hands from moving. A moan escapes the back of my throat and I sink a little further into his touch.

The crop moves down my neck and over my shoulder blades, coming to a stop at the back of my dress. Clive pinches the zipper and slowly guides it down. My instincts tell me to stop it before it falls off my breasts — but that's what he wants me to do. He wants me to raise my hands and grab it so he can punish me again.

I ignore the instinct, letting it fall, and I hear that same, amused grunt fall from his lips. He lays the crop down on the table beside me but I don't celebrate just yet. His hands start at my shoulders and move down my bare back. I close my eyes, feeling relaxed as his fingertips massage into me all the way down to the small of my back.

"You're fucking gorgeous," he says.

I smile. I can't hold it in. "Thank you," I say.

"Your skin..." He moves his palms up and down my spine. "It's like silk."

"Uh-huh..." I bite my lip, my nether churning with heat.

"I want to turn it pink."

He pushes the dress and it drops to my ankles.

"Would you like that?" he asks. He kisses the back of my neck, leaning in until I feel that thick bulge press into me again.

I sigh, the heat in me almost too much to control. "Yes," I whisper.

He snatches the crop off the table, making me flinch. "How about a brand?" he asks, tapping my lower back with the crop. "Just burn my initials right here..."

"*No,*" I say.

He chuckles. "As I expected. Have you thought of anything?"

"I can barely think at all," I admit.

"Why not?"

"Uh..." I clear my throat. "I'm standing in front of you practically naked... and you clearly have an erection."

"Does it bother you?"

"No, it's just... distracting."

"I can control my urges, Ms. Payne. Can you?"

"Yes," I say, playing it cool. "I can totally control my—"

His hand pushes between my thighs from behind and I tense up.

"Are you sure about that?" he asks.

I open my mouth but my words fade as his hand slowly inches upward. I lurch and my sweaty palms slip beneath my weight. I quickly straighten back up but I receive a hard rap on the knuckles for it and Clive chuckles softly to himself.

His hand reaches my panties. He lays a single finger along my crotch, lined up perfectly with my pussy lips.

"You're wet," he says.

"Yeah..."

"Were you expecting sex tonight?"

I shake my head. "I didn't know what to expect."

His finger moves back, gliding from my wetness to my ass. "Would you like me to fuck you, Ms. Payne?" he growls in my ear.

I hold my breath, feeling it rattling my lungs. My hands tremble and my toes curl. Blood pounds in my head as saliva builds beneath my tongue.

"Ms. Payne?"

"Yes," I answer.

"Yes, what?"

"Yes, Mr. Snow."

Clive forces me forward, bending me over the table. My hands push forward but I don't receive a whip for it. He lays the crop on the table and reaches for his zipper instead.

I lose myself, closing my eyes and counting the moments until I get what my body needs. I want him so badly, I could scream. I just might have to as soon as I feel him inside of me.

Oh, god. How much I want to scream.

Clive hooks my panties and pulls them down, exposing my ass completely. He guides the tip of his hard cock along my aching wetness, but he doesn't push inside. He remains in control, content on teasing me instead.

"Is this what you want?" he asks.

I nod.

"Say it."

His cock brushes against my anus and I let out a moan. "Yes, I want it."

"You want it like this?" he asks. "You want me to fuck you, use you like some object?"

No. No, I don't. I feel a resistance deep inside. I don't want to be used. I don't want to be thought of like that. I don't want *him* to think of me like that...

"No," I say.

He lays a warm hand on my back. "Good girl."

I feel him take a step back and he stuffs his erection back into his pants.

"Stand up," he tells me.

I push off the table, placing my palms back where they were from the start. "You don't want to fuck me?" I ask.

"I do," he says. "But not like this."

I twist back to look over my shoulder. "What do you mean?"

"Many Doms enjoy the view of their subs that way. Bent over and helpless."

I catch a solemn expression on his face out of the corner of my eye. "And you don't?" I ask.

"I have nothing against it as a rule, I just prefer something a little more... *personal*. When I do it that way, it always feels like I'm taking something from them, but when it's like this—"

He grabs my arm and yanks me around to face him. With one quick movement, he hoists me up to sit on the table and spreads my legs. I forget all about my hands and the rules. I stare into his deep eyes instead, falling head over heels with every word he says.

"Like this," he continues, "I can see every part of you. Your eyes, your breasts, your pussy... I'm not *taking* anything from you. You're *giving* yourself to me."

He cups my cheek and my tongue twitches as his thumb swipes my bottom lip. "Do you want to give yourself to me, Ms. Payne?" he whispers.

My chest heaves up and down. "Yes," I say, my voice shaking.

Clive kisses me. His tongue touches my lips, begging to be let in. I part them and we taste each other. My senses explode as his hands roam my body and I moan from the depths of my gut.

I run my hands up his body but he grasps my wrists and forces me down onto my back. He pins me against the table, his mouth dropping from my neck to my breasts. He digs his teeth into my nipples and I twinge from the heightened sensitivity. Christ, I could come right now, just looking down into his blue eyes as he licks my tits and touches my curves.

He stands up and pulls me closer to the table's edge. I gasp at the feel of his tented erection against my thigh. The tip pokes out of the elastic of his briefs, covering in pre-cum. I want to slide to the floor and lick him clean but I don't dare move from the position he put me in.

He looks down my body, admiring every inch of skin presented in front of him. I realize once again that I'm naked, completely naked, but I don't care at all.

Clive slides his hand into his briefs and he strokes himself. "What are you on?" he asks.

I blink. "What?"

"Birth control," he says.

"Oh — the pill."

"When were you last tested?"

"Uh..." I wince, trying hard to think of anything other than his huge cock pounding me. "Summer? All clear."

"Have you been with anyone since?"

I shake my head. "No."

"Are you sure?"

"Yes."

He lays a hand on my upper thigh, his thumb just an inch away from my throbbing clit. I bite my lip as my body surges with sweet, warm anticipation.

A hard knock strikes twice on the door.

Clive pauses, briefly glancing over his shoulder with a soft smile. "Time's up," he says, stepping back.

"What?" I ask.

He extends his hand for mine and I take it. "Time's up," he says again, pulling me up to sit. "Sorry, Ms. Payne. We'll have to finish this another time."

I blink. "But..."

Clive zips his pants and grabs the riding crop off the table. I watch him walk to the closet and he slides it right back into its place on the door.

"What?" I ask again.

He returns and bends over to grab my dress and panties. "Only paid for an hour."

PRETTY LITTLE THING   121

My jaw drops. "It's been an hour?!"

"Yeah."

"Nuh-uh!"

He laughs and hands me my clothes. "Hop up so I can wipe down the table."

I obey. Reluctantly.

While Clive grabs a towel and cleaner from beneath the sink in the kitchenette, I slide my panties back on. I shudder in disappointment as I step into my dress and guide the zipper up slowly. My arms feel weak and exhausted from the all the flexing and flinching on the table.

Clive cleans up and returns the supplies to their place.

"What do we do now?" I ask.

He grabs his jacket from the closet. "Now... I go back to work."

"Seriously?"

He lays a hand on my shoulder and turns me toward the door. "Sunset to 2 AM with an hour break... which I just took."

I frown with suspicion. "How many of your breaks do you spend up here?"

He smirks. "Not many."

"Wait, you work until two here, come into the office at nine, leave at five... and come right back here?"

"And on weekends, I work at a gym nearby." He slides his jacket on. "What, you never work multiple jobs before?"

I turn my lips down in sympathy. "No," I answer truthfully.

"Count your blessings, Nora," he says, pinching my chin. He leaves a kiss on the corner of my mouth. "Go home. Get some rest. Start thinking more about your limits."

I scoff. "Yeah, like I can sleep after *that*."

"You don't have to sleep," he says. "But you can't stay here."

I raise a brow. "Oh, really?"

He shakes his head. "No."

"Why not?"

"Because I don't want you to play with anyone else."

His voice is hard and strong, just short of an order, but I like it all the same.

"Are you the jealous type, Mr. Snow?" I ask.

"No, just possessive."

"What's the difference?"

"You don't want to know."

Okay, *that* sounded a little scary. I must have turned pure white or something because Clive exhales slowly and relaxes his face.

"I just don't want you to be taken advantage of," he says. "You're new around here. There are plenty of people down there who would try something outside of your comfort zone."

I nod. "All right."

He leans in again to kiss my cheek but I turn toward him at the last second to steal a kiss on the lips. We let it linger much longer than the quick peck it was meant to be, breathing each other in.

Clive breaks away from me. "Come on," he says, striding to the door.

There are a few people quietly chatting in the hall by the stairwell and they give Clive a quick nod as we pass.

My chest tightens. "Wait," I whisper to Clive, "they couldn't *hear us* in there, right?"

He smiles. "No, the whole floor is soundproofed."

I sigh. "Thank god."

FOURTEEN

NORA

We can't keep separating like this.

If I have to rush away and rub one off after every run-in with Clive Snow, then I'm going to become like one of Pavlov's pooches.

Just one glance at him in the office triggers my sex. My pussy salivates for him like a fucking dog and I can't do anything about it because this is work and he's my damn employee.

"Knock-knock, whore."

I turn my head up to find Trix in the doorway to my office. "Hey," I say, smiling and genuinely happy for the distraction. "What's up?"

"Oh, I'm just..." she frowns, *"hiding."*

"From whom?"

"Who," she falsely corrects on purpose. Trix has never been a fan of my uptight grammar rules. "Marcus," she sneers.

"Uh-oh." I laugh.

She raises a paper bag. "Sushi?"

I drop my pen on the desk, officially starting my lunch break. "Oh, that sounds amazing. Gimme!"

Trix walks in and plops into a chair by my desk. She tears the bag from the top down, shredding it to get at the three to-go containers inside. "We have a Philadelphia, a crunchy roll, and tuna sashimi. Go nuts."

My stomach growls. "You are my hero today, Trix."

"I know," she gloats.

I yank apart of a pair of chopsticks. "So, what's up with Marcus?" I ask, pinching a piece of tuna.

She sighs as she peels the lid off a small cup of soy sauce. "I think my dad might have told him to watch over me," she says.

"Why do you think that?"

"Because I found him parked on my street this morning."

I pause mid-chew. "How long was he there?"

"God. All night, maybe? I sure hope not but I can't be sure."

"Has your family received some kind of threat they haven't told you about?" I ask.

She shrugs. "It's possible. Honestly, I think it's more probable that Marcus is just being weird and possessive."

I pause. "Well, that's... something some guys do sometimes."

"I guess."

"Did you ask him?"

"No. I left out the back entrance so he wouldn't see me leave." She chuckles as she dunks her roll into the soy sauce. "He's probably still there right now."

"Naughty," I tease.

"I'll talk to him later. Never needed a personal body-guard before. Don't particularly want one now…"

My desk phone rings and I lay my sticks down. "Hold that thought." I swallow my mouthful of deliciousness before picking up the phone. "Nora Payne," I answer.

"Friend of yours?"

I shift in my chair as warmth rushes between my thighs. "Yes," I answer, playing cool.

"Does she know?"

I lick the flavor off my lips. "Know what?"

"Where you spend your nights now."

I glance over Trix's down-turned head, trying to find Clive, but I can't see him. "No," I say.

"Do any of your friends know?"

"Not yet."

He lets out that soft laugh. "Come to the club again tonight. Eight o'clock. I have something for you."

My body aches with anticipation. "Sounds good," I say. "Let me know how it goes."

"Bye, Ms. Payne."

"Bye."

I drop the phone back onto its cradle, looking up to try and catch Clive again but the angle is nowhere near his desk block.

"Anyway," Trix says with a thick sigh, "what are you wearing to Mel's thing tonight?"

I blink. "Thing? What thing?"

"Her book signing," she says. "We talked about it at brunch this week. And the week before that. And the week before that. I think. Not gonna lie, that one's a bit fuzzy…"

"Shit," I breathe.

"Did you forget?"

"No, I didn't forget. Just slipped my mind, I guess."

"I was thinking we could coordinate something and go as her cheerleaders," she says. "It sounds like this book is getting just as ripped apart in reviews as the last one. She'll need some tender loving care afterward, I bet."

"Absolutely. We'll do whatever she wants." I twinge with sympathy. "Poor thing. Wonder why she's struggling all of a sudden."

"Oh, come on." She tilts her head. "We both know *why*."

I shrug and shove another roll into my mouth.

FIFTEEN

CLIVE

"Hey, Clive. Are you finished with those payroll sheets yet?"

Ali speaks to me over the wall between our desk.

I type a little faster, inputting the last line of numbers to complete the task. "As… a… matter… of fact." I hit save and close it. "I just finished. Syncing with the server now."

Ali hops up to look at me over the wall. "Really?"

I nod. "Yeah."

"Not bad, temp. You're quick. Quicker than Ira, to be honest…"

"Thanks," I say.

She stretches her arms over her head. "All right. Just need to finalize, send to the boss lady, and we're done for the day. Might make it home before my kids for once."

Ali mumbles a little more to herself before scuttling off down the hall toward the restrooms.

Getting out of here early wouldn't be the worst thing in the world, truth be told.

Tonight, I have a sub to seduce.

My desk phone rings. I reach to answer it, quickly clearing my throat. "Accounting," I say.

"Hey, it's me."

I lean back. "What can I do for you, Ms. Payne? Ali just stepped out…"

"Yeah, I know. I've been waiting for her to go pee or something for like three hours."

"Okay…" I chuckle.

Nora sighs. "Look, I hate to do this, but I have to cancel tonight," she says.

I twirl my pen in my fingers. "Something come up?" I ask.

"No, not exactly. More like I made plans with you and almost stood up one of my closest friends by accident. She has a book signing tonight. Been planning it for weeks and I promised I'd be there. I'm sorry."

"It's all right." My gut twists with disappointment. "Book signing? That sounds fun."

"Yeah. They usually are."

"Is she a big deal, or…?"

Nora chuckles. "Actually, kind of. She's Melanie Rose."

I stop twirling my pen. "Melanie Rose?"

"Have you heard of her?"

I sit forward. "Yeah, I've heard of her."

"She's the one who recommended Red Brick to me, actually."

"You don't say?"

"So, I… guess we'll meet up tomorrow?" she asks.

Ali passes behind me and slides into her desk chair.

I shift to a more casual tone. "That works for me, ma'am."

Nora chuckles. "She's back, huh?"

"Yes."

"When she asks, just tell her it's me asking for the payroll reports."

I nod. "Right away, ma'am."

I hang up and Ali's head instantly pops up over the wall.

"Was that boss lady?" she asks.

I turn up my hands. "She wants those payroll reports," I say with a chuckle.

Her eyes roll. "If you're early, you're on-time. If you're on-time, you're late. Am I right, temp?"

"When you're right, you're right."

She falls out of sight again. I listen to the soft tapping of her keyboard behind the wall as I look straight ahead, my guts twisting in disappointment.

The quicker I finish this job, the better.

This time next week, I could be anywhere. I could do anything I want. That's the freedom money buys you. That's the freedom people with money take for granted. No work and all play. This time next week, that could be me. *Finally*.

I just have to get that client list.

To do that, I have to gain Nora's trust.

To gain Nora's trust, I have to earn it. I have to get her to let me in but I have to stay focused. She's not just any new sub, that's for sure.

No matter how much I might want her to be.

I had her in front of me. Naked, wet, and willing. She begged me for it, just how I like it. If our time hadn't have run out, I would have ruined her. There's no doubt about that. I told her I could control my urges but I'm not sure how true that will be once I get a real taste of her.

But even in the world's best-case scenario... I don't have a chance in hell with Nora Payne.

She's a certain type of woman and she expects a certain type of man and I'm not it. She'll figure it out eventually.

My only hope is that I'm long gone by the time she does.

SIXTEEN

NORA

No amount of success lasts forever.

You can be on top of the world at one second and be knocked to the ground the next. Things happen. Trends shift. If you don't adapt and change with the world, the world will leave you behind. It's a principal in all business but it's sad to see it happen with your own eyes, knowing that you can't do anything about it.

Melanie Rose is bright-eyed and smiling right now. Her fans are here. Her adoring readers have rushed out here on a cold, Friday night just for the chance to see her. Melanie lives for nights like this but the lines on her face are a bit stiffer than previous signings at bookstores.

I've seen crowds shut down streets in her name before.

Tonight, however…

We might not be here for very long.

Trix and I sit on either side of her in indigo t-shirts and gray pencil skirts — our coordinated cheerleading outfits to match the book cover's color scheme. Melanie threw on her little, black dress, as usual. And strappy shoes. That's another way I know she's feeling this night on the inside somewhere.

She only wears the strappy shoes when she feels like dirt.

"Oh, my god!" A woman rushes our table. "I'm so excited! I'm your biggest fan!"

Melanie grins at her. "Aww, thank you so much."

"Can you make it out to Jeanie?"

The woman sets her book down — but it's not the new release stacked up on tables all over the bookstore. It's one of her first bestsellers. The one Melanie can't ever seem to outrun no matter how hard she tries.

"Oh, sure," Melanie says, keeping her face.

"I don't think I'll ever find a better book boyfriend than Nathaniel Scott," the woman swoons. "Will there be a sequel?"

Melanie scribbles her name with a short dedication *for Jeanie* on the title page. "I have no plans for one, no. But I have a new release—"

"It's the most anticipated book in my book club!" she shouts. "They told me to tell you that. They said, *you tell that Mel Rose to stop dicking around and write the damn book.*" She cackles loudly.

"Maybe someday." Melanie holds up the book. "Thanks for coming. I appreciate it."

Jeanie snatches it out of Melanie's hand and admires the fresh, new dedication inside. "Oh, thank you! Thank you, thank you!"

She skips off with her book clenched to her chest, passing by stacks upon stacks of Melanie's new book.

Melanie exhales hard as soon as she's out of earshot but she keeps her smile going for the next person in line.

That's another truth in the business world. Sometimes, you can have an idea so great, create something that resonates so much with so many people, that it will be all they'll remember you for. It doesn't matter what you do. You'll never replicate that success again.

I look at Trix and she nods, thinking the same thing. Tender loving care for Melanie, coming right up.

Soon, and quickly, the line dies down. People pass by the table, passively glance over, and keep walking to the coffee shop across the store. Someone will trickle by here and there but they just so happened to be here at the right time while they were shopping. Their lucky night. *I didn't even know this was scheduled…*

Melanie flicks her strappy heel, gently kicking the support bar beneath her folding chair.

A man stops in front of the table holding a large bouquet of red roses wrapped tightly with a pink ribbon.

"Delivery for Ms. Rose," he says.

Melanie's face lights up. "Oh, another one!" She reaches for them and the man hands them off to her. "Thank you, kind sir."

He nods and walks off.

"Another one?" I ask.

She buries her nose in the bright red petals and inhales. "Yeah, I get these every so often," she says. "I haven't told you?"

I shake my head. "No."

"Is there a card?" Trix asks.

Melanie turns them over in her hands. "Here," she says, sliding the small, white envelope from the ribbon. "But it won't have a name. It never does."

I peel the envelope open and yank the card out. *"You look adorable tonight. Love, your SA,"* I read. "SA?"

"Secret admirer," she translates as she smells them again.

Trix leans in to catch a whiff. "How many bouquets have you gotten?"

"Six," Melanie answers. "One a month for the last half year." She fingers the ribbon. "Always a dozen with a one-inch ribbon. A different color each time. The last one was purple. Green before that."

I turn the card over, searching for evidence. "And you have no idea who's sending them?"

"Nope. None. But whoever it is knows my schedule, where I like to have lunch, my home address…"

"Melanie." I stare at her. "Don't you think you should report this? This person is stalking you."

"They couldn't do anything without a name or a face." She sets them down on the table beside her. "And even with that, you can't get a restraining order unless you can prove harmful intent and so far, all I've received is a bunch of roses now and then. Perfectly harmless. Chicago cops would probably just tell me to take it as a compliment anyway."

Trix glances around with wide eyes. "They could be here right now…"

"Most likely."

I nudge her arm. "Maybe it's Robbie."

"Pfft. Please." She rolls her eyes. "That man couldn't find my clitoris without a spotlight, there's no way he's tracking me around like this. No, this guy is smart and cunning. An obsessed fan, perhaps."

Trix chuckles. "That didn't end so well in *Misery,* Mel."

"Hey, if this ends with me getting to lay around in bed

all day while some devoted schmuck brings me food in exchange for smutty love stories, I wouldn't mind. Sign me up. No more bills. No more taxes. If he's moderately attractive and has a stable wi-fi connection..." She holds up her hands in surrender. "No cliffhangers. No cheating. Guaranteed happily ever after."

"What if it's a woman?" I ask.

She smirks. "You know, you'd think that would change my mind but I've done far stranger things for free food." She looks forward and her head instantly falls. "No," she groans. "No. No. No. No—"

I look up at the man approaching the table. Brown hair, cleft chin. Leather jacket and jeans.

Robbie. Speak of the devil.

"Hello, ladies," he says as he approaches. "You're all looking very nice tonight."

"What the fuck are you doing here?" Melanie spits.

He holds up her new book, gray and indigo cover and all. "I came to get my copy signed." He sets it down in front of her. "I *am* your biggest fan, after all."

"Yeah, I doubt that." She eyes the room. "Please tell me this place has a security team..."

"Or, you could just sign the book," he suggests, nudging it a little closer. "Wouldn't want to make a scene over nothing, Mel." He nods at the bouquet. "What's with the roses?"

"They're from a secret admirer," Trix says with suspicious eyes. "You wouldn't happen to know anything about that, would you, Rob?"

"Flowers aren't my style," he says, shaking his head.

"Strange," Melanie says. "I didn't realize drawing a penis on the bathroom mirror telling me to *come and get it, baby* was considered a style."

He winks. "It worked, didn't it?"

Melanie snaps the book open and scribbles on the title page. *"For Robbie,"* she says aloud. *"Thanks for all your support. Your pal, Mel Rose."* She slams it and holds it out to him. "There. You can go now."

Robbie takes it and flicks it open. *"Hey, Robbie,"* he reads, grinning wide. *"Eat a dick and die. Mel Rose.* Aww, that's cute. You drew a frowny face and everything."

Melanie feigns a smile. "Bye-bye!"

"Not so fast." He holds up his phone. "I paid for a selfie, too."

Her smile drops.

Robbie bends back over the table and holds up his phone. "Say cheese, Mel," he says, lining up the photo.

"I hate you," she says as the flash blinds her.

"Perfect." Robbie inspects it. "Now, that's a Christmas card."

"Go. Away."

"Relax. I'm on my way out." Robbie looks to me and Trix again and bows his head. "Ladies."

"Bye, Robbie!" I say with a wave.

"Love you, Robbie!" Trix adds.

"We miss you."

We both blow kisses at him and he returns a wink before disappearing into the nonexistent crowd.

Melanie groans. "I need new friends."

Trix pats Melanie's back.

I turn in my chair. "I'm heading to the ladies'," I say. "Be right back."

I stand up and head toward the restrooms in the far corner. I check over my shoulder, making sure Trix and Melanie aren't looking before hopping between the bookshelves and rushing toward the exit to catch up with Robbie.

I step outside, quickly looking from left to right in search of that familiar leather jacket. I spot him down the block just seconds away from hailing a cab.

"Hey, Rob. Wait up!"

He hears me and stops, instantly throwing his hands up as I catch up to him. "Hey, I was *nice,"* he says, defending himself.

"I know." I cross my arms to shield the cold. "You were. I just wanted to say thank you."

"It's her big night," he says with a shrug. "And from what you've undoubtedly already deduced, it's not as big as she wanted it to be. I can read a room, ya know."

"Not about that."

He pauses, studying me for a second before cracking a smile. "You went back to Judy's," he figures out.

"I did."

"Did you try the cross?" he asks.

"I..." I hesitate. "Yeah, I did. A little. Sort of."

Robbie nods with respect. "Well done, Nora Payne," he says. "You did what I couldn't do."

"Couldn't?" I ask.

"I guess I'm what your people would call a prude."

"You?" I lean closer. *"Prude?"*

He turns up his hands. "Life's complicated enough. I like to keep the bedroom simple. Melanie, on the other hand... she had her moments of panic. Won't get into it now — but I'm happy for you! You look good."

"Thanks." I smile. "I'm feeling pretty good about it."

"That's all that matters." He smirks. "So, what'd she say?"

"Say about what?"

His brow piques, hinting at something dirty.

"Oh." I exhale, remembering. "Yes. You were right. She thinks about you."

Robbie takes a smug breath, filling his lungs to the top. "Yeah, that's the stuff worth living for," he muses.

I tap my foot to spur some extra warmth. "How did you know I'd cave and ask her?"

He laughs. "Because any man who marries one of you marries *all* of you. I had to spend *way* too much time with you three. Now, I'm a perceptive young chap and I picked up on your personalities real quick so I can basically predict within a one-percent margin of error how you'll react to most situations."

I blink. "That's creepy."

"Yeah, that's me." He nods. "But, on the bright side, when shit hit the fan with Melanie, I knew that she'd be okay because she had you guys to take care of her. I never got the chance to tell you before but I appreciate everything you did for her then."

I tilt my head. "That's sweet."

"Yeah, that's me." He smiles. "Take care of her tonight, will ya? She'll need it."

"We will."

"See you around, Bubbles," he adds, raising his bandaged hand to his forehead.

"Bye, Robbie."

He performs a quick salute before he continues on down the sidewalk with his book by his side.

SEVENTEEN

NORA

Tender loving care in our world translates to two things: Calories and alcohol.

Trix supplied the wine by snatching a few imported bottles from her grandmother's pantry while I easily ordered a few pizzas to be delivered to Melanie's apartment the moment we arrived after the signing.

Melanie probably would have preferred to sulk alone but she'll get her chance to do that. Her eyes occasionally slip over to the stack of unsigned books left over from the signing. Trix and I do our best to distract her from that. That's future Melanie's problem.

Tonight is tipsy pizza night and it doesn't take long until the three of us are sprawled out in the living room with a few empty bottles and gnawed-on crusts.

I close the refrigerator door with a fresh bottle in hand, pausing for a second to admire the bunch of ribbons she has hanging from a magnetic clip beside the ice dispenser. There are six ribbons there, the newest pink edition hanging in the front with purple, green, gold, red, and silver following behind.

"Bitch, hurry up!" Trix shouts from the couch. "I'm drying out."

I walk back into the living room and set the bottle down on the coffee table in front of Trix, who promptly snatches it along with the corkscrew.

Melanie has crawled from her spot on the floor to her work desk in the corner again. She sits in the chair and stares at her laptop with a sunken look on her face.

I scold her. "Hey. No, no. No work." I snap my fingers. "Come back here."

"I'm just checking to see if anyone is talking shit about me," she says.

"*No.*" I look at Trix. "You were supposed to be watching her."

Trix twists the corkscrew. "She gave me a dollar," she says, popping the cork out.

I lower to the floor, plopping down to rest my back on the couch. "Well, whatever. I give up. Be sad." I shove the end of a pizza crust into my mouth, instantly regretting it. I'm already very full but I can't seem to stop munching.

Melanie groans and slinks back to the floor. "Fine," she says as she settles on her cushion by the coffee table. "You're right. You're totally right. I should not dwell."

Trix's phone vibrates against the end table. Again. She ignores it. Again.

Melanie squints. "Okay, who the hell is texting you so much?"

"Booty call bodyguard, huh?" I ask.

Trix nods. "Unfortunately."

"Ohh," Melanie muses. "Booty Call Bodyguard. That's a good title."

I chuckle. "Still haven't talked to him yet?"

"I will." Trix picks up her glass. "Tomorrow. Papa's lawyers are coming to talk to me so I'll probably run into him then."

"To Papa 'Gento," I toast.

They both raise their glasses and we all take a sip to the best damn mafia dad in the world.

Melanie chuckles behind her glass. "Remember the time he told Robbie to cut his fucking hair?"

"Well, to be fair," I laugh, "it was longer than yours back then."

Trix rolls a fist and gestures with it just like her father does. *"Oy! Young man,"* she says, immersed in an Italian accent. *"You got nice chin there. Why you gotta disrespect it with that mane?"*

Melanie grins. "He's never let it get longer than his earlobes since."

Trix's phone vibrates again and we groan.

I extend my hand. "Give it to me."

"No," Trix says.

"Give it to me. Give it to me. Trix. Give it to me."

She snorts. "Jesus, is this what sex with you is like?"

I pop off the floor but Trix is much too close. She grabs the phone before I do.

"Okay, okay!" she says, swiping the screen. "I'll tell him to back off."

"Tell him you are not interested in continuing a physical relationship with him, nor are you looking to begin an emotional one," I say, my words slurring. "You need to set some boundaries with him."

Melanie shakes her head. "If a guy is aggressive enough, that won't work. It just turns them on."

"Then, what do you suggest she do?"

She shrugs. "Kill him?"

"Well." Trix cringes. "That's a dick pic."

My head snaps toward Melanie at the same time she looks at me. We both bolt off the floor and rush to stand behind Trix's shoulders to get a closer look.

"Ladies," Trix sighs, "meet the very best part of all my bad decisions."

My jaw drops at his impressive girth. "Whoa."

Melanie giggles. "Not bad, Marky."

"Indeed." Trix clicks her tongue. "Too bad it's connected to an overbearing, possessive jerk."

I pat her inked shoulder on the way to my spot on the floor. *"Boundaries,"* I say.

"Yeah, I know." She taps out a message and sends it off. "We'll see how he takes that…"

Melanie plunks down on her cushion again. "I've never received a dick pic."

I blink. "Really?"

"Never," she says.

"My Black Book profile gets them all the time. I finally had to stop checking it and created a new one with a fake identity."

Trix leans up. "Wait, *Robbie* never sent you a picture of his junk? That can't be right."

Melanie shakes her head. "Never not once. However, the bathroom mirror drawings were a pretty accurate representation, I have to admit."

Trix exhales hard at the ceiling. "How are we *all* single? Can I just point out how utterly unfair that is?"

"You noticed that, too, huh?" I mutter.

"I honestly can't remember the last time we were all in relationships at the same time." She pauses. "Have we *ever* all been in relationships at the same time?"

"I don't think so," I say, thinking back.

"Well," Melanie grunts from the floor, "you gals can mope all you want. I, for one, *love* being single. I can do whatever I want, whenever I please. I can receive flowers from strangers without anyone pissing a bitch about it. It's great."

Trix looks at her. "There's nothing you miss about being in a relationship?"

Melanie wrinkles her nose. "We talking in general or with Robbie specifically?" she asks.

"Robbie, let's say. But only because I'm genuinely curious."

I raise a finger. "Me, too."

Melanie stares off for a moment. "I miss his vasectomy. Does that count?"

"No," Trix says.

"Oh. Then, no."

I snort and pick up my glass. "I miss the deep, soulful chats," I say, taking a sip. "Staying up all night just *talking* with sex being the furthest thing from your minds…"

"Yeah," Trix says with a sigh. "Those are nice."

"Multiple orgasms," Melanie says.

"Oh, yeah," I say. "Those are nice, too."

"No, I mean Robbie," she says. "He can have them."

I raise my head. "Robbie? *Seriously?*"

"No, he can't," Trix says. "Men can't do that. Can they do that?"

Melanie nods. "Oh, yes. Some can and he could." She

sighs. "That man could pull out, come all over my tits, go right back in, and pound me until we both came together. Now, *that*... that a girl might miss. But the rest of it?" She waves a hand. "Nah."

I blow a raspberry until I run out of air. "Sex. That is all."

"And not just any sex," Trix says. "Mind-blowing, body-tingling, need-to-rehydrate-mid-boning sex."

My mind wanders back to that room on the third floor. Naked and chilled to the core but I had sweat on my brow and heat rising off my skin. I could feel the outline of his cock pushed against my clit. Just five more minutes and I'm sure I would have been screaming his name.

Mr. Snow.

"No-ra!"

I snap to attention. "Huh?"

"I said, how's the stress going?" Melanie asks, her eyes squinting. "You okay?"

"Uh..." I swallow. "Yeah, I'm just... really fucking drunk."

"Good. I'm not the only one, then..."

We all raise our glasses once more, each one of us throwing back whatever was left inside and chugging it down our throats. A little wine dribbles over my chin. I wipe it away but the heat inside of me rages on.

Mr. Snow.

I can't wait any longer.

I glance at the clock. It's just after midnight. Clive works the club until two...

I feel for my phone in my pocket before pushing off the floor. "Be right back."

Melanie nods at Trix. "Any word from Big Dick Bodyguard?"

"No, not yet..."

I wander down the hall to the bathroom and close the door behind me. Their voices are barely audible, meaning I can probably get away with a whisper or two. I slide my phone from my pocket but quickly stop when I realize that I don't have Clive's number.

"Dammit..." I say to myself.

I set a hand on the counter to keep the floor from slipping out from under me.

Maybe the club has a number.

Yes, I'll call the club and ask for him.

I sit on the toilet seat lid and run a search. Thank god for auto-correct. I don't think a Red Crick Board exists in Chicago.

A girl answers. "Red Brick Road. What's your fantasy?"

"Clive," I say.

"I'm sorry?"

"Uh." I clear my throat and sit up straight, just like I do at work when I have to make official business calls. "I would like to speak to Clive Snow, please. Is he *avurlable?*"

"I think he's walking the floor right now. Do you mind holding?"

"I do not. Thank you very much, ma'am."

The line changes and soft hold music plays. I close my eyes, bouncing along to the smooth elevator music. Actually, I think that's the same music they play in elevators in my building.

"Clive here."

I startle. "Hello!"

"Nora?"

"Yes, hey. It's me. I'm Nora."

He chuckles. "And you're drunk."

"I am not. I'm just a little tipsy… and thinking about you."

"Oh, yeah?"

I lean back on the toilet. "And I want…"

"Want what?"

"Body-tingling, mind-blowing," I say, licking my lips. "Sex with lots of water drinking."

"You've never made a booty call before, have you?" he asks, amused.

I gasp. "I am not calling for booty… Okay, maybe a little."

"Nora, even if I could leave here right now, I wouldn't have sex with you tonight."

"Why not?" I ask, frowning.

"Because you're drunk," he says. "It wouldn't be right."

"Well, that's… respectful."

He laughs. "Sleep it off, Nora."

"Will we see each other tomorrow?" I ask.

"Yes."

"When?"

"Anytime after five. I work in the morning."

I smile. "You never take a day off, do you?"

"Look who's talking," he jokes. "Do you want to meet at the club?"

I imagine the dark, silent rooms on the third floor. Pink lights and time limits. "No," I answer. "Come to my place."

He pauses. "Are you sure?"

"Yeah, I'm sure." I bite my lip. "I want to submit to you. I want you to teach me how."

"Is that what you really want?" he asks, his voice low and wonderful.

"Come to my place," I say again. "I have a condo on Michigan Avenue."

He hums. "Of course you do."

I grin. "Six o'clock. The Bailey building. Unit 4."

"Again, Nora... are you sure?" he asks.

His voice curls around my spine.

"Yes, Mr. Snow," I say.

"Then, I'll be there."

"Six o'clock," I repeat.

"Six o'clock." He makes that sound; that delicious, quick laugh I can't get enough of. "I have to get back to work."

I shiver with anticipation. "Goodnight, Mr. Snow."

"Goodnight, Ms. Payne."

He hangs up but I sit in place for a few more seconds just listening to the silent hum in my ears. Once again I start salivating like a damn dog at the sound of his voice. Mind-blowing, body-tingling...

"Hey, Nora!" Melanie slaps the door. "You fall in or something?"

"No." I shove my phone into my skirt pocket. "I'm good."

"Hurry up. Trix just got another dick pic and I have opinions."

I laugh. "Be right out."

As I stand, I catch sight of myself in the mirror again. My cheeks are flushed red. My eyes are bright and shimmering. For one damn second, I actually look relaxed. No thoughts of work or responsibility. No weight on my shoulders or creases in my brow. Just pure, blissful relaxation.

"Yes, Mr. Snow," I say to my smile again.

EIGHTEEN

CLIVE

Tomorrow night. Six o'clock.

One step closer to Nora's client list.

I want to submit to you.

I can't stop replaying her voice in my head. It makes me feel powerful and wanted. I want to hear it again. I'm going to make her say it again…

"How's it going, Snow?"

My shoulder lurches forward as Roger smacks my back. I stand up straight against the door frame again. "Going fine," I say.

People pass by us on their way out. It's closing time. Roger the black blob, however, lingers in front of me.

"Didn't see the newbie here tonight," he says with a knowing laugh. "Trouble in paradise already?"

I sneer and point a stiff thumb over my shoulder toward the door. "Keep moving, Roger," I say.

He pats my shoulder again with his black-covered hand and carries on toward the exit.

Trouble in paradise? Not even close, Rog.

I want to submit to you.

And she will.

That should keep me warm tonight. Hopefully.

I walk upstairs to the third floor. All six pink lights are turned off but I check each room just in case. I wipe down the furniture and the sinks. I check the closets to make sure everything is in place.

Same goes for the second floor. Wipe down the crosses and the benches. Hang up any spare leashes or chains onto the wall hooks. Sweep the floors.

Once the water and juice bar is tidied up, I head for the front entrance. Judy sits behind the counter in her usual place, counting down the register and filling out her paperwork.

"Second and third floors are clear," I say, casting a wave. "I'm heading out. Goodnight, Judy."

She glances up and flashes me a smile. "Have a good night, honey," she says.

I step outside, pulling my coat a little tighter around me as I nudge the door closed. It's starting to get cold. I'm not too thrilled about that but it's just another thing in the world I have no control over.

I walk around the building to the back alleyway where my car is parked. As I draw closer, I fish into my pocket for my keys.

Tomorrow is Saturday. No plugging numbers at Little Black Book on weekends but I have an early shift at the gym. I'll make my way there now.

The roads are mostly clear so it only takes a few minutes for me to cross town. I round the building and park in a spot down from the entrance. My shift doesn't start until seven-thirty, so I have just under five hours to get a bit of sleep.

I lean over and grab the windshield visor from the floor by the passenger seat. I spread it over the dash and press it up to the window to block out as much of the annoying orange street lamps as possible.

My stomach growls and I look across the street at the twenty-four-hour convenience store. I won't be able to sleep unless I eat something, so I twist around, grab my extra jacket, and step outside.

The man behind the counter waves at me as I walk in. Whether he recognizes me or not, I'm not sure. Nor do I really care. I pass by the register and grab a turkey sandwich and a bottle of water from the first fridge after the display of lottery tickets.

"That your car?" he asks me. "Outside the gym?"

"Yeah," I say.

I set the items down on the counter and reach for my wallet.

He waves a sympathetic hand. "On me tonight, pal."

I pause. Guess he remembers me just fine.

I've encountered this kind of thing plenty before. In the end, it's best not to turn it down. It fills my stomach and makes them feel good about themselves. Win-win.

He eyes the patch on my jacket. "Thank you for your service," he says.

"Thanks."

I take the water and sandwich and walk out with them back to my car.

There's some trash on the backseat. I gather the empty bottles and food wrappers and toss them in the trashcan outside the gym. I grab an extra blanket from the trunk as well. Can't have too many of those.

I toss it onto my backseat on the way in and close the door behind me. Only a little bit of light from outside manages to slip in through the window covers. I won't need much anyway.

I set my watch to go off at seven as another hunger pang rattles my gut. I tear open the sandwich wrapper and take a quick bite of the corner. The bread is a bit moist but it's food. Free food. Won't complain.

I lay down on the seat with bent knees, resting my head on the small pillow against the door.

This time next week, I could be anywhere but here. It's hard not to get excited.

Even harder not to think about Nora Payne.

I want to submit to you.

Blood spreads a little faster through my limbs. Good. If those six little words get me through another day, then I'm happy. Six little words until six o'clock tomorrow. I can do that.

I've been through much worse.

NINETEEN

NORA

I feel like a damn high school girl waiting on her prom date to come pick her up.

Except this time, he's not going to come in, compliment my mother on our lovely home, and give my dad a handshake.

He's going to fuck me.

I tried on a dozen black dresses before choosing this one. I'm still not even sure it's the best option but if things go the way they're meant to tonight, I might not even wear it for very long.

Damn, I need a drink.

Shoes first.

I bend my knee, quickly raising my foot and slipping my red stiletto over my ankle.

The doorbell rings downstairs.

"Shit, shit, shit," I whisper as I shove on my other shoe.

All day. I have spent all day cleaning and tidying. It's finally six but how the hell did it get here so fast?

I look in the mirror one last time, quickly fluffing my

hair to make it look like I didn't spend an hour making it look like this, then rush down the stairs.

Late dusk shines in from the windows in the living room and I give mother nature an enthusiastic thumbs-up for the perfect mood lighting. At least she's looking out for me tonight.

I unlock the door — one last breath — and open it.

Clive Snow stands in the hallway and takes that breath away from me.

I expected jeans and a t-shirt, his usual work outfit at Red Brick. He wears a black suit with a red tie instead.

I gulp.

"Hey," he says, smiling.

"Hi," I say.

His eyes fall on my dress. "You look amazing."

"And you look…" I shake my head and move out of the way. "Like you're still out in my hallway. I'm sorry. Come in."

He chuckles and steps inside, instantly looking around my living room. "So, this is what Michigan Avenue looks like from this side."

I close the door and lock it out of habit. "To be honest, I never get tired of it." I sneak a peek at the mirror by the door. Still looking good. "Would you like a drink?" I ask him.

"Ice water, please," he says.

I cringe. "Right. No alcohol. That wouldn't… be right."

He smiles. "Nora, relax."

"What? No. I'm fine. I'm very, very relaxed…"

I walk past the stairwell to the kitchen down the hall-way. Clive follows behind me, taking slow and soft steps as he looks around. I try and tame my fidgeting hands as I reach into the cabinet by the sink for two drinking glasses but I nearly drop the damn things twice.

Get your shit together, Nora Payne.

I fill them with ice and water. "Okay—"

I gasp as I turn around and find Clive standing directly behind me.

"*Nora,*" he whispers. "Set the glasses down."

"'Kay."

I abandon them on the counter's edge. Clive reaches behind me and nudges them a little farther away from me before curling his arms around me and pulling me in for a hard kiss. I melt completely, giving in to the overwhelming pang for his attention deep inside of me.

"Relax," he tells me again as he draws a line along my cheek with his thumb.

I nod and catch my breath as his hands fall away from me. He picks up one of the water glasses and I do the same.

"Would you like a tour?" I ask.

He raises the glass to his lips. "Only if it ends in the bedroom," he says.

"Okay. Well…" I pour a large, cold portion of water down my burning throat. "This is the kitchen," I say, wiping my mouth.

I step around him toward the hallway. He follows close behind, a large, lingering shadow that could pounce on me at any moment.

"Bathroom here," I say, pointing into a room to the right of the kitchen. We enter the hall and I gesture to the closed door halfway down. "And this right here is my home office."

I keep walking, barely pausing to take another sip. "Living room," I choke. "With the wonderful view of—"

I twist around to find Clive halfway up the stairwell.

"And... that's how you get to the bedroom."

He peeks over his shoulder at me, his blue eyes pinched with devious intent.

I exhale hard and follow him upstairs. Clive waits for me on the landing and we walk to the bedroom together.

"I have something for you," he says over my shoulder.

"Oh, yeah," I recall. "You said you did." We enter the bedroom and I walk to the bedside table to set my glass down. "What is it?" I ask, excitedly.

Clive puts his water down next to mine. "Face the mirror," he tells me after a quick glance around. "And close your eyes."

I squint playfully at him before doing as he says. He walks up behind me and I feel his warm fingers gently push my hair to one side of my neck. His hands move out in front of me and my lips twitch as he lays something around my throat and fastens it.

"Open them," he says.

I look at our reflection. It's a thin, black choker made of leather with a small pearl dangling from the middle. Simple and classy. My style in almost every way.

My jaw drops. "Holy— is that a *real* pearl?" I ask.

"A *real* pearl?" he quips. "I work three jobs. Of course, it's not real. It's plastic."

I chuckle. "Well, still. It's so pretty. Thank you."

He spreads my hair down my shoulders again. "Thought you'd like something a little nicer than a hanky. And... it keeps others at arm's length from you." His eyes fall on my body in the mirror. "I want you to myself, Nora Payne."

I feel the smooth leather choker. "You want to own me," I say.

He grips my waist from behind. I shiver as his warm

breath spreads along my neck. "Yes," he answers as he kisses my shoulder. "But I know I have to earn that. If you'll let me."

He pinches the top of my zipper.

"Say that again," he says as he slowly slides it down my back. "Tell me the reason why you asked me to come here."

I lick my lips. "I want to submit to you."

"Again."

I let the dress fall to the floor. He admires my nearly naked form in the mirror, his hands crawling around me to feel my bra and panties.

"I want to submit to you," I say again.

He grabs my chin and guides my head back to crush his lips on mine. I kiss him back, parting for his tongue and reaching behind me to caress his neck. I push up on my toes and he leans down to meet me. I cup his chiseled face, press our bodies together, and I kiss him just like every other time before.

Clive slides his hands up my back and unclasps my bra. He guides the loose straps down my shoulders and I let it fall to the floor. His hands continues down my shoulders, firmly squeezing my breasts on their way down to my panties. I bite my lip as he guides them down and the throbbing between my thighs intensifies threefold.

"Sit on the bed," he says, stealing one more kiss from me.

I tremble at the words. "Yes, Mr. Snow."

He smiles as I walk away. I feel more tension fade from the room and by the time I sit down on my bed, it's gone completely. It's just me and him up here. Just me and my Dom.

And I want to learn.

Clive stands over me and reaches into his pocket. "Your right wrist, please."

I extend my hand as he withdraws a pair of handcuffs from his jacket pocket. I pause, just barely recoiling as he smiles at me.

"Just the one wrist first," he says. "To get used to it."

I let him cuff me, each metallic click of it sending bolts of heat throughout my core.

He slides his belt free and unzips his pants. "Ms. Payne," he growls.

My tongue twitches, salivating for him. I reach for him, hooking my fingers into the elastic liner of his briefs. He watches with lustful eyes as I pull them down to his thighs, exposing his hard cock. I open my mouth, wanting so badly to taste him again, but I take it slowly. I lick his tip, massaging it with several long strokes of my tongue as his fingers curl behind my neck.

"Good girl," he whispers with a heavy groan.

He reaches into his jacket pocket again but whatever he withdraws is locked in his enclosed fist.

"Lie back," he says. "Head on the pillows. Spread your legs."

I slide his cock out of my mouth and nod. "Yes, Mr. Snow," I say.

He finishes undressing himself as I move, taking his jacket and shirt off and letting his pants fall to the floor. I lay against my pillows with open legs, just like he requested, and he towers beside the bed in nothing but his socks.

"Hands above your head," he says.

I feel the handcuffs on my right wrist as I move them up to my headboard.

"I'm going to restrain you now," he says, his eyes on mine. "I'm the only one with the key. If you're a good girl, you will be freed when I'm done with you. Do you understand?"

I twitch, completely enthralled by the deep growl in his voice. "Yes," I whisper.

"You will have no control," he adds. "You will submit to me completely. Body and mind. Do you understand?"

Oh, hell yes.

This is what I wanted. What I *needed*. A chance to give up control. No more orders or meetings or deadlines. Just a few damn hours to submit to someone else's demands, just like Melanie said.

I'm not the boss in here. He is.

And it feels so fucking good.

TWENTY

NORA

I smile at Clive. "Yes, Mr. Snow."

His gaze glides down my body before he leans over and slips the cuffs around the bars of my headboard. He waits for a moment, softly staring into my eyes, giving me one last chance to back out. I do nothing.

He closes the other cuff around my left wrist, locking them in place above my head.

Clive climbs onto the bed and settles between my spread legs. I look down at our naked bodies, admiring his hard cock as it rests on my mound.

He moves forward and balances on his arms above me. "Kiss me," he says.

I part my lips and raise my head to meet his mouth. It's a soft, slow kiss, but full of heat and need. He massages our tongues together, turning me on even more. His cock presses harder against me. I want to satisfy him so badly. I want him to take me hard and fast but the look in his eyes tells me that he will make this last.

As Clive sits back, my eyes rush down his body again.

His sock has rolled down his right foot, revealing the skin beneath and my silent breath catches. A deep, jagged scar is carved up his calf above his ankle. Dark red and menacing. It's a wonder he even walks at all.

I pull my eyes away from it before he notices me staring. He sets his hands on my thighs and gazes down at me.

"Do you trust me?" he asks.

I twist my wrists, locked in place, but I feel no nerves about it. I nod. "Yes, Mr. Snow."

He reaches for his water on the bedside table and takes a sip, widening his mouth to capture an ice cube between his teeth. He sets the glass down and turns back to me with squinting, devious eyes as he leans downward toward my breasts.

I gasp slightly as Clive rolls the ice over my right nipple like a frozen tongue. My nipple piques and I chuckle as the melted water falls down my belly. He moves to my left nipple, performing the same slow circles until that one stands to hard attention as well.

Clive drops the cube into my lap and leaves it there to melt. He pinches my nipples softly — at least, it feels that way.

"Does that hurt?" he asks.

I shake my head. "No."

"No pain at all?"

"None."

Clive smirks and opens his fist, revealing the object from his pants pocket I already forgot about. Two metal pinchers with rubber tips connected together by a short chain.

Nipple clamps.

I tense up. He notices, of course.

"I'm sorry—" I laugh. "I just have *really* sensitive nipples."

"Good," he says, bringing one of the clamps close to my breasts.

I recoil on impulse. "Wait, wait, wait—"

"Nora, sit still." He looks at me and that hard stare settles with sympathy. "I want to know your limits," he says, leaning in. *"Don't you?"*

"Well, yeah, but—"

"You'll never know for sure unless you push yourself a little." He kisses me again, soft and slow. *"Right?"*

I swallow. "Right."

"Close your eyes," he whispers. "Count to ten."

My eyes flutter closed as he gives me another sweet kiss.

"Be a good girl for me," he says, backing away.

I inhale slowly. "One, two, three…"

I have to relax. That was the whole point, right? Relax. Let go. Release the stress. Submit to Clive, let him guide me.

"Six, seven…"

It's been working so far. Him and me. I feel amazing. Absolutely amazing. It's the most satisfying relationship I've ever been in… and we haven't even had sex yet.

"Nine, ten."

I open my eyes to find Clive staring back at me. He smiles and kisses the tip of my nose.

"There," he says. "That wasn't so bad, was it?"

I furrow my brow and look down. My nipples are clamped. I didn't even feel it.

"Whoa," I whisper.

Clive hooks a finger in the chain. "You're numb," he says. "You won't feel everything but—"

He gives the chain a light tug and I twinge with pain.

"Ah!" I cry out and laugh at the same time.

He smirks. "You'll feel *some*things."

"Won't I gain feeling back soon?" I ask, exhaling the last bit of discomfort.

"That's part of the fun," he says. "You'll want to sit still and not move, but…"

My lips twitch. "You'll make that impossible."

Clive kisses me again. "Good girl."

He leans back onto his knees and lays his hands on my thighs again. My eyes fall to his erection, still as hard and ready as before. My tongue taps the roof of my mouth, remembering his taste.

"You still in?" he asks, his hands gently rubbing my sides.

I watch on pins and needles as his hands travel upward. "Uh-huh…" I murmur with suspicion.

His hands move beneath the hanging chain and he rests his fingers along the curve of my breasts. He looks at me as he massages me gently, studying my face as I twitch. It doesn't hurt — yet. But there's a deep feeling of suspense — like he could rip the chain off at any second, but I know he won't. Still, my body responds with heat, making my pussy throb as my eyes bounce to his cock yet again.

"Is that what you want?" he asks, reading my every thought. "Do you want me to fuck you?"

I quiver at the tone of his voice. Soothing and tender Clive is gone. This is Dom Clive, the one who expects me to obey… and beg.

I want to say yes so badly but I know I'll be in pain if he touches me again.

He hooks an index finger under the chain. "Answer *now*."

"I don't know," I say, my voice shaking with the hope that he'll drop that chain.

"Why did you take so long to answer?" he asks, holding on. "When I ask you a question, I expect an immediate response."

"I'm sorry, Mr. Snow," I say quickly. "I'm... conflicted."

"Why? You don't want me to fuck you?"

"I do…"

"You do?"

"Yes."

"How long have you wanted to fuck me?"

I pause. "What?"

Clive tugs the chain and I gasp. "You're not allowed to ask me questions," he says, growling. "If you have a question, you will request permission to ask it first."

"Mr. Snow, may I please ask a question?"

He smiles, impressed. "Go ahead."

"… uh…" I go blank. "Crap, I forgot what I was gonna say."

His character breaks and he lets out a laugh before quickly flattening his lips again. "Ms. Payne…" he warns.

I try not to laugh either. "I'm sorry, I'm sorry—"

"We're having a very serious discussion right now," he says.

"Very serious," I repeat, barely keeping it together.

He flicks the chain and I wince at the new, piercing pain.

"Ow…" I say.

Clive stares at me, his bright eyes shifting dark, and I take a deep breath.

"How long have you wanted me?" he asks me again.

I swallow the last of my laugh. "Weeks," I answer, truthfully.

He pauses, his lips curling. "You wanted me before you ever set foot in Red Brick," he says slowly. "Didn't you?"

I eye his finger still wrapped around the chain. "Yes," I say.

He sits still for what feels like forever before he rests the chain against my skin again. I exhale with relief, but the movement of my chest still makes the clamps pinch me harder. The more I move, the more it hurts. Every second a little more feeling comes back. A sweat breaks on my brow. I'm completely torn between fighting pain and receiving pleasure I've long ached for.

"I wanted you, too."

I open my eyes and look up at him.

Clive adjusts his position, taking hold of his cock in his right hand. "I like to watch you," he begins. He guides his tip down toward my slit. "You walk with confidence and grace. Strength and poise, like nothing bothers you." He rubs his tip between my folds, separating them to expose my throbbing clit. "I want to bend you over your fucking desk."

I sigh with pleasure, instantly imagining it.

He rubs his tip along my clit. "I want to make you moan for me," he says.

Pleasure aches through me, forcing me to move and shake. It twinges my nipples, mixing delicious pain into it. I hate it and love it at the same time. I don't want it to stop.

Clive continues rubbing me with his dick, refusing to slow down. "I told myself, *one of these days…*" He chuckles. "*I'll fuck her brains out.*"

I moan, the tension building inside.

"*She'll scream for me. Submit to me.*"

His fingers curl around the chain.

"I'll make her body feel things... she never thought were possible."

I cringe in agony but the pain doesn't overrun my pleasure. It becomes it.

"Mr. Snow," I beg.

He flicks his finger, bouncing the chain and gently pulling at my nipples. I moan louder, barely on the edge of climax. Every time I wince in pain, he focuses on my pleasure. He makes me feel both at once until I can hardly even tell the difference at all.

"Come for me, Ms. Payne," he says, rubbing and flicking. "Be my good girl."

My body breaks in two, forced to obey. I dig my nails into my restraints as I cry out. My back arches. My toes curl. Every part of me shakes in orgasm. Tears spring to my eyes as pain takes me away.

Clive lays one strong hand on my belly to hold me still. He takes his other hand and caresses my cheek. "Nora..." he whispers. "Have you had enough?"

I don't answer right away. I can't, even though I try. He doesn't scold me for it this time. He waits with a gentle gaze, genuinely concerned that he's pushed me too far.

I smile. "No."

He smiles back with a slight tilt to his head. "Are you sure?" he asks.

"I'm sure," I say, "Mr. Snow."

Clive leans down and crushes his lips on mine. I kiss him back, tilting my head to accept his tongue as it owns me.

"Do you remember your safe word?" he asks.

"Yes."

His fingers curl around my hair. "I want you to use it,"

he tells me, tilting my head back. "I want you to hold on..." He kisses me. Hard. "For as long as you can. Do you understand?"

I nod. "Yes, Mr. Snow."

"Test your limits. Will you do that for me?"

I quiver as the pleasure in my core fades and the pain in my breasts takes over. "I will," I say.

He leans upward and grips his hardness again. The tip grazes my sensitive clit, purposefully tapping me to remind me what he can do to me. He gazes at me, gently stroking himself as a bead of pre-cum seeps out of his tip.

"I'm going to fuck you," he says, "just like you wanted me to. I'm going to use your body... just like I've wanted to since the moment I saw you."

He grabs my waist and pulls me closer. I gasp with need. My cuffs stretch taut and my chest heaves. He pushes his dick down to my entrance, pressing the tip into place.

"You're mine, Ms. Payne," he growls. "Say it."

"I'm yours," I say, my voice breaking.

He thrusts in slowly. My mouth sags open as he fills me. He doesn't stop until he can't go anymore and his pubic bone presses into mine. I take a breath, almost forgetting to breathe all over again.

Clive eyes me, his face contorted with pleasure and greed. "Your cunt is so tight," he says.

He pulls halfway out and thrusts me again, hard and fast. He rests his steady hands on my waist and rocks back and forth, purposefully moving me in short, quick bursts. My breasts bounce, bringing me sharp pains but it's not enough to break me. I promised I'd hold on. And I will.

"Mr. Snow," I say, bringing a deeper smile to his mouth.

"That's a good girl," he says, his breath quickening.

His eyes fall and he watches his cock sliding in and out of me for several strokes. I watch him move, admiring his body and technique. I'd give anything to lick down his abs and grips his ass. I want to touch him and embrace him but that's not my role right now.

I'm a submissive.

But I don't feel like he's taking from me. I'm giving him everything. All my pleasure and pain are his to mold and control. My very life is in his hands.

Each thrust brings me closer to the edge but I can't tell if I'm going to cry or scream when I get there. My eyes water as I tighten around his surging cock. I try to say his name but I've forgotten how. It's all too much…

Clive flicks the chain again, pushing me to the brink. I come hard again, my body betraying every nerve ending in my body. Tears stream down my face and I finally regain control of my tongue.

"*Stop!*" I cry out, shaking with bliss and pain. "Stop, please…"

Clive halts and lays his hands on me, spurring an almost immediate calmness in me. "*Shh, shh,*" he whispers. "It's all right. It's over."

He pulls out of me and my tired legs fall to the bed. I inhale a deep breath as my thighs relax and my toes uncurl.

I wince as Clive removes the nipple clamps.

"*Shh,*" he soothes, laying a comforting hand on my chest. He reaches over me to release my cuffs one wrist at a time. As one falls free, he lowers it to my side and sets it there. "It's all over now," he says again.

I roll onto my side, somehow finding my way into his arms. "Clive…" My voice trembles.

"I'm right here." He brushes the tears off my cheeks and kisses my forehead.

I cling to him. My body still buzzes back and forth between satisfaction and agony. It hurts so much but I love it. I'm so turned on but I hate it. I can hardly see straight and I can't stop the feeling that I've done something wrong—

"Nora." His lips brush my cheek.

I tilt my head up and he kisses me softly.

"It's all right," he whispers in my ear. "That was beautiful."

And just like that, I smile.

TWENTY-ONE

CLIVE

Nora chuckles softly, but I didn't say anything funny. She lays on her side with her back to me. The bed sheet rests up on us. I lean over with a hand on her naked waist beneath the sheet and kiss her shoulder.

"What?" I ask.

"Nothing," she says.

"You're laughing at nothing?"

"No, not nothing." She turns her head back and I brush the blonde hair off her temple to see her better. "This is nice," she says.

"You didn't think it'd be nice?"

"I didn't expect it to be so quiet and sweet afterward."

I chuckle, once again pressing my lips against her soft skin. "You never cuddle after sex before?" I quip.

"I have, obviously. I just didn't expect it after *that*."

I run my hand up her bare shoulder. "It's called aftercare."

"Oh?"

"If a scene gets too intense, a Dom will often comfort

their sub after. Hold them, talk it out, let them know that are not, in fact, a worthless cum-slut created to be used and disposed of."

Thankfully, she laughs. "Oh, good, because I was wondering..."

"It fosters intimacy, strengthens the bond."

She touches my hand in front of her, gently sliding her nail along the back of my wrist. "Is that why you held me when I passed out at Red Brick?" she asks.

I nod. "Yes... and I really was worried you'd fall and hit your head."

"I might have," she says. "I could barely stand."

"I know. I caught you, though."

"You certainly did." Her smile widens. "That's really nice, actually. I didn't know BDSM had that sweet side to it..."

"It's important," I say. "Doms comfort their sub and subs reassure their Dom that they did nothing wrong and they enjoyed the experience."

Nora turns onto her back to get an easier look at me. "Is that what I should be doing now?"

"If it's true. If I did something wrong, I'd like to know that as well."

She reaches up to touch my cheek. "Well, I had fun," she says, smiling. "And I do not, in fact, believe I am a worthless cum-slut."

I laugh. "Good."

Nora's eyes glide downward, stopping at the edge of the sheet just below my abs. "So..." Her voice falls, along with the question obviously lingering on it.

"What?" I ask.

"Do Doms and subs ever have, like... regular sex? Or is it always so intense?"

"Depends on the relationship," I answer. "I know a woman who has never had sex with her sub. They've been together ten years."

Her eyes widen. "Ten years and no sex?"

"None."

"At all? Not even... the tip?"

I chuckle, letting my lips graze her forehead. "For some people, it's not about sex."

She looks down again. "Is it about sex for you?"

"Yes. When a sub submits to me, I expect every part of her in that trade."

"Every part?"

"Every part."

"But does it always have to be..."

"Intense?" I finish.

She nods. "Yeah."

I smile at the blush on her cheeks. "No."

Her lips press together. "So..." She shifts up and the sheet falls. "If I were to just..." She mounts me, settling her legs on either side of my waist. "You wouldn't shove me off or anything?"

I look her up and down her perfectly bruised breasts and milky curves. "Lordy, no."

She leans in to kiss me. "Good."

Our lips crush together, softly and slowly, as Nora gently rocks her body on mine. I feel her pussy lips rubbing my dick and it tingles with blood, instantly growing hard for her. I relish in the last few seconds of her breasts touching my chest and her scented hair teasing my nose before she leans up. She reaches between us, quickly aligning herself and I settle in for a damn fine view.

Nora guides my cock inside of her. I watch the changes in her face and that sudden gasp of air as she takes me in just a little deeper. I lay my hands on her waist, but she guides them to her breasts instead. Not gonna argue with that.

She grinds her little hips on me, making me hit her exactly the way she wants inside. I keep watching her face, waiting for the moment when she finds the perfect grind to get herself off. She moans, her voice sharp. I feel the sudden twitch of her pussy and I buck slowly, timing my movements to hers and her breath quickens in reaction. She could easily get herself off without my aid but I'm not about to sit this one out.

I take my right hand off her breasts and lick my fingertips to moisten them first before putting pressure on her clit. Nora reaches down and pushes me to a better spot, one that instantly makes her jaw drop.

"Right there," she gasps. "Like that."

I groan as she squeezes my cock from the inside. Nora fucking Payne. She's like a well-oiled machine, inside and out. My balls tighten just thinking about the type of sub she'll be once I get her broken in.

I gently pinch her bruised nipple, giving her the slightest tick of pain. To my pleasure, she moans a little louder. Good. Nipple play is some of my favorite play and hers are just too perfect not to clamp.

"Don't stop," she whimpers. "Oh, god..."

"No," I say, rubbing her faster. "Don't say his name. Say mine."

She laughs. "Don't stop, *Mr. Snow.*"

"That's my girl."

Her hand falls to my chest as she struggles to keep her balance. Moans fall one after the other and her inner muscles convulse. Her face twists and her body turns. She leans back again and places her hands on my knees, touching me there without hesitation or restraint, just like I told her to.

I release her clit and lay my hands on her sides to keep her from rolling off me. My god, I hope I never get tired of watching this woman come. I don't see how I ever could...

Nora collapses on my chest, her warm breath rushing out onto my skin. I take hold of her limp body and roll her onto her back. She instantly wraps her legs around my waist, keeping herself wide open to me.

I thrust back inside of her, filling her dripping cunt as much as I can. Her wild, tired breaths get pushed aside in favor of deep, hungry moans as I rock her against the headboard. She extends her arms upward, locking her elbows and taking every buck of my hips like a goddamn champion.

"Mr. Snow," she moans, strands of her hair invading her mouth.

I bury my face in her shoulder, pinning her down and listening to every noise that tumbles out of her mouth. "Fuck, Nora," I growl. "You make me want to tear you apart."

She scratches my back, laughing. "What's stopping you?"

I raise my head to crush my lips on hers. She plucks my bottom lip between her teeth and sucks on it, a move that nearly makes me explode.

I groan as everything tightens. "Can I come in you?" I ask.

She moans. "Yes."

I let my head fall again. I close my eyes, focusing hard on the feeling between us. My cock bursts and I pump a few times until I just can't anymore. Fuck, she feels good. Inside and out, Nora Payne is exactly the pretty, little plaything I've always wanted.

I stop to breathe. Her hands roam my body, moving up my sides and down my back. She runs her fingers through my hair and kisses my forehead. It's a perfect cocoon of warmth and comfort, one unlike anything I've ever felt before.

I slide out of her, instantly missing her tight clench but it won't be the last time. I'm sure of it.

I look up and her face looks about as dumbfounded as I feel. "What is it?" I ask, still out of breath.

"That was just..." Her voice falls away.

"What?"

She smiles. *"Intense."*

I laugh. "Come here."

Nora leans in, meeting me halfway with another kiss.

TWENTY-TWO

NORA

I already feel it before I even open my eyes; that deep muscle pain which comes from bending and twisting in ways you never have before. A smile creeps up my face and I roll over, completely delighted with the stretch of my thighs and the twinge in my abs.

I'm alone on the bed, but I wasn't always — that's for sure. The duvet is somewhere on the floor, probably. My dress lies in front of the mirror next to a man's dress shirt and tie.

"Clive?"

No answer. I sit up, letting the lonely sheet fall free as I drop my feet to the floor. My thighs clench as I stand, stretched and tingling with vague memory. I bend down and scoop Clive's shirt off the floor to put on. As I slide it over my shoulders, I stop in front of the full-length mirror by the doorway.

My jaw slowly opens as I gaze at the fresh marks on my breasts. Deep, purple bites left behind. I gently pinch them, wincing at the tenderness, but smiling at the memory.

I button up and head downstairs.

I see him before he notices I'm there. Clive wanders around my condo in nothing but his black pants and socks. I delight in the crunch of his abs and the deep, v-lines on his back. His hair is wild and haphazard with a natural bed-head.

I quickly realize that I was so preoccupied with my nipples before that I didn't check my own hair. I comb my fingers through to kill any tangles that might be there. He continues his slow walk from my sitting room to my office and I follow him with curiosity.

I peek in at him from the hallway. Clive scans the walls of my office, checking every nook and cranny as if he's searching for something.

"Good morning," I say.

Clive startles and twists around in surprise. He instantly smiles at the shirt I'm wearing and exhales a deep breath. "You move very quietly," he says.

"The perks of being petite." I step inside. "You looking for something?"

"No," he says. "Not at all. I'm just..." His eyes flick back and forth. "You have a very nice place."

"Thank you."

"A little, black book did all this, eh?"

I nod. "It did."

"That's kind of amazing."

My shoulders bounce as I look away. "I just got lucky, I think."

"Turning a full house in Vegas is lucky," he says. "You worked your ass off and you know it."

I blush. "Well, I don't like to brag."

"Brag. You earned it."

I pause, sensing a shift in his tone, almost as if he's demanding it. "All right," I say. "I am amazing."

He smiles. "You also snore."

My face falls. "No, I don't."

He pinches the air. "Just a little."

"Fuck me..."

"Don't worry about it." He steps closer and I look up from my view of his smooth, exposed pecs into his deep, blue eyes. "How did you sleep?" he asks.

I take a breath. "Honestly... I don't remember the last time I woke up this good."

His brow furrows. "Me, neither."

"Yeah?"

"Oh, yeah."

"My snoring didn't keep you up?"

He chuckles. "I zoned it out after a while."

"Thank god."

His hands rise to cup my face. My cheeks tingle as he leans down to kiss me.

Clive bends suddenly and hoists me off the floor. I gasp and wrap my arms around his neck as he carries me toward the stairs.

"And just where do you think you're taking me?" I ask.

"Wherever I want," he says, his lips locking on mine.

My pulse pounds as he ascends with me. I feel like I'm floating on air, so safe and warm, just like that night at the club. I could pass out all over again, though, I wish I wouldn't.

We reach the landing and he takes me to the bedroom. I kiss him over and over again, letting myself enjoy the ride. His arms suddenly fall away and I drop like a rock onto my bed. I laugh hard but my cackling is cut short fast as he towers over me and shoves his tongue down my throat.

I flinch away. "What time is it?"

Clive blinks. "Uh..."

I look at the clock on my bedside table. It's eleven-thirty. "Oh, shit," I say. "It's almost noon."

"It's *Sunday,*" he says, leaning in again. "Sunday's are made for sleeping in. Even *I* don't have to be at the gym until three..."

He kisses me again, his lips firm and demanding.

"Yeah, but I..."

My lips surrender to his and I kiss him back as he pulls me against him.

"I have..." I sigh, pausing as his mouth falls to my neck. "I have somewhere to be."

He guides me backward until my head hits the pillows. "Where?" he asks.

"I'm meeting my friends for brunch," I answer.

"Brunch?"

"Yeah, we..." I shiver as his hands crawl up the bottom of the shirt. "We've done it for like five years," I say. "We have a reserved table every Sunday at twelve at Moira's Cafe. We sit down, get blitzed on mimosas, and just... leave our troubles at the door."

Clive looks at me and nods. "Sounds like fun."

"Until recently, it was the best part of my week."

"Oh, really?" He cocks an eyebrow. "What changed?"

I smile. "Nothing really."

"Nothing, huh?"

He reaches beneath me, giving my rear a quick spank. I laugh as my legs slowly curl around his waist. He's semi-hard and his dick pushes against my inner thigh, bringing back memories from last night.

I try and pull myself out of it. "I should really go..." I say.

"No," he says.

"No?"

Clive pins my wrists above my head with one strong hand and reaches for his belt with the other. I look down and watch as he unzips, pulls his cock out, and strokes himself.

"Where do you want it?" he asks.

"Huh?"

His breath quickens. "I'm going to come on you," he says. "I want you to walk around today... with my seed on your body."

My pussy pulses with need, utterly turned-on by the request and I haven't the slightest idea why. I just love that it's coming from him.

"Better choose quickly," he says, his fist stroking faster. "Breasts? Bellybutton?" He arches a brow. "Face?"

I swallow the building moisture on my tongue, listening to the quiet groans in the back of his throat. "Inside," I whisper.

"No, that's cheating," he says. "I want it on your skin."

I bite my lip as a crippling wave of heat tingles me from head to toe.

"Last chance," he says. "Don't make me choose for you."

"Belly," I say. "I want it there."

Clive releases my hands and sits up, giving himself a more stable aim at my navel. He flips my shirt open, still stroking himself with a tight grip. His muscles tense up and I brace for that warm spray to touch my skin.

He comes on me with satisfying pleasure on his face as

he lets out one long, agonizing grunt. Thick, white ropes leave a small pool of semen along my navel. I feel dirty already, but in the best of ways.

Clive drops his spent cock and stares at my body, from my curling toes to my heaving breasts. "What do we say?" he asks me.

I exhale, trying to calm my throbbing sex. "Thank you, Mr. Snow," I tell him.

"You're welcome, Ms. Payne." Again, his eyes fall over my curves. "You look gorgeous."

I try another breath but my body rumbles. "Uh-huh."

He scolds me with soft, warm eyes. "You want to come, too," he says. "Don't you?"

I nod my head. "Yes, please," I say.

Clive slides off the bed and kneels on the floor. With both hands, he takes hold of my knees and yanks me along, positioning me on the edge of the mattress in front of him.

His eyes look up at me, fueling my trembling need, as he purses his lips against my inner thigh. "Is this what you want?" he asks, his breath tingling my skin.

"Yes," I moan.

He guides my legs straight up into the air and kisses the back of my knees. "I don't think you want it badly enough," he says, peeking at me.

"I do."

"Then, why aren't you *begging?*"

I quiver as his tongue draws a line down my right leg, continuing all the way along my exposed crack. "Please, Mr. Snow," I beg. "Make me come."

His tongue brushes my anus, making my ankles jerk in the air. He holds my legs in place and flicks me again.

"Yes," I moan. "More, please."

Clive spreads my knees and gently settles my legs up over his shoulders. As my rear shifts down, he keeps his tongue on me, slowly licking upward to my dripping slit.

"I want that ass, Ms. Payne."

I nod, wanting him to take it. "Yes..."

"Are you going to give it to me?"

He taps my clit with his tongue and I shudder with pleasure.

"Yes," I answer.

"Good girl." He laps at me, bringing me so close to the edge I grow tense in anticipation. "Will I be the first?" he asks.

I hesitate. "No."

Clive withdraws his lips and I ache with regret. "What was that?"

"No, Mr. Snow," I say, breathing hard. "You won't be the first."

"How many other men have been in your ass?" he asks, staring up at me with dark, intense eyes.

"Two," I answer truthfully.

He forces my knees together again. "Legs up," he says, drawing my ankles into the air. "Don't move."

I hold them there as he stands up off the floor. He stares down at me with hard, unblinking eyes as he pulls his belt from of his belt loops.

"Two men," he says, folding the belt in half. "Two lashes."

I shiver in place, rocked to the core but still intrigued. "I'm sorry—"

"It's too late for sorry. Don't move."

He grips my ankles with his left hand, easily holding them together with his strong fingers.

I look into his eyes. So wild and intense, unlike anything I've seen in him before. He's displeased, that's for sure, and that's my fault.

My tongue twitches for the safe word but I bite it instead. The heat building on my skin screams even louder. I'm still throbbing for release and I know the only way to get it is through this. I want to know where this leads. I want to know how it feels to be truly punished.

Clive raises the belt over his head. His eyes shift to look at me for a brief second before he takes aim at my lifted ass.

The belt descends, slapping my skin with a quick, smooth whip.

"Ah!" I cry out, arching my back in pain.

"One," he counts.

I dig my nails into the bed, riding out the red fire shooting up to my knees. It hurt. *Really* hurt. But part of me doesn't care. Part of me knows that it's halfway over. One more and he'll forgive me. One more and he'll be satisfied. One more... and he'll give me pleasure.

Clive hits me again, this one faster and more biting than the first one. I don't cry out this time. I grit my teeth and hold my breath, letting the discomfort ride through me.

"Two," he says, dropping the belt to the floor.

I open my mouth, letting my breath out through my trembling lips. A warm tear creeps out of the corner of my closed eye, sparking a sense of bliss deep within my chest.

"Nora."

Clive's hand touches my cheek, prompting my eyes to open. He stares at me the same wild intensity as before, but the opposite emotion. Kind and gentle. Sympathetic comfort. He thinks he's gone too far but I've never felt more relaxed in my life.

I smile. "Yes, Mr. Snow?"

He smiles back and leans down to kiss me. I meet his lips and cup his face to reassure him that I'm still here. I'm still *his*.

"Please," I whisper again. "Make me come."

One more kiss and he lowers down to the floor again, taking my fatigued legs along with him. His face slips out of sight and he leaves gentle kisses up my thighs again before burying his face in my pussy.

I gasp and laugh, fawning over his impressive tongue. It burrows in me, lapping and sucking and fucking until he feels my legs twitching around his shoulders.

"Fuck," I moan, biting my lip.

Clive looks up, his eyes smiling and nose wet. He reaches up and swipes my belly, coating his fingertip with semen. "Open. *No swearing*," he scolds.

I open my mouth and he slides his finger inside, making me suck it. He latches his lips on my clit and gives it a long, slow suck. I gnaw on his knuckles to try and keep myself together but the pressure inside is just too much.

I come hard on his face, my knees pushing up his shoulders and slipping upward to lock around his head. He doesn't release my clit. It's almost if he refuses to. He continues his fierce, flicking assault on me as I squirm and shift on the bed.

I slap his forehead, giggling like mad. *"Stop! Stop, stop, stop."*

Clive releases me with a wide, happy smile. "Yes, Ms. Payne," he says, licking and wiping his mouth.

I breathe hard at the ceiling, unable to move.

He stands up and towers over me as he quickly secures his belt. "Are you all right?" he asks.

I give him a thumbs-up. "Yeah, I'm good. Think I'll just… rest my eyes a little…"

"Aren't you late for brunch?"

My eyes snap open. "Ah, crap."

Clive laughs and extends his hand. "Come on."

I take it and he helps me up. I wobble a bit on my quivering legs, feeling a rush of blood to… well, everywhere.

He cups my face and draws me closer for one smooth kiss. "Guess I'll see you at the office tomorrow morning," he says.

"Right." I take a breath, filling my lungs with him. "Tomorrow."

We kiss again. His hands slide from my face to my shoulders, pushing my shirt down my arms.

I chuckle. "I thought you were leaving…"

"I am," he says. "This is my shirt."

"Oh!" I roll my eyes and hand it to him. "Sorry."

He takes a step back and throws it on as I head toward the closet for my robe. "But before I go…"

"Yeah?"

"Was there anything about last night you want to talk about?" he asks as he buttons his shirt.

I think back, getting lost in the memories for a moment. "No," I answer, smiling. "Last night was perfect, Mr. Snow."

Clive nods. "I agree, Ms. Payne."

TWENTY-THREE

NORA

I round the corner and our usual table comes into view. Trix and Melanie are already here — as they probably showed up on time.

Melanie spots me and throws up her hands. "And just where have you been, young lady?"

"Sorry," I say, sliding my jacket off. "I got a little... held down."

I sit a little too fast and my sore cheeks twinge. At least the chairs are padded.

Trix sighs. "Well, now that you're here, let me tell you about this motherfucking prosecutor trying to put my dad in prison."

A mimosa drops down in front of me and I glance up into the youthful eyes of our usual server. I flash him a wink in thanks and his lips twitch before he takes off once again.

I reach for the glass, shifting my attention back to Trix as I take a sip.

"*Lance Tyler,*" she says, squinting. "What the fuck kind of name is that?"

"Very American," I answer.

"Yeah, well, he and this Max Monahan guy can suck my ass because..."

I glance at Melanie and I realize she's been staring at me since I sat down. Or, more specifically, at my neck.

"What?" I ask her.

She points at me. "What's that about?" she asks, talking over Trix.

I shrug. "What's what about?"

Trix goes quiet.

"The choker," Melanie says, leaning in. "You're wearing a choker. In 2017."

My hand snaps to my neck. *Fuck.* I forgot I was still wearing it.

"Uh..." I shift in my chair. "It's an old necklace. I found it in my closet. Thought it looked cute..."

Melanie shakes her head with suspicion. "You went back to Judy's, didn't you?" she asks.

I drop my jaw. "No! I didn't."

Her palm slams on the table. "You went back and you found yourself a Big Daddy Dom, didn't you?! You're *collared!*"

My throat clenches. Fuck me and my stunning inability to lie.

"*Nongh itz...*" I sigh. "Yes. *Fine.* I went back. But it's not what you think!"

Trix gasps at me. "You little slut!"

"Oh, be careful now," Melanie says, grinning. "She might like that."

"Stop it!" I glance around, hoping the sudden outburst didn't draw eyes to our table. "It's really not what you think," I say again.

"Who is it?" Melanie sits back with crossed arms, looking smug. "I want *names.*"

"No."

"Why not?"

"Because… you probably don't even know him."

She shrugs. "Try me."

I sigh. "Clive. His name is—"

"Clive?" she repeats. "Clive *Snow?*"

"… Yes."

"The bouncer, right?"

I pause. "Yeah… you know him?"

She laughs. "I interviewed him."

My eyes widen. "For what?"

"I love to pick apart the staff at Judy's," she explains. "Those people have the *best* stories. I get some good, filthy material from them for my books."

Trix grins. "Do you still have your notes on this *Clive Snow?*" she asks with devious eyes.

Melanie snatches her phone off the table. "Oh, I'm sure I do."

"Guys, come on…" I say. "Can we not make such a big deal out of this, please?"

She turns her wrist, presenting the speaker forward.

"First question," her voice begins from a recording. *"What's your favorite masturbatory fantasy?"*

A man laughs, instantly making the hairs stand up on my neck. That's definitely Clive.

"Wow, you really jump in there, don't you?" he asks.

Trix visibly shivers. "Well, hello, Mr. Sexy Voice Man."

Melanie nods. Repeatedly.

"It's my favorite ice-breaker," she says. *"Trust me, we'll get to favorite colors in a minute."*

"Okay…" He chuckles. *"My favorite masturbatory fantasy…?"*

"Yeah, the one that makes you instantly come. I'm talking buckets here."

I glare at Melanie but her smirk never fades.

"Oh, that's an easy one," he says.

My cheeks burn. "Maybe we shouldn't listen to this," I say.

Trix snaps her fingers at me. "Shush."

Clive continues and I can almost hear the smile in his voice. *"It's a woman lying on the edge of a bed, on her back with her head just barely tilted over the side."*

"Naked?" Melanie asks.

"Definitely — or in some really nice lingerie. So, she's lying there, head back, eyes open, looking right at me, and she begs me to come on her face."

They both silently turn to me. I sit back.

"Oh, that's a good one!" Melanie says.

"I certainly like to think so," he says, awkwardly laughing.

"Do you ever get the chance to do it for real?"

He hesitates. *"Ehh… not really."*

Trix nudges my arm. "Have you guys done it?"

"No!" I bite my cheek. "Melanie, come on. Turn it off."

Melanie raises a sinister brow. "Don't you want to know how to please your new Daddy?"

"He's not my Daddy!" I lower my voice, blushing hard. "We don't play like that."

"Oh, but you *do* play."

Trix squints at me. "I thought you looked different…"

I close my eyes, blocking their teases out, and my ears naturally focus on his voice coming from the phone instead.

"I don't want to say exactly what drew me to Red Brick, if that's

okay," he says. *"The now hiring sign was particularly appealing, I'll admit that much."*

"Had you ever been here before that?" Melanie asks.

"A little, yeah."

"How often do you pick up girls and take them home with you?"

"Never."

"Never?"

"My place isn't very big at the moment," he says. *"Three seats and a steering wheel. Lots of trunk space, though."*

I open my eyes. "Wait, turn it up."

Melanie frowns. "Oh, I forgot about this…"

"Hard times, huh?" she asks him.

"You can say that."

Trix leans forward. "Did Daddy just say he lives out of his car?"

My heart stops. "He's *homeless?*" I ask.

"Yeah…" Melanie taps the recording off. "We'll just… put that away now."

"No, wait." I reach out. "I want to hear that."

"This was like half a year ago," she says. "He's probably picked himself up by now. I mean, you've been to his place, right?"

I sit back. "No, I haven't."

I picture him this morning, walking around my condo with wide eyes. I thought he was just reacting how everyone reacts to a place on Michigan Avenue — but maybe last night was the first time in a long time he's actually slept in a *bed.*

Melanie snaps her fingers at me. *"Stop that."*

"Stop what?" I blink.

"You're over-thinking," she says. "You're flashing back

and over-analyzing every little moment together, aren't you?"

"No, I'm not," I say quickly.

He works three jobs but doesn't have a cell phone.

"Nora."

He wears the same outfit to work every single day.

"Nora."

"Oh, my god." I cover my mouth. "I'm fucking a homeless guy."

Melanie twists in her chair and grabs my hands. "Nora, do you like him?" she asks.

"Yes," I answer.

"Does he treat you well?"

"Yeah. Very well."

"Does he smell like a dumpster?"

"No. God, no."

"Then, who cares?" She squeezes my fingers. "Shit happens. That doesn't make him a bad person."

Trix frowns. "Has he been to your condo?" she asks me.

I swallow. "Yes."

"You should do an inventory when you get back." She picks up her drink. "Just sayin'..."

Melanie scoffs. "Poor doesn't equal thief, Trix."

"Hey, Aladdin lived out of a hole in the wall and was hot as fuck. Dude still stole some bread."

I fall forward, groaning to myself as I smack my forehead on the table.

Melanie nudges my shoulder. "Nora, this is not a big deal. Okay? And it's not the type of thing you can just drop into a conversation either — especially not with somebody like *Nora Payne*, if you know what I mean. Also, you love helping the less fortunate, right?"

I raise my head a few inches. "Yeah, I do. I do like to do that."

"Just think of this as a charitable cause," she says. "You're helping a man find solace in a cruel and horrible world."

Trix cringes. "With her vagina, though?"

Melanie fires her a glare before turning back to me. "And he's helping you with your new sexual awakening. You look better right now than you have in weeks."

"I do?" My voice squeaks.

Trix reluctantly nods. "Yeah, you do."

Melanie pokes my cheek. "So, there you go. No harm done. World not over. And you look cute as fuck in a choker."

I sit back in my chair as another round of mimosas appear on the table and the server's shadow disappears behind me.

"You're right," I say. "Who cares if he's homeless?"

Trix briefly raises her hand but Melanie forces it back down.

"He's clean," I continue. "And gorgeous and funny. And he likes me. And I like him. And yeah, it's a little awkward since he's my employee, but—"

"Whoa, what?" Melanie says over me. *"Employee? What is this?"*

"He works at Black Book. Did I not mention that?"

"Uh... *no.* What does he do?"

"He's..." I pause, thinking twice about telling them but it's too late now. "He's my new, hot temp."

Trix blinks twice. "You're fucking your homeless, Daddy Dom *employee?"*

"Yeah." Melanie frowns. "I might have to change my

vote here..."

"What? Why?" I ask. "Two seconds ago you were all for it."

"Nora, you cannot bang a guy on your payroll," she scolds.

"Oh, come on. No one cares about that kind of thing anymore," I argue. "Our personal relationship doesn't even touch our work relationship. I barely even see him throughout the day and as soon as Ira comes back, he'll be gone anyway."

"So, there's been no hidden, lingering glances?" she asks. "No private chats or secret messages? Promises of post-work hook-ups?"

I hesitate. "... No?"

Melanie sighs and reaches for her phone.

"Nora," Trix says, "how long have you *really* thought about this and all the ways it could possibly go wrong?"

I stare across the restaurant, my mind hung in a state of temporary blankness.

Shit, they're right. I haven't thought about this enough. I've only considered how *good* he made me feel.

Trix snatches Melanie's phone away from her. *"No,"* she snaps.

"Hey, give that back."

"Only if you promise to stop taking notes on our love lives for your naughty romance novels. Steal your ideas from K-dramas just like everybody else."

"Okay, fine." Melanie takes it back and sets it down. "I'll stop."

I keep staring forward, my hand running on autopilot to deposit multiple sips of my drink down my throat. I made up excuses to say no but they instantly dissolved the second

Clive's tongue touched mine. *Damn the consequences,* or so I thought…

"Nora? You still in there?"

I'm not sure which one said it but I glance between their sympathetic eyes. "Hmm," I hum.

"Look," Melanie says, "we are but two opinions. Ultimately, it's up to you. What do you want?"

I flex my jaw. "I want my sexy, homeless street rat," I say.

"Then, go get him." She smiles. "Who am I to judge? I'm probably just jealous anyway. I haven't gotten laid in months."

Trix nods. "That would explain the writer's block."

Melanie agrees. "I do write my best when I get nightly dick."

"You could always call Robbie."

"You shut your whore mouth."

"Meow." Trix hisses. "Grouchy."

Melanie balances her chin on her palm. "So, how's Marcus?" she asks.

"Ugh. Touché."

I look at Melanie. "You really think he's picked himself up by now?"

She shrugs. "Probably. You could ask him."

"I wouldn't even know how to bring up something like this," I say.

Trix smiles. "*'Hey, Daddy. You homeless?'* is probably a good start."

I furrow my brow and pour the rest of my mimosa down in one smooth gulp.

TWENTY-FOUR

NORA

We leave Moira's Cafe shortly before two. I cringe at the bright sunlight beaming down on me so I search my purse for a pair of sunglasses.

Trix pauses on the sidewalk. "You guys want to hit up a movie or something?"

I laugh. "Anything to keep you from going home, right?"

"You don't understand," she says. "My rejection of his little Kodak package is just making it worse. Might have to throw doggy a bone before shuffling him off to the pound."

"Yeah, don't do that."

Melanie points across the street. "Hey, isn't that Clive?"

I spin around. "Where?"

"The laundromat."

Trix nudges between us. "Lemme see!"

I follow Melanie's pointed finger and there's Clive stepping out of the laundromat at the opposite corner.

"Yeah," I say, my insides twisting with warmth. "That's him."

Trix swoons. *"Daaaamn."*

"Uh-huh."

"Maybe *I* should go to Judy's..."

Melanie nods. "Good, ole Judy," she says. "She changes lives."

Clive steps off the curb and pauses by the trunk of an old, beat-up car with a garment bag draped over his arm.

"Is that the mythical house-on-wheels?" Trix asks.

"I don't know," I answer truthfully. "It's possible he's not homeless anymore, you guys. Mel, you did say your interview was half a year ago."

"This is truth," Melanie says.

Trix squints. "We should get closer."

I twitch. "Why?"

"Well, if he's got blankets and pillows in the back, then we'll know where he sleeps."

"There are loads of reasons why someone might have pillows and blankets in their car," I argue.

"Oh, yeah? Name one."

I stutter. "Camping?"

"Does Daddy seem like the camping type?"

I scoff. "Stop it. I don't call him that."

Clive pops his trunk and I can't help but push up onto the tips of my toes to try and get a better look inside.

"Let's follow him," Melanie says.

I snap in her direction. "Are you serious?"

"Why not?"

"Because it's rude!"

Trix smiles. "I can be rude."

"Well, I can't!" I say.

"Two against one." Melanie grabs my arm. "We're doing this."

"No, wait, guys—!"

She tugs me along with her around the building to the parking lot.

"We'll take my car," Trix says, grabbing her valet stub. "It's the least conspicuous and I'm the best getaway driver in case he pulls evasive maneuvers."

"No one's pulling evasive maneuvers!" I say. "You guys, come on."

Trix gives her stub to the valet. "Lightning fast, please. I'll slip you a fifty if the car is in front of me in fifteen seconds."

He grabs her keys and races into the lot.

Clive closes the trunk and rounds the car toward the driver's side door.

I breathe through the rising panic in my chest. "Clive will be long gone by then," I say. "Can we just go to the movies instead?"

"No, he won't," Melanie says, raising a finger. "Daddy's still right there."

I force her hand down. "Will you please stop pointing at him?"

"Nora," she takes a breath, "do you want to know if he's still homeless or not?"

"Well, yeah, but—"

"And do you feel, beyond the shadow of a doubt, that he'd tell you the truth if you walked up and asked him right now?"

I pause. "I dunno."

Trix's car screeches to a halt beside us.

Melanie smiles. "Then, get in the fucking car."

I deflate. They're going to do this with or without me. I might as well tag along and make sure they don't confront him directly. Or worse.

"Fine," I say, lowering into the backseat. "But I'm doing this under protest."

She winks. "Sure, you are."

Melanie hops into the front seat next to Trix, who immediately slams on the gas as soon as her door is closed.

I clutch the seat beneath me as I click my seatbelt and hope for the best.

Melanie points down the block. "He's at the light. Hurry."

"Slow down, Mel..." Trix says, calm and collected. "We need to establish a safe distance first."

I frown. "How many times have you done this?"

"Enough," she answers.

"He's turning!" Melanie points again. "He's turning!"

"I see him..." Trix says, slightly annoyed.

Clive takes a right turn and disappears down the street. We make it to the intersection in time to see him stop at a light a block away.

"Don't lose him," Melanie says.

Trix merely sighs and ignores her.

I sit back with crossed arms, feeling absolutely wretched. Maybe I should have just asked him directly on the street. Or, better yet, maybe I shouldn't bring it up at all. He'll tell me when he's ready.

I look up into the rearview mirror. The pearl on my choker waves back and forth as Trix weaves between lanes. I smile slightly, remembering everything about last night and this morning. Safe and warm. I don't want to lose that...

But still, my eyes keep flicking ahead. I don't want to lose him right now either. Curiosity clenches my gut. There's still so much I don't know about Clive Snow.

Clive turns off the street into a parking lot. Trix slows

down and slides into an empty parking spot just off the street and barely out of sight of Clive's vehicle.

Trix tosses her seatbelt off. "All right, ladies. Light feet."

They throw open their doors and I roll my eyes as I reluctantly join them. We walk to the edge of the building to get a view of Clive's car in the parking lot, me stepping normally while the two of them slide against the wall with their backs hunched over like sinister cats. I'm glad they're having fun with this because I'm about ready to turn around and—

"It's a gym," Melanie says.

"Daddy getting his swole on," Trix muses. "Is he as ripped as he looks, Nora?"

I ease forward slightly to catch sight of Clive as he opens his trunk and withdraws a red gym bag.

"Yeah, he's in pretty good shape," I answer. "He also *works* at a gym on weekends and, low and behold, it's *Sunday.* So, now that we know he didn't drive to a box under a bridge, can we please go?"

Melanie gasps. "Maybe this is where he showers!"

Trix slaps her shoulder. "You think?"

"Yeah! Gym memberships don't cost nearly as much as rent and it'd cost even less with an employee discount. If I were homeless, this is how I'd stay clean."

I sigh. I want to argue but she makes a decent point.

"What are we looking at?"

I jump at the familiar male voice in my ear. I spin around, coming face-to-face with Robbie.

"God, Rob!" I smack the arm of his leather jacket. "You scared the shit out of me..."

Trix smiles. "Hi, Robbie!"

Melanie groans at him. "What do you want?"

"I saw you guys slinking around," he says with a shrug. "Thought I'd come say hi."

Melanie crosses her arms. "You know, for a city with almost three million people in it, we tend to bump into each other an awful lot."

"Yeah, it's almost like you're obsessed with me or something," he says, smirking. "So, whatcha up to? Casting spells from the Book of Shadows you found in your attic after your grandmother died?"

"Did you literally look up a bunch of witch references just to whip out and insult me with?" Melanie asks.

He nods. "Yes, I did."

She rolls her eyes.

Trix waves him closer. "We're spying on Nora's Dom!"

His jaw drops at me. "You have a *Dom?!*"

I sulk in annoyance. "Trix…"

"Wait, I thought *you* were a Dom," he says.

"No." I shake my head. "I'm a submissive."

"Well, that's disappointing," he says. "I pictured you in a corset with a little whip. It was so cute."

Melanie raises a brow. "You pictured her in a corset?"

"Hey," he waves his left hand, "do you see a ring on this finger?"

She sneers with disgust and turns away from him.

His grin returns and he pushes forward to stand with Trix. "So, where is he? I wanna see him."

She sighs. "He went inside."

"Oh, the gym." He nods with respect. "Nothing like that mid-Sunday pump."

"Hey —" Trix nudges him. "Will you go in and see if he's using the shower?"

Robbie rises an inch. "Will I what?"

Melanie nods. "Yes!"

I glare at her. "How are *you* agreeing with this?"

"Because my momentary desire to solve this mystery briefly outweighs my eternal hatred for Robbie," she says.

"Oh, this must be good, then," he says. "What mystery?"

I groan in defeat. "He may have been homeless six months ago..."

He pauses. "Okay..."

"So, we're following him to see if he's still homeless now."

"Why, does he smell?"

"No," I answer.

"Then, who cares?"

Trix snorts. "You and Mel agree on something."

He smirks at Melanie. "Oh, Melanie and I have agreed many, *many* times."

Melanie stays quiet, her eyes squinting.

He turns back to me. "So, you want me to go in there to see if he's... using the shower?"

Trix nods. "Yep."

"Instead of, I don't know, asking him yourself if he's homeless?"

I cringe. "Yeah."

"Why can't one of you do it?"

Melanie points at me. "Well, he knows her. He'd probably recognize me, too."

"Why can't Trix do it, then?" he asks.

She sneers. "Because I don't wanna."

Robbie looks between the three of us and sighs. "What does he look like?" he asks.

"He's your height," I say, looking up at him. "Brown

hair, short but not buzzed. Bright, blue eyes. He was wearing jeans and a blue t-shirt with a black jacket."

"No," Melanie says. "He wore black pants and a blue jacket."

"Pretty sure it was jeans."

Trix wrinkles her nose. "I thought he had a dark gray polo."

"Ladies," Robbie says. "Do the world a favor: Never witness a murder. Mm'kay?"

Melanie takes out her phone. "Okay, hold on. I should have a picture of him."

I blink. "Why do you have a picture of him?"

"I took it during our interview," she says, swiping the screen. "Ah — here!"

She hands it to Robbie and he takes a look.

"Hello, gorgeous!" He winks at me. "Good job, Nor."

My lips twitch as I blush. "Thanks."

"Wait, when was this interview?" he asks.

"Five months ago-ish?" Melanie answers.

"So, you were taking pictures of gorgeous men *while you were still married to me* but for me to *mentally picture* Nora in a corset now is— you know what?" He gives the phone back. "Never mind. I'm just gonna let that one marinate. Be right back."

He spins around and walks off toward the gym.

"Thanks, Robbie!" Trix shouts after him, prompting a casual wave with his good hand.

Melanie exhales hard with a raised brow. "He has a point, doesn't he?"

I nod. "We won't tell, though."

"Thank you."

Trix heaves a happy sigh. "This is way better than a movie."

I sink a little deeper, feeling a heavy weight on my shoulders. This feels wrong. I trust him. He trusts me. That bond is forming, albeit slowly, but it's there and I can feel it. I don't want to sneak around and follow him like some—

"Oh—!" Trix slaps my arm. "He's coming back."

My heart leaps as Robbie shuffles his way back toward our hiding place.

"Well, I was right," he says, stopping in front of us.

We lean in.

"Right about what?" I ask with wide eyes.

"If you walk up to the counter and say, 'Hey, I know I don't go here, but can I check your showers for a man with bright, blue eyes?' they *will* ask you to leave."

I deflate. "You didn't see him?"

He shakes his head. "I did not. Sorry, Nora."

"Thanks anyway, Rob."

"Don't mention it." He shifts back a step. "Now, if you ladies will excuse me, I have to get back to work."

Melanie snorts. "Sure ya do."

He smirks. "What part of that do you find so unbelievable, Mel?"

"All of it," she says. "Just… the whole thing."

"You know, most men wouldn't say this, but I wish you were more like your mother."

She grits her teeth in offense. "What did you just say?"

Trix rolls her eyes at me. "Oh, boy."

"You heard me," Robbie says, twisting to face Melanie. "Glenn and Francie don't doubt me at all. They encourage and support me, unlike you. In fact, I'm going to tell them about this next weekend."

"N... next weekend?" she repeats.

"That's right." He nods.

"What's next weekend?"

"My monthly dinner with your parents."

Her face turns beet red. "Your *what?*"

"I have dinner with your parents once a month," he says with a shrug. "You didn't know?"

"No, I didn't know!" she seethes. "Why do you still have dinner with my parents?"

"Because they're *awesome.*"

"Bullshit." She points a finger at him. "What are you up to?"

"I'm not up to anything, Mel. I've always had a good relationship with your parents. Don't make this some kind of conspiracy. I like hanging out with them and they enjoy keeping in touch with me, so we have dinner."

"Not after the divorce is finalized! After that, you're supposed to *go away.*"

"Says who?" he asks.

"Says everybody!"

I break away from the group and walk toward Clive's car as their argument surges on behind me.

Robbie chuckles. "Well, luckily, I've never been one to blindly follow what society tells me I'm supposed to do, so I'm just gonna keep doing what makes me happy."

"No." Melanie stomps her foot in defiance. "This stops now."

"You're free to start tagging along, if you want," he offers.

"No, thank you."

"Fine. We'll all just see each other at Christmas, then."

"You're coming to my family's *Christmas?!*" she shrieks.

"Yes."

"No, you're not."

"And miss Francie's peppermint snickerdoodles?" He scoffs. "Not a chance."

"Robbie, where are you going?"

"Work."

"Bullshit."

I stare into the backseat of Clive's car, or what bits of it I can see into. The windows are covered with makeshift blockers to keep the sun out — or unwanted attention. Like exactly what I'm doing right now.

There's a pillow on the seat. Food wrappers and empty water bottles. Not enough evidence to prove it but just enough to make me believe it.

Trix enters my reflection in the window and wraps her arm around my shoulder. "You want to catch that movie?" she asks, giving me a reassuring squeeze.

I force a light smile. "No, I think I'll just head home."

"I'll drive you back to your car." She looks over her shoulder. "Once we separate those two, obviously…"

I chuckle and follow her gaze toward the empty street. "Where did they go, exactly?" I ask.

She grimaces. "Ah, crap."

We rush off down the street to catch up with them.

TWENTY-FIVE

CLIVE

I shove the towel cart around the corner, pausing by the hamper outside the locker rooms to gather the last dirty ones on this floor. Then, it's an hour of quiet downstairs while I wash and dry and fold. Of all my jobs, I can honestly say this one is the most relaxing — not that it will matter much today after what happened last night.

Last night was... well, to put it bluntly, fucking amazing. It didn't quite sink in for me until I left her condo this morning. It's been so long since I met a woman who meshed so well with me.

Actually, I take that back.

I've *never* met a woman who meshed so well with me.

I head downstairs to the laundry room, replaying the moments over and over again. Latching that collar around her neck. The warmth of her mouth when she sucked my dick. That beautiful ruin on her face every time the nipple clamps did their job and *that absolutely perfect way she said she wanted to submit.*

I'd do it all again. I *will* do it all again.

"Hey, Clive!"

I look up from the washing machine to find Alex standing behind me.

"Hi," I say, turning up my hands.

"Why didn't you answer me?" I ask. "I called out to you three times."

I focus on the machine. "I'm just busy," I say.

"Yeah, I bet." He smirks. "Busy got a name and her name is Payne. Am I right?"

I gawk at him. "No."

He slaps my shoulder and hops up to sit on the next machine down. "Seriously, though. You find that drive yet?"

"No," I answer.

"You got into her place, right?" He furrows his brow. *"Tell me* you got into her place by now. Otherwise, the world of good pussy is doomed for all of us."

"Yes, I got in."

He leans in with excitement. "So, where is it?"

"I'm not sure," I say, dumping the rest of the towels into the washer. "I didn't find it out in the open and she woke up before I could really dig into her office but there is a small safe built into her bedside table. I think it might be in there."

Alex grins. "Now, that's progress."

I nod. "I need more time."

He cringes. "I'll keep stalling, but..."

"Then, keep stalling."

"But this buyer wants his product."

I glare at him and he holds up his hands.

"All right. Stall mode activated." He pats my shoulder again. "But tell me. How did it go otherwise?"

My heart skips as I imagine her mewling on top of me in the dark.

"It went fine," I say.

He sighs in disappointment. "You're the only guy I know who doesn't kiss and tell, man."

"No, you just hang out with a lot of douchebags, Alex."

He throws his head back and laughs. "Ain't gonna argue with that."

I shift my focus to the dryer as it shuts off. "Anyway, I gotta…"

Alex slides off the washer. "All right, man. Keep me updated. But, uh… you know. Hurry up. The rest of our lives is waiting for us."

I ignore it until he disappears down the hall.

The rest of our lives. It was so easy to imagine before. On the road with a brand new car, plenty of food, and extra cash to spend. A smooth, easy-going existence to anywhere but here. It's been so long since I looked forward to anything, but now…

I can't wait for Monday morning.

Can't say I've ever thought that before.

Monday morning. Little Black Book. Nine-to-five shift.

I've been working here for only a few weeks and I've never felt so excited to walk into this building. Even the lonely, old security guy up front seems to notice the special hop in my step. Instead of the usual wave, he gives me a salute. I'll take it. Hell, I'll even salute him right back.

The sooner I get up to the fifteenth floor, the sooner I get to see Nora.

The elevator comes into sight and it dings, ready to close on me but I don't want to delay getting upstairs any longer than I have to.

"Wait!" I say. "Hold the elevator!"

A small hand reaches through and blocks the doors from closing at the last second. They slide back open and I pick up my pace to make it before they decide to close again.

I step on. "Thanks—"

And it's Nora Payne.

Her hair is held up in a tight bun. She stands tall in a nice suit — or what her petite stature's version of tall is — with her briefcase and purse held down in front of her. My eyes fall to the plastic pearl dangling above the hollow of her throat. She's wearing her collar for me.

My cock twitches in my briefs.

"Good morning, Clive," she says, offering a professional smile.

I nod and stand beside her. "Good morning, Ms. Payne," I say.

I tap the button to the fifteenth floor, praying silently that the doors hurry up and close before someone else manages to get on.

We stand still, staring straight ahead, until the doors close.

I slap the stop button and the car halts mid-floor.

Nora drops her things as I rush at her. Our lips merge together and she performs a little hop as I hoist her up and pin her little body to the corner wall.

"Good girl," I groan. I kiss from her lips to her cheek and down to her collared neck. *Very* good girl."

"I wasn't sure if I should wear it to work," she says, laughing. "We didn't really discuss the rules…"

I bend down to kiss her hidden cleavage. "The rules are…" I grip her chin. "You wear it proudly or not at all. Do you understand?"

She licks her wild lips. "Yes, Mr. Snow."

"To not wear it is a show of disrespect toward me," I say, holding her eyes. "And you do not want to disrespect me." I run my thumb along her bottom lip. "Do you understand?"

Nora smiles. "Yes, I understand."

I kiss her once more before releasing her from the wall. She lowers her feet to the floor and looks into the mirrored wall to check her shirt for wrinkles while I wipe her lipstick off my lips and fix the mess she made of my hair.

"Do you work tonight?" she asks me, catching her breath.

"Actually, I have one of those strange happenstances I keep hearing about called a night off."

"Really?" She smiles at me, her eyes twitching with thought.

I reach out to straighten her necklace. "Why?" I ask.

She nods a thank you. "I thought that maybe…" She picks up her purse and briefcase. "Maybe you'd like to grab a cup of coffee. With me."

I lean over to enable the elevator again. The car bounces an inch and continues its ascent.

"Coffee?" I ask.

"Uh-huh," she says.

"*Coffee…*"

"Yeah, you know, it's like tea but better," she quips. "Or worse, depending on your perspective."

I shift on my feet. "Hmm."

"What?"

"It just occurred to me that we've never gotten coffee before."

"I came to a similar realization myself," she says. "Figured I'd do something about it. Also, it gives us a chance to talk. One-on-one. Face-to-face. About something other than... well, you know."

"Talk?" I ask.

"Uh-huh."

"Talk..."

She squints in confusion. "Yeah, you know, it's like thinking... but you say it out loud."

I laugh. "Okay. Sure. If you want."

Her eyes shine with the slightest, most innocent, twinkle. "I want."

"Then," I stand taller, "let's get some coffee... and talk."

Nora bites her lip. "Meet me at the coffee shop next to Red Brick at six?"

I nod. "I can do that."

"Great," she says, her face relaxed but still smiley.

The elevator opens and Nora walks onto the floor with confidence the way she always does.

I stand still until the last possible moment before the doors decide to close.

Talking over coffee.

Talking over coffee... about something other than... *well, you know*.

Nora Payne just asked me out.

I step off the elevator and make a hard turn toward the accounting block.

This was the whole point, right? To gain Nora's trust. To earn access to her life and get close enough to... Christ, I don't even remember anymore.

That's a lie. I remember exactly why I'm here and it sure as shit isn't to plug payroll numbers all day.

I lower into my desk and stare at the wall beside my computer monitor.

This is getting too out-of-hand. It was different when it was a possible one-night-stand. It was different when Nora Payne was just another rich bitch from the wealthy district. Just a damn representative of the elite one-percent with enough money to throw at all of her problems — anything Alex and I planned to accomplish included.

I never expected a connection.

I never expected real trust.

I never expected to fall for her.

That's what this is, isn't it? That gripping nausea in my gut twenty-four hours a day? That sick feeling that never goes away until I'm in her presence again. Then, I feel like a million fucking bucks. I feel indestructible. All because she looks up at me and says my name.

She's my sub. I have a responsibility to protect her... inside and outside of the bedroom.

But how long could we possibly last? Not long, that's for damn sure. She'll move on and I'll be left with nothing. That's the only way this can end.

I have to finish the job I started.

TWENTY-SIX

NORA

I look over my shoulder toward the entrance again. It's not even six yet but I can't stop counting the moments.

Talking over coffee. It's the oldest date in the book. I've done it a dozen times before but I've never felt this many butterflies.

The entrance chimes again and I perform a quick look, hoping for that ruggedly handsome and familiar face to walk in and whisk me off my feet, but... no.

It's just Robbie.

I see him before he sees me. He walks in with dirt caked on his jeans and t-shirt but that leather jacket is in pristine condition, as usual. He spots me and I give him a friendly wave. He raises his bandaged hand to acknowledge me as he heads toward the counter to order.

I pick up my phone to distract myself from checking the time again but I just end up checking the time anyway. Five fifty-five. He still has five minutes. *Calm down, girl...*

Robbie plops into the booth across from me and sets his coffee down in front of him. "Hey, Bubbles," he greets, nodding softly. A few tattered, sweat-covered strands of his hair plop down along his forehead.

"Hey, Rob," I say. "You look… tired."

"Just another manic Monday," he answers, raising his coffee to his mouth. "You, on the other hand, look cute as hell, well-rested, and ready for a night out."

"Maybe." I blush. "If he shows up."

"Nora, nobody, and I mean *nobody*, will ever live up to your impossible standards for timeliness and punctuality," he jokes. "Give Daddy a break."

I tilt my head in annoyance. "You, too?"

"Blame Trix. She texted me."

I deflate. "Jeez…"

He chuckles but quickly throws on a more serious face. "For real, though. Are you happy?" he asks. "You look happy."

My smile spreads. "I think I might be."

"And you're safe, right?"

"Uhh…" I laugh. "Yeah, we're *safe.*"

"I don't mean *condoms,*" he quips. "Obviously don't have to ask *you* that. I mean, do you *feel* safe with him? He's not violent or anything?"

I shake my head. "No, he's not. He's dominating, sure, but I've never felt safer. You don't have to worry."

"Are you *sure?*" he asks. "Because there is a very tall, very blue-eyed father figure by the register that looks about ready to beat me up."

I look over my shoulder. Clive stands at the counter across the shop, gently leaning against it as he waits for the barista to make his coffee. A smile touches my lips but he continues staring fire daggers at Robbie.

I turn back to Robbie. "He's a sweetheart, Rob. He just

sees a strange guy talking to his date. Do I need to remind you what happened to the last guy you thought was hitting on Melanie right in front of you?"

He rolls his eyes. "You punch *one* priest and the world never lets you forget it."

I raise a brow while I take a sip from my cup.

"Hey, Nora."

Clive appears over me, his hand instantly falling to rest on my shoulder.

"Hey, Clive." I gesture across the table. "This is my friend, Robbie. Robbie, this is Clive."

"Yo, Clive," Robbie says. He extends his bandaged hand by accident. "Whoa — wait. Hope you don't mind going lefty."

He switches to his left hand and Clive extends his own.

"Nice to meet you," Clive says.

Their handshake lasts a second too long. I look down to find both of them squeezing each other with white-knuckle grips.

Men.

"Anyway…" Robbie takes his hand back. "Good to see you again, Nor."

I nod. "You, too, Rob."

Robbie stands up, purposefully extending his height as tall as he can but Clive clearly towers over him by five inches. He slides his sunglasses free from his pocket and scoots them up his nose. "I'll see y'all around," he says, giving Clive a head nod.

"Bye," Clive says.

Robbie takes off and Clive sits down in the booth across from me.

"What was that about?" he asks me.

"That was just… Robbie," I answer.

He wrinkles his forehead. "Seemed like he was coming on to you," he says, gripping his cup.

I set my coffee down. "Clive, no. Trust me. He's my best friend's ex-husband. We've been friends for a very long time and that's all we've ever been. He's more like a big brother to me than anything."

His shoulders relax a little. "And he's never…?"

"*Never.* Okay — full disclosure — I *have* seen him naked but that was a very strange Easter Sunday parade that he will never live down." I laugh.

"Okay." He cracks a smile. "*Ex*-husband?"

"Yeah."

"What happened there?"

I sigh. "Melanie Rose, despite her profession, isn't the romantic type and Robbie Wheeler is the tattooed bad boy from the other side of town who knows exactly how to push her buttons. They met out of nowhere one night, a few years ago, and it was like a powder-keg. When they weren't fighting, they were fucking, and every moment in-between, they were madly in love. In all my years of setting people up, I've never known two people more entwined than Mel and Rob."

"So, what changed?"

"Robbie is an alcoholic," I say, thinking back. "And after a year of urging him to get help and making excuses for him and his behavior, she had enough."

He raises his coffee. "Seems harsh," he says, taking a sip.

I nod. "It's hard to stand by your man when he can't even stand up on his own. But she tried. We all tried. One day, she kicked him out. They had a huge fight. They both said some things they couldn't take back. She filed the next morning and he signed the papers."

"He didn't try and fight it?" he asks. "If I was that much in love, I don't think I'd give up so easily."

"Oh, Robbie's never given up on Melanie," I say, smiling. "When Melanie decides she wants something, she usually gets it. But Robbie is far more patient than she is. He'll wait." I shake my head. "It's only a matter of time until that keg sparks again. I guarantee it."

Clive's brow bounces once. "You really are good at the whole dating thing."

"Only when it comes to others. My own track record is…" I chuckle into my coffee. "Well, *fail* is such a strong word."

"And it doesn't apply," he says. "I don't think dating and relationships are things you *fail* at. There's far too much chance involved for there to be a definitive formula. Not to throw your livelihood under the bus, of course."

"You might be right." I tilt my head. "Just don't advertise that I said that."

He laughs. "I won't."

I admire him across the table. It's almost strange seeing him somewhere other than the office or standing in the shadowed corners of Red Brick. This is just… Clive Snow. Casual, coffee-drinking Clive Snow.

"Well, enough about me and my friends," I say. "I want to know about you."

"About me?" he asks.

"Yeah." I glance around. "Here we are. Talking over coffee for the first time. It kind of feels like a first date."

He nods, smiling. "A little."

"You want me to trust you, right?" I ask. "I want to, too."

"What do you want to know?" he asks, staring into his coffee.

I shrug. "Where are you from?"

"Here," he answers. "Born and raised."

"Oh, yeah? Where did you go to high school?"

"Amundsen."

I blink. "Me, too."

He leans forward. "Yeah?"

"Class of 2005."

"I was 2010."

"We just missed each other, then." I laugh. "So, that makes you…"

"Twenty-five," he answers.

I bite my lip. "I remember twenty-five."

"Not too long ago for you."

"Feels like a million years," I say, chuckling. "What'd you do after you graduated?"

"I tried more school for a semester or two," he says. "That didn't work out, so… I joined the Army."

"Ahh," I raise my cup, "now here's the good stuff."

Clive shakes his head. "That didn't work out, either."

"What do you mean?"

He pauses. "I went through basic and then they chucked me onto a plane to some desert first chance they could."

"Afghanistan?" I ask.

"Iraq," he corrects. "A few months later, I was injured and they tossed me right on back home."

I hesitate. "Must have been some injury, then."

"It was enough to discharge me for good."

"So…" I look at the table between us. "That scar on your leg is…?"

He fixes his jaw. "You noticed," he says.

"Hard not to."

His eyes go dark for a moment. "I nearly lost it," he says. "I wish I had some amazing story of heroics to go along with it, but I don't. A squad mate of mine panicked under pressure, hugged his rifle a little too hard, and I just happened to step in the way at the wrong time."

I breathe out, my heart breaking. "That's… a letdown."

"It really was." He taps the table. "Anyway, they sent me home and I moved back in with my mother for a while until I could walk again."

"What does she do?" I ask, happy to shift the subject.

"She was a teacher — at our high school, actually."

I lean forward. "Wait, what does she teach?"

"English Lit."

"Mrs. Snow?" My jaw drops as my brain places her. "Your mom is Mrs. Snow?!"

He nods, smiling. "That's Mom."

"I loved Mrs. Snow!"

"Oh, yeah?"

"Wow." I blink with nostalgia. "I haven't thought about English Lit since… English Lit."

Clive laughs. "I'm sure she'd understand."

"I wonder if she remembers me."

His eyes fall again. "She died last year."

I lean back, my guts churning with grief. "Oh, god. I'm so sorry," I say.

"It's all right." He waves a hand. "She worshiped her students. I'm sure she would have remembered you."

Fuck.

How many times am I going to shove my foot in my mouth here?

Still, at least I feel like I know him just a little bit better now. The timeline isn't exactly complete yet but he's already revealed so much. And not an ounce of it is fair. I'm not about to make him tell me more. I'm not even sure I want to hear it, in case my heart rips apart.

I exhale hard. "Clive, I am so sorry," I say again.

"Really, Nora. It's fine."

"No, it's not." I drop my head. "We've been here five minutes and I've paved over the worst possible subjects in your life…"

Still, he smiles. "I guess, in your case, we can probably re-visit the concept of *failure* in dating."

I breathe a laugh. "Fuck. Maybe you're right."

Clive extends his hand across the table and rests it on mine. "Nora, I mean it. If I didn't want to talk to you about these things, I wouldn't have answered. Okay?"

I nod, feeling his warmth climb up to my elbow. "Okay," I say.

He rubs the back of my hand with his thumb and sits back. "So, you're the expert. What do normal couples usually do after the first coffee date crashes and burns?" he asks.

"Well," I grin, sensing opportunity, "according to my expertise, the general consensus is that the man takes the woman back to his place and… he spanks her."

He raises a brow. "Does he?"

"He does."

His head tilts. "Something about that just doesn't seem right…"

I raise my hands. "Hey, you asked the expert."

He stares across the table at me with a subtle hesitation in his blue eyes. "My place, huh?" he asks.

"Yeah," I say.

He sucks in his bottom lip, pausing for a moment before his mouth curls again. "I'll do you one better. Come with me."

I blink as Clive stands with his cup. "Go with you where?"

"Just come on."

I bolt up with excitement, tossing my empty cup in the trash as he leads me outside.

TWENTY-SEVEN

NORA

Clive takes my hand and walks me down the block. We take a right turn into the first alleyway we pass. I look back with suspicion, covering my nose over the stench of garbage while Clive's fingers tighten around mine. Please, don't let me step in a puddle or… worse.

We turn again and I find myself at the coffee shop's alley exit. The next door down is bright red with white grid lines painted from top to bottom.

The Red Brick Road.

Clive reaches into his pocket and withdraws a set of keys. "Be real quiet, okay?" he says.

I bite my cheek in suspense. "Why?"

He unlocks the door and pushes it open. "After you."

I don't hesitate. I walk past him inside, mostly just to get out of this smelly alleyway. He closes the door behind us, plunging the room into darkness but that doesn't seem to slow him down at all. His hand locks on mine in the dark and he leads me down a shadowed corridor cut off from the club's floor. I hear the deep, moody music and the faint hum of voices on the other side of the wall.

"Employees only area," he whispers.

"I figured."

"Watch your step. Going up."

My toes tap the edge of the first step but I find the banister beside me to keep from falling. After a few steps up, I move easier but I keep my tight grip on his hand.

Clive turns a knob and pushes another door wide-open. I blink to adjust to the soft lights inside but my jaw drops as I realize where we are now.

It's a tight corridor, barely large enough for two adults walking side-by-side, with three large windows looking out onto the club's second floor. My head tilts in confusion, thinking that I don't recall those windows being here on the other side, but then—

"Two-way mirrors?" I ask.

Clive pauses by the first window viewing a St. Andrew's cross and smiles. "Yes."

I stand beside him, taking in the view of a young girl tightly restrained to the cross. It's that same couple from my first visits here. Her Dom stands behind her with his belt in one hand and her ponytail in the other, gently tilting back to growl something in her ear. She smiles, just like always.

My skin shifts. "Isn't this…" I pause, feeling the beautiful ache in my neck as he tugs the girl's hair back. "Isn't this like, really wrong?"

"What is?" Clive asks.

"Aren't we invading their privacy? They don't know we're here…"

"In here, out there." He shrugs. "What's the difference?"

I bite my lip, still not sure if I agree. "There are no fake mirrors on the top floor, are there?"

"Oh, no. Those rooms are one-hundred percent private. I wouldn't have taken you up there if they weren't." He points at the windows. "These are just an added measure for keeping people safe. If we suspect someone of bad behavior, we can get a closer look through these."

"Bad behavior?" I chuckle. "Isn't all of this *bad behavior*?"

He winks. "I mean rule-breaking, specifically. Not honoring safe words, things like that."

"Have you ever caught anybody doing that?"

"Once or twice," he answers. "We have a zero-tolerance policy, and yes, it's very satisfying to kick them out."

I nod, feeling a little better about it. "So, why are we here *now*?" I ask.

Clive looks at me, his eyes dropping down to my chest. "I have a fantasy," he says, "and I thought that maybe you'd be willing to help me fulfill it."

"What fantasy?"

"It's kinda naughty."

My lips twitch. "Can we get in trouble for it?"

"Only if we get caught."

"Will we get *arrested* if we get caught?"

He chuckles. "No."

"Okay. What is it?"

Clive bites his lip and takes a quick, cautionary glance over his shoulder. "Stand in front of me," he says.

He puts a hand on my waist and pulls me closer, guiding me in front of him to look through the window. I tense up, feeling paranoid as I look right into the eyes of the girl on the cross, but she doesn't see me looking at her. It feels so dirty… but I like it.

Clive pushes my hair to one side and kisses my neck above my collar. "I want to fuck you while we watch," he whispers in my ear.

I breathe a laugh. "That's it?"

His hand crawls up my thigh, raising my skirt. "That's it."

"I expected something a little more complicated."

"Oh, it might get complicated." He bites my earlobe. "This room isn't soundproofed… and we have no idea when another employee might walk in here."

I shiver, feeling his erection press against me through his jeans. "We'd have to be quick," I say.

"And quiet." His hand crawls into the front of my panties. "What do you say?"

I look forward as the girl's face contorts into a feeling that's so painfully familiar by now. She wants it from her Dom but she can't have it. He won't let her have it. Not until he wills it.

I reach behind my back, quickly finding Clive's belt. "Yes," I whisper, pushing his zipper down.

He lowers my panties to my ankles as he bends me over in the corridor. I put my hands on the wall, split on either side of the window. My breath quickens and my sex aches as I watch the Dom in front of me rake his teeth along the girl's neck. His lips move, whispering god-knows-what that brings that smile to her face. I hear her moaning softly through the glass and I bite my lip to keep from doing the same.

Clive's cock stands on end between my thighs. He rubs

his tip on my entrance, enticing me to open but I'm already so wet for him.

He thrusts inside and I gasp with pleasure.

"Shh," he whispers behind me. He lays one strong hand on my shoulder and the other on my hip to hold me in place. "Don't make a sound…"

It's a struggle already. His dick slides in and out of me and my toes curl from the pressures inside. The added visual stimulation from the couple in front of us isn't helping either.

"Ms. Payne," Clive whispers in my ear, his breath rushing out. "I want to put you on that cross again."

I nod, wanting it, too.

"Now that I know…" His hand moves from my shoulder to the back of my head. "That you…" He curls his fingers to grab my hair. "Are such a good girl—"

The girl through the glass yelps in pain as her Dom's belt hits her ass.

Clive lays his other palm on my rear as my desire builds. "When you're ready… this is what I'll do to you."

The Dom pulls back his arm, gearing up to slap her with the belt again. I cringe with the same anticipation as Clive's hand hovers over my ass. The belt connects with her back, creating a loud slapping noise, and Clive slaps my ass at the same exact time.

I whimper in pleasure.

"I'll push you until you break…" He readies his hand again. "And then, just when you think you can't take anymore…" The belt swings down and they both strike us again. "I'll fuck you as hard as I can."

I cry out in painful ecstasy but Clive slaps his hand over my mouth to cut off the sound.

"Shh," he scolds. "Bad girl."

He quickens his thrusts, pounding harder. I moan into his hand, unable to help myself as pleasure spurs in my sex.

"Is that what you want?" he growls in my ear. "To be my bad girl? Do you want me to punish you? Is that it?"

I shake my head as my body betrays me by shoving me toward the edge.

"Don't come," he says. "Only good girls get to come."

I hold back, clenching every muscle in my body to try and quell the relief begging to undo me. *"Please…"* I beg.

He continues with quick, steady thrusts. "Please what?"

"Please let me come, Mr. Snow," I whisper.

"If I do…" He draws my chin back. "Then, you have to do something for me."

I nod. "Yes."

Clive taps my lips. "If you come, then you have to let me come in your mouth," he says. "And you're not allowed to swallow me until we leave this place." He kisses the corner of my mouth. "Do you understand?"

I shudder, completely taken in. "Yes, Mr. Snow."

He holds me tighter. "After you, Ms. Payne."

I dig my nails into the wall along the mirror. Clive moves in me, fucking and grinding me until I'm almost screaming through his hand.

I look through the glass and watch that couple. He's released his sub from her restraints and he's holding her the same way Clive held me after. She's shaking but his tender touch brings warmth to her eyes. I think of that release and how good it felt to be loved in that way. To be held and respected and cared for.

I come hard in Clive's arms. Every muscle twitches and

his solid grip never loosens on me. It's so safe and secure. I never want to leave his arms.

He kisses the edge of my mouth again. "Kneel," he whispers.

I fall to my knees, using all of my strength to lift my head and present my tongue to him.

Clive takes hold of his cock and strokes himself. He lays his other hand beneath my chin to tilt me into place.

He comes quickly and my tongue twitches the instant his semen touches my taste buds. I catch every drop of it, forcing myself not to swallow. I wrap my lips around his tip, sucking him clean as he brushes the hair out of my face.

"Good girl," he says.

He extends his hand to help me off my knees. I pick up my panties and quickly slide them back on as he tucks himself back into his pants. There's a feeling of urgency. Anyone could walk in here. We've done the hard part. Now we just have to get out.

Clive leads me back to the stairwell. We rush down with light feet but voices coming our way bring us pause. I hold my jaw clenched, tasting more of his sweetness with every flinch of my tongue. He pulls me into a dark corner behind the stairs and we wait silently for the employees to wander by.

Once they're gone, Clive guides me to the back exit again.

We burst out into the alleyway and he instantly holds up a finger to me.

"Wait..." he says. "Show me."

I carefully open my mouth to prove I've been good.

He smiles. "You can swallow now."

I close my mouth and force it back, feeling it tingle all the way down my throat.

"Thank you, Mr. Snow," I say.

Clive pulls me in and kisses my wet lips. "Let's go back to your place," he says.

I bite my inner cheek. It's not what I was hoping for but I can't say no, either.

I take his hand and we rush out of the alley, quickly blending into the crowd.

TWENTY-EIGHT

NORA

I t hurts.

I thought it'd stop once we made it back to my place and I fell into his arms.

I thought it'd stop after he cuffed my hands behind my back and had his way with me.

I thought it'd stop once we fell asleep with our limbs entwined and I sure as hell didn't expect it to still hurt when I woke up in his arms this morning.

This just fucking hurts.

I walk into Melanie's apartment building shortly before nine. I'll be late for work, that's for sure, but I can't bring myself to care about that as much this morning.

I roll my fist and tap twice on her door.

"Enter!" Melanie shouts from inside.

I turn the knob but the door doesn't budge. "It's locked, Mel!" I shout.

I wait for several moments until the lock finally slips free and the door swings open on Melanie in all her messy bun glory. Off the shoulder shirt. Baggy pants. The faint smell of alcohol. Yep, she's been up all night writing.

"Hiya," she says.

I throw a sympathetic pout. "Rough night?"

"These characters... will not fuck," she says, stepping backward and leaving the door open for me. "Unlike *you,* I bet."

I close the door behind me. "Well, you're not wrong."

Melanie shuffles toward her writing desk in the corner and plops onto her old desk chair. "Of course I'm not." She points at me. "Hey, since your life is basically a porno now, can I start a weekly serial based on you and your erotic adventures?"

"Uh..." I toss my jacket over the back of the couch. "No."

"*Nora Payne and the Kink Club Cumshot,*" she says. "*Nora Payne and the Sex-Crazed Stud Muffin.* I could do this all day..."

"Please don't."

Trix pops up on the couch behind me with a bag of cheddar popcorn in her lap. "*Nora Payne and the Backseat Blowjob.*"

I gasp in surprise. "Jeez, Trix—" I pause, clutching my heart. "Wait, how'd you know about that?"

"I didn't, ya big whore." She stuffs popcorn into her grinning mouth and crunches it between her teeth.

I roll my eyes. "What are you doing here?" I ask.

She swallows. "Still hiding."

"From Marcus?"

"Yeah. I've been here all night. Mel and I might still be little wine-drunk, so if you're here for advice, *it's gonna be awesome.*"

Melanie chuckles. "What's up, Nora?"

I exhale hard. "Well… he's a vet. He's a goddamn home-less *vet.*"

Trix beams. "Aww, I love animals."

I glare at her.

"Oh. Never mind. You mean the other kind." She slinks down behind the seat again in shame.

"I don't know what to do," I say. "My heart is bleeding. He joined the Army. He almost lost his leg. He came home and his mom died. Oh—! And I knew his mom!"

Melanie squints. "How did you know his mom?"

"She was my English Lit teacher in high school. She made me read *Gatsby* and now I'm fucking her son."

"Aww, that's cute," Trix says behind me.

Melanie nods. "It is kinda poetic."

I hold my face in my hands. "He's so pretty and smart and sexy and his story is so sad and depressing but he's so pretty *and I don't know what to do.*"

"See, now," Melanie's face screws up, "I'd like to help you, Nor, but I don't understand the problem…"

"Yeah." Trix talks with her mouth full of popcorn. "It sounds like you and your patriotic vagina already got this one."

Melanie snaps her fingers. *"Nora Payne and the Chick Lit Clit Cadet."*

"Good one!" Trix flicks a thumbs-up.

"Thank you."

I fall into the armchair beside Melanie's desk. "The *problem* is that I'm really starting to feel things for this guy."

"Oh, no," Melanie says, completely deadpan. "You're falling for an attractive guy who seems to really like you. How dare you."

"I just mean…" I sit forward. "I want to help him but I

don't know how to do that without it seeming like I pity him."

"Pfft!" Trix snorts. "Fuck that. If we were *men,* do you think we'd all be sitting around wondering whether or not your mistress thinks her new diamond necklace makes her feel *pitied?*"

"Well, no, but—"

"Do you think our mighty man-penises give a flying fuck about her and her dainty *masculinity?*"

I look at Melanie. "How much wine did you let her have?"

She tilts her head. "Girl has a point, though."

"*Nora…*" Trix scolds me. "This man should bow down to your womanly altar. He should thank his lucky stars you allow him to be in your heavenly presence *at all.* He should accept your generosity with style and grace and…" She takes a breath. "I should lie down."

She disappears behind the couch again.

Melanie clears her throat. "What Beatrix here is *trying* to say is that Sugar Mama got the goods, and if Daddy wants those goods, then Daddy better put up." She glances at the couch. "Right?"

Trix's thumb shoots up again. "That'll do."

I sigh. "I got the goods, huh?"

Melanie nods. "Ya really do. And I get it, I do. I used to wonder the same thing about Robbie, remember?"

I think back. "Yeah."

"In the end, it was a non-issue because any hang-ups he may have had over me being the breadwinner were vastly outweighed by how *proud* he was of me for my successes." She shakes her head. "If Clive's insecurity about his failures means more to him than being proud of you and sharing your successes then I don't think this relationship can go much further."

"You're right," I say, nodding. "You're totally right. If spoiling him makes both of us feel good, then I shouldn't feel bad about that."

"Exactly."

"Thank you," I tell her.

She smirks. "I learned it from watching you."

Trix shoots up on the couch again. "Wait! I got it. *Nora Payne and the Star-Spangled Gangbang.*"

Melanie raises a fist. "Nailed it!"

"That'll be three-thousand dollars," Trix says, looking smug.

I frown. "I need new friends."

TWENTY-NINE

CLIVE

"Hey, temp."

I look up at Ali's hovering head between our desks. "Yeah?"

She shines a mischievous smile. "Boss lady wants to see you."

I pause. "She does?"

"Mmm-hmm." She holds up a folder with my name stamped on it and passes it over to me. "It's your four-week performance evaluation today."

I stare at the folder in my hand, wondering where the hell the time went. "You're kidding."

She shrugs. "She said anytime but you might as well get it over with now. Payne can be... pretty rough."

My lips twitch. "You don't say?"

Ali disappears behind the wall. I feel a quick tease of adrenaline in my veins. Nora and I have to be careful around here. It's rare that I find a genuine reason to go into her office.

I take the folder with me and make my way over, trying to act as normal and casual as possible.

Nora sits at her desk with her reading glasses on. She's immersed in something — logo designs, by the looks of it — and she doesn't notice me in the doorway. I take a moment to admire the view of her. Her milk-white skin and blood-red lips. Her blonde hair pulled back in a loose, but somehow elegantly professional, up-do. Her perfectly manicured French-tipped nails. And the collar, of course.

I look through the glass top desk at her outfit. It's a gray suit jacket with a white blouse and...

I furrow my brow. Nora's wearing a skirt. Nora Payne *never* wears a skirt to work.

I tap the door frame. "You wanted to see me, Ms. Payne?"

Her little eyes flick in my direction and for a second, I wonder if she really did know I was here the whole time and she was just... *playing.*

"Come on in, Clive," she says. "Close the door behind you."

I do as she says. She is the boss, after all.

I close the door and lay the folder down on her desk.

"Sit down," she says.

I take a seat as she flicks the folder open. "Four weeks," she muses, turning over my resume.

"Yes, ma'am," I say.

"Ali seems to like you."

I nod. "I guess so."

She glances at me over the thick rims of her glasses. "Do you enjoy the work you do here, Clive?" she asks.

"I enjoy working for you, Ms. Payne."

"That's not what I asked."

"No," I answer truthfully. "It's not the kind of work I would prefer, but it is work and I'm happy to do it."

She flops the folder onto her desk. "What kind of work would you prefer to be doing?"

I pause. "I'm not sure."

Nora slowly uncrosses her legs. "I have something in mind for you," she says. "I would highly recommend you consider it if you value your future place at this company... Mr. Snow."

I raise a brow. "What did you have in mind, Ms. Payne?"

She looks at me, her eyes dropping down to my chest. "I have a fantasy," she says, "and I thought that maybe you'd be willing to help me fulfill it."

I smile. "What fantasy?"

"It's kinda naughty..."

"Name it."

She chews on her red lip as her nervous eyes flick behind me. "Get on your knees," she says.

I slowly slide from my chair onto the floor.

"Not there," she says, gently turning. "Here."

She spreads her knees, hiking up her skirt to reveal herself. I look forward beneath the glass-top desk, instantly salivating at the smooth skin of her thighs and the pretty, pink pussy on display just for me.

I drop onto my hands and crawl toward her beneath the desk. "Like this?" I ask.

"Mm-hmm," she hums, nodding her head as my lips peck at her knees. "I want my employee to do *anything* to keep his job."

I laugh. "Anything?"

"Yes."

"That *is* naughty."

She winces with playful eyes, her character breaking. "I'd never do something like this for real... but since I helped you with your naughty workplace fantasy..."

I kiss her inner thigh and she releases a passionate breath. "You want me to do the same."

"I know it's probably not what you had in mind when you asked me to be your sub, but—"

"Nora," I interrupt, "I love your pussy so much, you couldn't pay me not to eat it whenever you wanted it."

I bury my face between her legs, parting my lips and sticking out my dripping tongue.

Nora gasps, her voice muted and suppressed. She opens her legs wider and hoists them up over my shoulders as I slide my hands beneath her ass to pull her even closer to me. I coat my tongue with her flavor, letting it overwhelm me like a damn animal.

"That's it," she whispers. *"Right there."*

I lap her clit, using soft and slow moves to make her purr for me. It might not be the best use of time — anyone could knock or open the door at any moment — but this is her fantasy and I don't want to rush it. Hell, I might have daydreamed about this once or twice myself.

Her fingers comb through my hair, twitching softly against my scalp. "I haven't been very impressed by your performance recently, Clive," she says through heavy breathing.

I chuckle against her thigh. "I'm sorry, Ms. Payne." I suck on her clit once. "I promise I'll be a very, *very* good boy from now on."

Her head rolls back. "Yes..."

"You can double my workload," I say, staring up at her. "I'll stay late... if it means you'll sit on my face."

She lets herself moan, quiet but deep. "That would be a good start," she teases.

I unleash a flurry of tongue-lashings along her clit and her knees knock against my ears.

"I'll give you one-hundred and ten percent... of my cock."

She slaps her hands over her mouth to smother her laugh. "Clive..."

"I don't even know how that's possible but I'm sure the creative team can help me think of something."

"Shut up," she says, flicking my forehead.

I grin. "Yes, ma'am."

I latch my mouth around her clit, giving it a hard suck between my teeth. Nora fights the scream in her chest as she grabs me by the hair again.

"Just like that," she moans. *"Fuck."*

A wave of wetness covers my tongue. I lap it up, refusing to abandon even just a little bit of it. I groan for her as she twitches with pleasure and gasps for breath. I look up at her, admiring her flushed cheeks and rising breasts. There's nothing I don't love about this view. Her silky skin and juicy lips. Those reading glasses that make her look like the hottest fucking librarian in the whole Midwest. My dick throbs for release but I control my urges in favor of giving her what she needs.

"Clive," she says, convulsing in her chair. *"I'm coming."*

My jaw burns but I keep going. Her nails dig into my scalp as she comes and I bite the flesh of her thigh to stop myself from crying out, too. She gasps and flinches but she doesn't stop the beautiful ruin taking over her.

I continue eating her, focusing on her entrance to give

her sensitive clit a break. She'll stop me when she's ready...
but I'm not ready to stop yet.

Nora gazes down at me, breathing hard as her lips curl.
"Not bad, temp," she says.

I plunge my tongue inside of her and she slaps my
forehead.

"No, no..." she scolds, still smiling. "If you don't stop
now, I might never let you..."

I pull out and kiss her inner thighs. "I suppose it would
look suspicious if I spent all day in here," I say.

She hums with pleasure as she caresses my cheeks.
"Whatever happened to *it's the 21st century?* No one cares
about that kind of thing anymore..."

"Nora, I was so desperate to get into your pants, I would
have said anything."

Her jaw drops. "I knew it! You filthy, little liar."

I laugh and catch her wrist before she can slap me. "I'm
only here for another few weeks," I point out as I leave a
few kisses on her knuckles. "Then, I won't be your
employee anymore. No one..." I spread her knees a little
wider, "will give..." and kiss her thighs again, "a single
fuck."

She combs her fingers through my hair, encouraging me
to continue my trek back to her dripping slit.

"What if..." she says, "your employment at Black Book
wasn't so temporary?"

I raise my head. "What do you mean?"

"I mean that our company sees great value in keeping
you around on a more permanent basis," she says, her lips
curling. "Accounting, for instance, is always in need of a
second pair of eyes."

"Are you sure?" I smirk. "We both know that I'm not the best at doing that."

"What about the creative department?" she offers instead. "We're starting development on a sister app. One more focused on matching people based on sexual kink."

I lean away slightly. "You are?"

She nods. "We need an expert to help determine what kinks go best together with certain lifestyles." She runs her finger along my brow. "Naturally, I thought of you."

"Oh, I'm an expert now?" I ask, amused.

"You know more than I do. You have connections with others who might know more than that." She smiles. "Just think about it, okay?"

I sit back on my knees. "Are you serious about this?"

Nora lowers her feet to the floor. "Yes," she answers.

"You're really offering me a full-time job here?"

"Salaried with benefits. Yes."

I close my mouth, suddenly realizing it was hanging open. "Why?" I ask.

She presses her red lips together. "I like having you around. You're like…" She smiles. "Okay. When I was a kid, I only ever had vanilla ice cream."

I laugh. "Oh, I see where this is going…"

She grins. "And all of my friends kept telling me about chocolate. And strawberry."

"And rocky road?" I ask.

"And rocky road!"

"So, I'm your naughty, corrupting, devil ice cream," I joke. "Is that it?"

"You're that sweet, delicious, wonderful treat that I should have let myself have *ages ago*." She runs her thumb along my cheek. "And I don't want to give you up."

"Even if I make you fat?"

"Especially if you make me fat." She laughs. "How's that for a performance evaluation?"

I shake my head in disbelief. "I don't know what to say."

"Say you'll take it," she says. "Or, at the very least, that you'll think about it."

"In that case..." I push forward, stopping just short of her lips. "I'll think about it."

Nora gently purses those perfect red lips against mine.

"Good boy," she says.

THIRTY

CLIVE

Nora digs her nails into my chest and I know she's seconds away from coming. She rounds her hips on me, riding and grinding my cock while I lie back and enjoy the view.

I'll never get tired of this damn view.

You would think starting each day by giving your boss an orgasm would be a frowned-upon practice but I'm certainly not filing anything with human resources just yet.

She collapses onto my chest, breathing hard. A laugh shakes her shoulders, small at first but then grows even louder.

"I guess you enjoyed that," I say, pushing her hair out of her face.

She hums in satisfaction before rolling off me.

I sit up and watch as she walks away, admiring her perfect body as it disappears into the bathroom.

"We're gonna be late again," she says.

I stretch out on the bed. "It's Friday. Everyone's a little late on Fridays."

She pokes her head in and raises a stern brow. "Do I need to review your time logs, Clive?"

I laugh. "I hope not."

She smiles and steps back into the bathroom. The sink turns on, followed quickly by the usual sounds of teeth brushing.

I sit up and throw my feet onto the floor. If I don't hop up now, she'll start scolding me. That'll just turn me on and we'll be right back at square one.

"*Clive…*" she begins.

"I'm up!" I say with a chuckle.

I stand and make my way into the bathroom. After a quick rinse off in the shower, I start gathering my clothes off the floor. Nora's already done her make-up and fixed her hair, leaving nothing left to do but slip into the outfit she's already laid out for herself. I could probably learn a thing or two from her about preparation.

"It's payday," she says as she steps into her pants.

I nod as I button my shirt. "The best day."

"Got any fun plans?"

"Oh, paying a bill or two, I imagine," I say, keeping it vague. I spot her briefcase lying on the bed. "Do you mind if I use your laptop to check my balance?"

She smiles and turns back into the bathroom. "No, go ahead," she says, her heels clicking along the hard floor.

I zip it open and pause.

LBB. The little, black harddrive.

It's right here.

I look at the bathroom. It would take three seconds for me to pocket it and disappear. Meet up with Alex. Sell it and pocket a million dollars.

I reach in and pull out the laptop instead.

Nora walks back in as I sit down. I open the internet browser, feeling the urge to angle the screen away from her as I check my account balance.

Wait...

Well, this isn't right.

I was definitely paid today but this isn't my usual office temp pay.

"Something wrong?" Nora asks.

I refresh the page in case there was a glitch but it's still wrong. "Yeah," I mutter. "I think Ali might have messed up somewhere."

"Why? Were you not paid?"

"No, I was paid, but this is..." I pause and look up into her knowing eyes. "Did you do this?"

"Do what?"

"This is *three times* my usual pay," I say.

She doesn't look the least bit concerned. "Weird."

"Nora." I close the laptop and stand up. "What are you doing? I haven't accepted your job offer yet."

"I know," she says, smiling. "But you've been working very hard lately. We agreed that a nice bonus was in order."

"We?"

"Yes, we."

"Who's we?"

"Me, your boss."

"Don't you find this a tad bit inappropriate?" I ask.

She tilts her head in amusement. "And how many nights have you spent here this week?"

"Using my dick as an alarm clock is one thing, Nor," I argue. "Giving me a raise *in exchange for it* hoists up some red flags."

She puts on her suit jacket. "It's not a permanent raise,

Clive. I just have a little idea how much money you make and it's not enough for tonight."

I frown. "And what's tonight?"

"Dinner," she says as she slides her laptop back into her case and zips it up. "You're taking me someplace very, very nice for dinner tonight."

"Uh..." I shake my head. "No, I'm not. I have a shift at Red Brick."

"No, you don't. I took care of it. Meet me on the roof at four."

I blink. "You took care of it?"

Nora smiles and speaks slower. "You're taking me to dinner instead."

"No, *you're* taking you to dinner. This is like giving a kid a twenty and letting him hand it to the cashier. It's *your* money — and why the roof?"

Her smile doesn't fade. "You'll see." She takes one last look in the mirror. Stunning perfection. "Four o'clock. Don't be late. Want some coffee?"

I stumble over my tongue. "Sure."

I listen to the determined tap of her shoes, easily picturing the exact way she walks through the condo. Wide, confident strides. Head up, shoulders down, with murder in her eyes.

Something isn't right here.

But it doesn't feel all that wrong, either.

―――――――――

I knew my answer the second the job offer fell from her mouth. Long before I had the chance to grab that harddrive and take off. Long before I sat down in this old, damn car and drove out here to the gym.

A salaried position at Little Black Book isn't something anyone turns down, homeless or otherwise. I could work normal hours. Take nights off for something — anything — else. I could have hobbies. A life.

A life with Nora Payne.

That doesn't sound all that bad.

I walk through the gym, scanning the faces for Alex. A few regulars notice me and acknowledge me with a head nod and I do the same.

Strange. This might be the last time I do that.

I hear him before I see him. He's chatting up some woman who clearly just wants to use the treadmill in peace.

"Alex," I say.

He twists around and smiles at me. I wave him over, gesturing for him to follow me into the locker room — and leave the poor girl alone. He's not supposed to stop and talk to the customers in his jumpsuit anyway.

I wait in a quiet corner among the lockers. Private but not too private. I don't think he'll react to this very well.

Alex springs into the room with a mop and bucket. He rolls it in my direction and raises his lip at my suit and tie. "Hey, Mr. Fancy Pants. I didn't think you worked here today."

"I don't."

He wrings out the mop and plops it on the floor. "Come for a run? Because I must request you do it somewhere *away* from the redhead out there," he jokes. "If she sees you, she'll never look at me again."

"Listen, Alex," I say, keeping an even tone. "We need to talk."

He barely looks up from his mop. "About what?"

"This job. I can't do it anymore."

He snorts. "It's just cleaning toilets, man."

"You know what I mean."

His head finally rises. "You don't mean *the job* job, right? Not that job?"

I nod. "That job."

Alex tosses the mop back into the bucket. "What do you mean you can't do it? Just swipe the damn thing while she's sleeping. Easy peasy."

"I can't," I say again.

His brow furrows in confusion for a moment before shifting to a frown. "Oh, this isn't *can't*, is it? This is *won't*."

"She's a good girl," I argue.

"She's a *what?*"

"I mean, she's *a good person,*" I correct myself. "And she doesn't deserve this."

"What the fuck do you care about some rich bitch?" he asks, growing furious. "She'll *manage*. Meanwhile, poor, hardworking men like you and me get shit on. It's time for us to get ours, Clive."

I shake my head. "Not like this."

He fumes. "What the hell's gotten into you?"

"Look, I'm sorry, all right," I say. "But I have to think ahead here and do the right thing."

"The right thing?" he repeats. "The right thing for who? For you? For *her?* Sure as shit ain't the right thing for me, man. What about me? I'm the one playing footsie with a bunch of criminals who would rather slit my throat than forget about this. While you, what? Fuck some hot chick? Is this cunt really worth throwing away a friendship for?"

I roll my fists. "You're out of line, Alex."

"No, *you're* out of line!" He points at me. "I'm not about to let five million dollars slip through the cracks because your dick had an attack of conscience."

I blink. *"Five* million?"

His face turns white. "No, not five, I meant—"

"You told me the deal was for *two* million. Remember?" I point between us. "One for you. One for me."

"It *was!* I mean, it *is,* I just got confused," he stutters.

He looks down, lying through his fucking teeth.

"You were going to stiff me out of my cut, weren't you?" I ask. "You were going to hand over one million and pocket the other four."

He wags his head. "No, no. I wasn't—"

"Yes, you were." My guts churn. "This was never about *making it up to me,* was it? You wanted a payday and you *used me* to get into Black Book because you couldn't get in yourself."

He twitches. "Clive, I—"

"You know what, Alex?" I flex my jaw. "I forgive you."

He looks up. "What?"

"I forgive you," I repeat. "I forgive you for losing your fucking shit in Iraq. I forgive you for nearly shooting my goddamn leg off. I forgive you for setting me up and trying to steal one-point-five million dollars from me—"

"Clive, come on, we can still split it. Two-point-five for you. Two-point-five for me."

I bear my teeth. "I forgive you, Alex. Now, *get out of my life.* If I ever see you again, I will kill you myself. Do you understand?"

He recoils and drops his head again. "Wait. Clive—"

I ignore him.

Hell, I forget he even exists by the time I step outside.

Four o'clock. Don't be late.

I board the elevator at three fifty-five, feeling more than a little uneasy. And excited. But mostly uneasy. I have no idea what's going to happen when I reach the roof. I can't remember the last time something like this happened to me.

Yes, I can. Never. It's *never* happened to me.

The elevator opens on the top floor and I spot a door down the hall marked *roof.* My heart pounds harder with each step I take toward it. Just one quick flight upward and I reach the roof access door.

I open it and my skin chills, instantly touched by the thin, cold air up here.

"You're late."

I smile. "No, I'm not."

Nora smirks at me from the center of the helicopter pad. My eyes bounce between her, the amazing view from the top of Chicago, and — of course — the giant fucking helicopter parked behind her.

I walk up to her and the amusement deepens on her face. "What is this?" I ask her.

"Our ride to the airport," she answers. "The restaurant is a little outside of town."

My guts churn. It's been a long time since I've been in one of these. "How far outside of town?" I ask.

Nora smiles.

THIRTY-ONE

CLIVE

New York City. That's how far outside of town.

I stare out the window of our hotel suite, trading one brilliant skyline for another, wondering whose life I'm living right now. It's not mine, that's for sure. This suit that just happened to be here for me to change into when we got here isn't mine, either. These shiny shoes. That chilled bottle of champagne on the cart by the door. I don't own a single damn thing in this room.

"Are you lost, honey?"

I follow Nora's voice behind me. She stands in the bathroom doorway in midnight blue cocktail dress and a black clutch purse. Her hair is up, perfectly-styled off the neck to give that collar its time to shine.

"What?" I ask.

"That's what Judy said to me my first night at Red Brick," she says, smiling.

I chuckle at the window. "Yeah, I might be."

She wanders up behind me and wraps her arms around

my waist. "Soak it in, Clive. It's gonna be a good night," she says.

Her hands fall away. I try and do just that. Let it all soak in. But a resistance keeps me from putting both feet on the ground.

Something about the look in her eyes. Like she knows how out of my element I am here. The fancy clothes, the new shoes. She's dangling this life in front of my face like a shiny object.

Like a distraction from the hell I usually live in.

"Ready to head upstairs?" she asks.

I look at her and nod.

The hotel restaurant sits on the very top floor. We ride the elevator up and the doors open on a few dozen tables and a three-sixty view of Manhattan.

"Good evening, Ms. Payne," the hostess greets as we step off. "Your table is ready."

Nora smiles at her. "Thank you."

She takes my hand and we follow through the restaurant to the opposite corner.

The hostess sits us down with a wine list and two glasses of water. "Your server will be with you soon. Enjoy the views," she says.

I sit quietly, almost afraid to touch anything. This chair alone probably costs more than my car is worth.

"So, what do you think?" Nora asks me.

"Uhh…" I laugh. "Kind of blank up here right now."

She takes a sip of her water. "I know what you mean."

"Do you?"

"Of course. I wasn't born wealthy."

I nod. "Right."

Nora takes a moment to look out the windows herself.

"So, have you considered my job offer?" she asks, her eyes reflecting candlelight.

"I have," I say slowly.

She waits for an answer, her head tilted in suspense.

"And…" I wet my dry lips. "I'm leaning toward a yes."

"Leaning?" she asks.

"Leaning," I repeat.

"Anything I can say to tip you over?"

I laugh but it fades quickly. "Why are we really here, Nor?" I ask.

She adjusts her hands in her lap. "Because I wanted to spend time with you," she answers. "We can't do that publicly outside of the club and coffee shops just yet, so…"

"So, you figured… New York City?"

She shrugs, chuckling lightly. "Why not?"

"Feels…" My voice falls.

"Feels like what?"

"Like I'm a dirty, little secret."

She smiles. "You are. Is that so bad?"

"You sure there's nothing else? No other reason why you would splurge like this?"

Her brow furrows. "What else is there?"

I study her bright face. For the slightest second, her eyes twitch with nerves. "You know, don't you?" I ask.

"Know what?"

"Come on, Nora." I shift in my chair. "The hints about hooking up at *my* place? Sneaking extra money into my account? Offering me a permanent job that you know I'm in *no way* qualified for?"

She looks down. "I don't know what you're talking about. I just thought it'd be fun to—"

"I'm homeless," I say. "I'm a poor, homeless soldier that you *feel sorry for.*"

Her mouth sags open. "No, Clive. That's not—"

"How did you know?" I ask.

She hesitates, pressing her red lips together before speaking. "A friend told me," she answers.

"What friend?"

"Melanie Rose."

I nod. "Of course."

"I dropped your name at brunch and she said she knew you from an interview you gave her…"

"Christ…" I sigh.

"She still had her notes on all the things you told her, including how you were living out of your car at the time and I saw that your car still had signs of *living in it* and I just—"

"When did you see my car?" I interrupt.

She winces. "Ah, jeez."

"When, Nora?" I ask again.

"Sunday," she says. "At the gym you work at."

"How did you know what gym I worked at?"

She deflates. "I kind of… *feroed yue,*" she mumbles.

I lean forward. "You what?"

"I followed you," she says again, her face full of shame.

"You followed me?"

"We saw you at the laundromat," she admits. "I didn't want to follow you. I said it was wrong but Trix and Melanie were gonna do it anyway so I tagged along and I waited for you to go inside before checking your car and—" She exhales hard. "Are you mad?"

"No, just very…" I shake my head at the table. "Actually,

yeah. Maybe a little. I don't know. I'm embarrassed, that's for sure. Mad might sneak in later."

"But you don't have to be!" she says. "It doesn't matter to me. Really."

"It matters to me," I say. "Nora, it matters to me."

"Okay, but…"

She shrinks in her chair, looking even smaller than she usually does.

"Nora, I don't think you realize how intimidating you are," I say. "I mean, Jesus, you're the wealthiest woman in Chicago."

"Well… not technically," she says, raising a finger. "Wealthiest woman *under thirty*, sure, or I was last year… but that's not important! It's not! I don't care about money."

"Spoken like someone who has it," I bite.

"Oh, come on, Clive. Don't be like that."

"How am I supposed to be?" I ask. "Reverse this. Imagine being in my shoes right now. How would you feel if I tripled your pay and literally flew you across state lines to some flashy place just to impress you after I gossiped about your private business behind your back with my friends?"

"I'd…" Her face wrinkles. "I'd be pretty pissed off."

"Uh-huh."

"And embarrassed and insulted." She hangs her head, briefly touching her cheeks. "God, Clive. I'm sorry."

What the hell was I thinking? I knew this would happen from the start. I knew that once she knew who I really was things would change between us.

"Honestly, Nora," I say, forcing the words to come out. "I think we should think twice about this."

Nora looks up. "Think twice about what?"

"About…" I gesture between us. "Us. You and me."

"I made an awkward judgment call," she says. "Let's not jump onto the first knee-jerk reaction."

"This isn't a knee-jerk reaction," I argue. "This is about fundamental lifestyle differences."

Her eyes narrow. "Lifestyle differences?"

"You have every opportunity, Nora. You deserve a man with just as much influence and ability to provide—"

"So, a woman's not allowed to date beneath her tax bracket?" she asks.

"I… didn't say that."

Her eyes flare up. "No, that's exactly what you're saying. I'm a rich girl. You're a poor boy. Kate and Leo covered this already. We don't have to sneak below deck for third class dance parties anymore."

I set my hands on the table. "What can I possibly give you that you don't already have? Or that you can't just go out and buy?"

"Clive…" She exhales. "Clive, you own something no amount of money could *ever* buy."

"Yeah, what's that?"

She tilts her head, the answer so painfully obvious. *"Me,"* she says.

I look at the pearl hanging from her neck. "It's just plastic," I say.

"I don't care."

"But you will," I claim. "Someday. You will."

She extends her hand across the table and lays it down with her palm up.

"I feel safe with you," she says. *"I don't care about money, and yes, it's because I have it and I'll probably never want for it again, but that doesn't fulfill me."*

I sigh. "Nora…"

"I was a barren shell until you held me and asked me if I was okay. Now, I'm prepared to do the same for you." She heaves a frustrated breath. "And dammit, I don't care if you think it's charity because — fuck it — *it is*. Life wasn't fair to you, I can change that, and I won't take no for an answer."

I lean away from her open hand. "Nora—"

"I love you, Clive."

My heart stops in my chest. "You *what?*"

She furrows her brow. "I think…"

"You *think?*"

"I don't know. It just came out."

"It just *came out?*"

Nora lays her hand over her heart. "I think I forgot to breathe again…" She fills her lungs to the top. "Yep. Seeing spots now."

I rise halfway out of my chair. "Nora, are you—"

She holds up a hand. "It's fine. I'm cool. Let's just move on."

I stay put, hovering and ready to stand. "Are you sure?"

"Salmon."

I blink. "What?"

She picks up a menu. "Feeling salmon tonight. Do you like salmon—?"

"*Nora.*" I sit down. "Do you love me?"

"Maybe go for the classic steak and potatoes. The meat here is so soft, you can cut it with a spoon—"

I snatch the menu out of her hand. "Nora, do you love me?" I ask again.

"Oh, you heard that?" she squeaks.

I let out a laugh. "Yes. I did."

She looks down. "Well, I just…" She pokes her inner

cheek with her tongue and taps her nail against the bottom of her water glass. "I mean…"

I shake my head. Tense and speechless Nora Payne…

"I love you, too," I say.

Nora stares at her hands for so long, I think that maybe she didn't hear it. Finally, her head turns up and she looks across the table at me.

"You do?" she asks.

I nod. "Yes."

She doesn't move. Even her eyes stay fixed in their sockets.

"Breathe," I remind her.

She inhales deep. Her cheeks flush and her lips twitch as she pushes the air out again. She bites her lip and nods over and over until she gets up the nerve to look at me again with those big, glistening eyes.

"I love you," she says again.

I extend my hand across the table and lay it open with my palm up. She takes it and I hold it until her fingers stop shaking.

"So, what do normal couples usually do after saying I love you?" I ask her.

She laughs. "Well, according to my expertise, the general consensus is that the man carries his woman down to their hotel room and he fucks her brains out."

We lock eyes and her lips curl upward into a sweet, sinful smile.

Yes, Ms. Payne.

I raise a hand. "Check, please."

Nora glances around after a few seconds of silence. "I don't think they heard you," she says, amused.

I whisper across the table. "Yeah, that seemed weird

when I saw it in the movies. What waiter is *always* around to hear that? They've got shit to do."

She laughs and grabs her clutch. "Actually, we only got water so far, so I think we can just *leave.*"

"All right."

We stand up quickly and I grab her hand as we beeline across the restaurant back to the elevator. She taps the call button repeatedly while we dodge the curious eyes of the host staff.

Finally, the doors open and we pounce onto the empty elevator. The doors barely slide closed again before my urges take over and I pull her body against mine.

We kiss, and this time, it feels deeper than before. Cosmically charged and delicately real. She feels almost softer, smoother, but no less tough-as-nails.

I pin her to the wall and she instantly hops up to wrap her legs around my waist. I hold her there, feeling the heat on her skin as my hands travel beneath her dress. I touch even more skin, along with the heat and natural wetness between her legs.

"Nora…"

"Yes?" she replies with a moan on her breath.

"Where are your panties?"

She chuckles. "Not wearing any."

"And you didn't mention this, because…?"

"Well, it was *supposed* to come up sometime between the main course and dessert, but then *somebody* had to—"

"Yeah, yeah—"

I crush our lips together, killing the accusation before it even gets out.

The doors slide open and someone gasps behind us. I

turn to look over my shoulder at the elderly couple standing outside wanting to get on.

I clear my throat. "Excuse us," I tell them.

I bend over and toss Nora's petite body over my shoulder. She yelps in surprise and gently hits me on the back with her clutch.

"Clive, what are you—"

"You said the man carries his woman, right?"

I playfully slap her bare ass as I step off the elevator. The old woman covers her mouth, shocked as hell, while the man does little to hide his smirk.

Nora's words get lost in her giggles as I carry her down the hall toward our room.

THIRTY-TWO

CLIVE

I lower her down and she slides our room key into the lock.

"Good girl," I say.

I move to pick her up again, this time hoisting her up and cradling her in my arms.

My heart throbs. This was how I held her the first time.

She seems to think back to the same moment and smiles as she turns the knob and pushes the door open.

It closes behind us. Nora curls her arms around my neck and we kiss until I reach the bed. My first thought is to drop her like a rock and listen for the high-pitched laugh from her that's sure to follow, but I don't.

I lean over and lay her down gently. Our lips barely part for longer than a second as I climb over her. We kick off our shoes. She loosens my tie. I feel behind her dress for her zipper and she leans up to help me slide it off her. I take it the rest of the way down to her ankles and drop it to the floor.

I stay there to admire the naked goddess lying in front of

me. Her heavy breathing breaks the silence and she barely moves, save the tips of her toes gently rubbing upward between my thighs. I toss my jacket off and let it slip to the floor along with my shirt and tie. Nora watches me undress, her tongue poking out from between her lips as I reach for my belt.

"Come here," I whisper.

She sits up and scoots forward to align her mouth with my zipper. I give her no further instructions. She knows what to do.

She pulls my pants down to free my hard cock and instantly sticks it in her mouth. Her suction is hard and fast, nearly knocking me off balance as I watch her bob back and forth.

"*Clive,*" she lets out a breathy moan, "*come on my face.*"

I tilt my head. "What?"

"Please." She licks me from base to tip. "Come on my face."

Nora turns around and lays down on the bed with her head slightly tilted over the side of the mattress. I gulp hard as she draws my cock close and shoves me back into her little mouth again. My balls tighten and my glands throb. Her tongue, her cheeks, her vibrating moan...

So fucking perfect.

Nora cups her breasts and I watch as she touches up and down her own body. Her hand pushes between her thighs and she lets her little fingers do the dirty work. She moans around my cock, taking me in a little deeper while she rubs circles around her clit. This view is almost enough to make me explode but I want to hear her beg me again.

I pull out of her mouth and stroke myself.

She takes a deep, smiling breath. "Please," she moans. "Please come on my face."

I stroke tighter and faster.

"I want it." She licks her lips and moans, her hand still dominating her clit. "I want it so badly, Mr. Snow. Please."

"Open your dirty, little mouth," I tell her.

She obeys, dropping her jaw and showing me the perfect, pink tongue inside.

"Again," I say, balancing on the edge.

"Come on my face." She lets out one final begging gasp as orgasm takes her body.

I come with her, releasing a heavy stream of cum onto her cheeks. It strings out onto her nose and chin, painting her face and I do my best to keep it out of her eyes.

I let my last release dance on her tongue and she wraps her lips around me to suck me clean while adorable moans still rattle her throat.

"Holy fucking shit, Nora," I groan, out of breath and satisfied.

I pull out of her mouth and she laughs to herself while I struggle to stay standing. She licks her lips, hesitating to move from her position in case she drips all over the extravagant bedding.

"Hold on," I say, reaching for the box of tissues by the bed. I pull a few free and kneel beside her. "Don't move."

I clear a bit from beneath her eye and wipe the rest off her cheeks. She looks at me with that devious glint while I clear the rest from her nose and chin with a second tissue.

"Thank you, Mr. Snow," she says.

I shake my head, my heart still pounding. "You are..."

Nora chuckles. "I know."

"Turn over." I toss the tissues aside. "On your back. Legs spread."

She moves slowly — painfully and purposefully slow — until I grab her and force her down myself. I drop to my knees and throw her legs over my shoulders as I yank her to the edge of the bed.

She giggles. "Have I been a good girl, Mr. Snow?"

"A good fucking girl."

I stick my tongue inside of her, coating it with her wetness. She grips my hair and pulls me so close I can't breathe but I can sure as hell keep fucking her.

Nora's moans run wild. Each breath she takes sounds quicker and shallower than the last. Her thighs squeeze around my head. I move to her throbbing clit and clamp my lips around it, making her back arch and her toes curl.

I slide a finger inside to fuck her some more.

She looks down at me over the peaks of her breast. I can tell she wants to speak, to say something sexy or fun, but I don't recognize a word she says. I can't say for sure it's English.

"Co—me!" she cries out.

I understood that one.

Her cunt squeezes my finger. I lap up the deluge of moisture that flows from her and get my fingers nice and wet before pulling out.

I slide them down to her ass.

She clenches in surprise as I touch her back entrance.

"Relax…" I massage her tight, little ring. "I'll make you feel good."

Nora runs her fingers along my brow, still quivering from her last orgasm. I lay long, soft kisses on her clit to keep it warm while I tease her anus. Wetness drips down from her pussy, giving me ample lubricant to make her ass ready for me.

I slide a finger in, just down to the first knuckle.

Nora gasps but she lies still, taking calming breaths. I lick her slowly, giving her clit a smooth touch while I move my finger in and out. The beautiful, aching expressions on her face are enough to get me hard again. Blood surges into my cock but I ignore it. I'll fuck her brains out soon.

But I'm going to enjoy this first.

I push a second finger in. It slides in just as easily as the first one but makes her moan twice as loud.

Nora bites her lip, driving my desire for her even more. That passion-filled face. That blissful agony making her twist for me. She's giving me so much... and I'll thank her body over and over for it.

Her thighs tighten around me again. One quick jerk and the woman could easily break my neck but I keep attacking her clit. I want to hear that scream...

Nora gives me what I want. She orgasms hard beneath me. She grabs the bedspread until the claws of her hands turn white. Her body's in ruin and her voice is broken. She can barely move.

But I'm not done yet.

I release her and stand up, letting her numb legs fall down. She lies there and I hear her quiet, blissful hums as I grab my tie off the floor. I secure it to the headboard, leaving the ends stretched down among the pillows.

"Ms. Payne..." I say as I climb onto the bed.

"Mmm..."

I pinch her chin. "Ms. Payne."

She opens her eyes and smiles at me.

"Have you had enough?" I ask.

Her eyes wander down my chest to my hard cock. "No, Mr. Snow..." she says, licking her lips.

I grab her by the waist and push her back to the head-board. She lets me do it, surrendering herself and her body to what I want. I move her hands over her head and she crosses her wrists the way I taught her to. She wants to submit. She wants to be mine...

I'll have to reward her for that.

I sit back to admire her naked body. "Give yourself to me, Ms. Payne."

"Every part," she says.

I lean over to kiss her. "Yes," I say, brushing my lips against hers.

I touch her restrained hands, caressing all the way down her arms to her shoulders. She flinches as I graze her armpits but sighs as I move on down to her breasts. I pause to kiss them and nibble her hard nipples. I bite at her flesh and run my tongue down her navel. I settle between her parted legs and pull her closer to align my cock with her. The tie stretches taut. Her legs wrap around me. Every part of her, open and mine for the taking.

I guide my cock inside of her. She's still so tight and wet. It feels like heaven and always has. I don't bother being gentle. I grip her waist and fuck her hard, listening to every moan of pleasure she gives me.

A few times, I think she might say *wait*. I think she might mutter *stop* and bring an end to this. But she doesn't. She holds on. She pushes her limits for me and for her.

I come so close to finishing. I force myself to slow down and pull out. Her pinched eyes open to look at me. I move down to kiss her, taking comfort in her lips and her warm breath on my cheek. My heart aches for her. My pretty, little thing.

"I love you, Nora."

She smiles and lets out a soft chuckle. "I love you, Clive."

I kiss her again, leaving smaller kisses on her forehead and the tip of her nose.

"Are you all right?" she asks.

I nod. "This just… everything feels so perfect."

"Does that mean you'll accept the job offer?"

I kiss her neck, gently tonguing the hanging pearl on her collar. "Yes," I say.

"Good." She pecks my forehead. "Now, hurry up and fuck my ass."

I crack up, laughing hard against her skin. "Oh, Nora…"

"What?" She grins.

I sit back, yanking her body closer and aligning us again. "I'm going to tear you apart."

She bites her lip. "Let's hope so."

I enter her pussy again, giving it a few healthy strokes to stay hard and lubed. She raises her legs, angling her ass up as I slide out and push my tip toward her anus.

Nora relaxes completely, letting me slip inside. I close my eyes as I gently fuck her just an inch at a time. I concentrate on her reactions, testing her body and slowing down when she needs it. She moans as I do, both of us taken in by the taboo sensations.

I lean forward to place my hands on either side of her. I hump and grind, feeling a whole new part of her. She'll easily bring me down if I keep going like this…

"You're gonna make me come…" she mumbles.

I slide a hand up her body, feeling her curves and her breasts. "Come with me, Ms. Payne," I tell her.

Her smile tears me down. "Yes, Mr. Snow…"

I let go, feeling the sudden surge of release. Her climax strikes her first and I watch the expression change on her face as I shoot inside of her. I put my weight on my arms, flexing hard to hold myself up when all I want to do is collapse on her.

Nora lifts her head and kisses any piece of me she can reach. I shift over to kiss her back as I reach up to loosen the tie around her wrists.

She slips free and cups my cheek. "Good boy," she teases.

I laugh as I wrap an arm around her. "Good girl…"

I pick her up off the bed and carry her with me to the bathroom.

THIRTY-THREE

NORA

"Y ou know, a girl could really get used to this aftercare thing."

I lean back in the bathtub with my glass of champagne. Bubbles float all around me in the hot water, filling the air with the lightest popping sounds.

And Clive — oh, sweet Clive — sits at the other end of the large tub with my foot in his hands.

"Have thirty minutes of rough sex," I say. "Receive hours of pampering."

Clive runs his thumb up the arch of my foot. "Nora, exactly what kind of shitty boyfriends have you had?" he asks.

I roll my eyes. "You don't want to know."

He chuckles and gestures for my other foot, which I promptly set in his very capable hands. "Well, it's nice to know where I stand in your little, black book."

"Very highly," I assure him.

I lay my head back against a rolled-up towel on the tub's edge and moan to myself.

"Sub life," I sing.

Clive laughs and keeps rubbing my foot.

I take a deep breath, smelling the warm, scent air. "Hey, Clive."

"Yes?"

"Why did you become a Dom?"

"What do you mean?"

"Well, obviously," I raise my head, "why does anyone have any preference, but I mean… I stumbled on Red Brick to explore ways of relieving stress. Why did you go there, at first?"

His eyes fall on the water between us. "My leg," he answers.

I say nothing, hoping that he'll continue himself.

"My mother, she…" He pauses. "My father disappeared when I was fifteen. He left behind a mountain of debt that my mother had no idea existed. We were already making just enough to get by and now we had to dump whatever spare cent we had into his damn debt or we'd lose everything. I didn't want to go to college but she, being a teacher, pushed me to go. When I saw how hard it was for her to pay for my school, make her ends meet, and pay down that debt, I couldn't in good conscience continue so I dropped out and I joined the Army. Every dime I made, I sent home to her.

"After my injury, I felt so awful being a burden to her again. I couldn't hold down a decent job and the jobs I could get didn't pay much — mostly just enough to afford painkillers, but still, every dime I made, I gave to her. I lived with the pain instead. I needed something else, something that would help me manage it, and that's when I found Red Brick."

"You took it out on subs?" I ask.

"No, it wasn't like that. It was…" He pauses, gathering his thoughts. "Inflicting pain on a lover, even *controlled* pain, it was something we shared. I watched them overcome it, no matter how much it hurt. I thought if *they* could do it, then… Experiencing pain and pleasure as one in the same is the only thing that helped me. Eventually, I healed but I keep going back because it's just who I am now." He looks at me. "Does that make sense?"

"Yeah," I say. "It does."

"Life doesn't have a safe word. Pain either fades away or we adapt and learn to live with it. Sometimes, you can't even tell the difference."

My lip trembles. "How did she die?" I ask.

"Car accident," he says. "Died on impact. I remember thinking how lucky she was. She didn't have to fight anymore. Without her around, I stopped fighting for a while, too, and… well, shit happens." He breathes a short laugh. "Before we met, I had just started earning enough for a studio apartment. How's that for timing, eh?"

"Ugh," I grunt.

"What?"

"Nora Payne," I say. "Master conversationalist."

He laughs. "It's all right."

I abandon my champagne glass on the tub's edge. "Yeah, I think I'm just gonna…" I sink into the water, "drown myself now."

Clive slides forward and pulls me up into his lap. Water splashes over the edges onto the floor as he wraps his arms around me to hold me against him.

"Don't you dare," he says. He kisses my jaw. "It's good to finally talk about it with someone I trust."

I rest my forehead on his and cup his cheek. "You're an amazing man, Clive Snow," I tell him.

He says nothing. He just makes that quick, happy sound from the back of his throat and kisses me.

My phone vibrates on the table by the door but there's no way in hell I'm getting out of this bed to answer it.

The sun has barely risen over Manhattan. The sky outside is still a dark blue but it's slowly brightening every minute. Saturday morning in New York City. It's probably still bustling down there from last night but this hotel room could not be calmer.

I feel Clive stir beside me. His arms stretch over his head but his legs stay entwined with mine. I take the opportunity to slink a little closer, trapping myself between his body and his arm before he manages to lower it again. It works and he hugs me tighter without even opening his eyes.

"Good morning," he says.

I chuckle. "Understatement."

He kisses my head and inhales deep. "What time is it?"

"I have no idea nor do I care."

He laughs. "You know, I have to work today."

I raise my head. *"Noooo—"*

"Yes."

"Just quit."

"I planned on putting in my two weeks as soon as I got there."

I groan and drop my head to his chest again. "Fine, be a responsible and model employee," I quip. "When is your shift?"

"Noon. So, we might want to get moving now so we can fly back in time."

"But…" I cling to his body, "I don't wanna."

He runs a hand along my arm. "Just a few more minutes."

"Okay…"

I settle in, resting my hand on his abs. His skin spurs heat through my fingertips and I caress him south toward his—

Clive grabs my wrist. "Nothing about what you're doing right now means *a few more minutes…*"

I feign offense. "I wasn't doing anything!"

"You were doing exactly what it looked like you were doing."

"Well…" I sigh, "I guess you'll have to punish me, then…"

He shoots up and forces me onto my back. "You, Ms. Payne, are being a very, very bad—"

The phone vibrates again.

I scoff. "Someone is really desperate to reach me today…" Clive pushes off me and hops off the bed. "Wait! I must be punished!"

"Punishment *later*," he says, heading toward the bathroom. "Now, clothes and breakfast and flights home."

I throw on a pout. "Fine."

Clive smiles and twists back in my direction. I set my feet on the floor and he tilts my face upward to kiss me.

"Good morning," he says again.

"Good morning," I say, smiling back.

He turns away and I watch that glorious ass saunter away into the bathroom.

I look at my phone and my smile becomes a sneer. I

hoist myself up, throw on a bathrobe, and walk toward it, *so not ready* to embrace the real world just yet.

Uh-oh. Nine missed calls.

I call back the unrecognized number.

"Chicago Police Department."

I blink. "Hi, this is Nora Payne. I'm sorry you've been trying to contact me but I've been traveling."

"Yes, Ms. Payne. Let me transfer you to Robberies and Homicides."

The line cuts off.

"Wha…" I wince. "But which one?"

Clive returns with a towel wrapped around his waist. He stops cold the moment he looks at me. "Whoa, what's going on?" he asks. "You okay?"

"I'm being transferred to Robberies and Homicides."

His brow rises. "… which one?"

"I don't know! They should be more specific, right?"

"Yeah, there's a huge difference there…"

"Ms. Payne?" a man says in my ear.

"Yes, I'm Nora Payne." I hold my breath. "What's going on?"

"I'm Detective Zimmer. I'm sorry to bother you so early but there's been a break-in at your condo tonight."

"Was anyone hurt?"

"No, ma'am."

I exhale at Clive. "So, just the robbery part, then…"

He nods and lingers by my ear.

"Well, what did they take?" I ask. "Is there damage? How bad are we talking here?"

"No damage other than the front door, which your super is taking care of right now. Nothing was stolen, either. A neighbor heard the door breaking and called the police, so the suspect was apprehended on-site."

"Oh." I sigh with relief. "That's… lucky."

Clive lays a hand on my shoulder and I look up at him, finding a little more comfort in his eyes.

"Do you know a man named Alex Preston, Ms. Payne?" Zimmer asks.

"Alex Preston?" I repeat.

Clive flinches.

"No," I say. "I don't know anybody by that name…"

His hand falls from my shoulder as he takes a step back.

"He walked right to the safe by your bed," Zimmer says. "Seems like something only a friend or acquaintance would know about. Can you think of anyone who might know of its location in your home? Recent house guests or repairmen?"

"No, not even my closest friends know…"

I study Clive's downturn eyes. He won't even look at me.

Why won't he look at me?

"Ms. Payne, would you stop by the station at your earliest convenience?" Zimmer asks. "I assume you'd like to press charges."

Clive picks his shirt up off the floor. His movements are slow and stiff, almost sickly, as he slides it on.

"Yes," I answer. "Of course. Thank you."

I hang up and lower the phone to my side.

He still won't look at me. He just puts on his clothes one piece at a time. He tosses his towel over the chair. He doesn't say a word.

I pinch my robe closed. "Clive, who is Alex Preston?" I ask.

THIRTY-FOUR

CLIVE

"Nora, I'm sorry."

She takes a short step back and adjusts her robe, tightening it around her like armor to protect herself. From me.

"Sorry about what?" she asks.

"I didn't think he'd…"

I pause, wanting nothing more than to hold her but she'd never let me get close. Not right now. Not with that rage boiling beneath her eyelashes.

"Do you know this guy?" she asks.

I could lie. I could say Alex was just some co-worker of mine who got jealous over her. I could say he was a disgruntled customer banned from Red Brick looking for revenge of some sort. Some insane lunatic. But why bother protecting a man who lied to me, too? Why dig myself in deeper when I could just come clean and hope she believes me?

"Alex and I were in the Army together," I say. "He's the man who shot up my leg and ruined my career."

Nora squints in confusion. "So... what does he want with me?"

"A few months back, I got a job working janitorial and maintenance at the gym. Little did I know, Alex worked there, too. We got to talking and catching up since Iraq and he found out about my situation. He wanted to help. He blamed himself and told me he'd make it up to me. Some weeks later, he tells me about this data entry job. He'd apply for it himself but he didn't qualify with his criminal record, but I did."

"Black Book?" she asks.

I nod. "I got the job. I was really happy about it. Thought it would lead to something better down the line. But when I told Alex, he told me the real reason why he wanted the job. Apparently, he had a buyer. Someone with deep pockets in the market for a lot of user-generated personal information. He asked... he asked me to get it for him and we'd split the money fifty-fifty."

Nora looks down, her eyes heavy with thought. "You... you were going to steal from me?"

"But I couldn't go through with it." I step forward. "Nora—"

"Don't come near me."

I stop. "Please, hear me out. Okay?"

"Clive, a data breach of that level would have *destroyed* me. I would have lost *everything.*"

"I know."

"So, what? You just didn't care?"

"I didn't know you," I say.

"Okay, so thievery is *excusable* when you don't actually know the person?"

I exhale. "I was in a bad place, Nora. I wasn't thinking

straight. You know. You weren't born into wealth, either. Imagine someone dangling a million dollars in front of you when you weren't even sure where your next meal would come from."

"So, when I walked in on you in my office, *that's* what you were really doing?" she asks. "Trying to rip off my client list?"

"Yes." My voice breaks. "But I couldn't get it because you… you take it home with you."

"Oh, my god." She touches her stomach and recoils in disgust.

"Nora, I—"

"You *violated* me."

A tear rolls down her cheek, stabbing me in the heart.

"No," I whisper. "No, my feelings for you are *real,* Nora."

"Bullshit."

"It's true. I got close to you at first to try and find that list, but I backed out of it when I fell for you. That's the truth." I touch my chest. "This is real. Last night was *real."*

She shakes her head and looks at the floor as more tears fall. "You're a liar," she says. "A filthy, lying *hypocrite.* You made me feel awful about trying to help you and give you a better life, when all this time—"

"I know. And I'm sorry."

"I trusted you. I gave you *every part of me."*

She sobs into her hands, barely holding together.

"I had the chance, Nora," I say, grasping at anything I can. "I could have gone through with it but I didn't. I got to know you and trust you. And love you. I saw a life with you. I should have told you what was going on. I'll own up to that."

She looks up. "Were you ever going to tell me?"

"Honestly, I hoped I would never have to," I say. "I hoped Alex would move on. I really never thought he'd—"

Nora turns away and walks to the other end of the room to pick up her clothes. She moves quickly, keeping her back to me while she steps into her dress and drops her robe.

I shift towards her. "Nora?"

"Your services will no longer be needed at Little Black Book."

She takes a wide step around me and gathers her shoes.

My chest tightens. "Nora, don't do this."

"Any due wages will be deposited into your account within the next twenty-four hours."

Her voice sounds so cold and repressed, like she's seconds away from screaming.

I step in front of her as she heads for the door.

"Nora, *please.*"

"Do not attempt to re-enter the building or you will be escorted out by security. Any personal belongings left behind will be mailed to your home address, or… dumped on the sidewalk, in your case."

"Stay here with me just a little bit longer and we'll talk this out."

"Clive…" She looks up at me, her face wet and utterly broken. *"Stop."*

It crushes me. One word from her mouth ends it in an instant.

Nora grabs her purse from the shelf and throws the door open, leaving me behind to fend for my own bleeding heart.

No. No, I can't let her go like this.

I rush out into the hallway as she steps onto the elevator.

"Nora!"

She looks up but she doesn't move other than to wipe the tears from her cheeks.

I pick up my pace, breaking into a sprint to try and beat the doors before they close. If I can get to her, I can beg. I can drop to my knees and plead for forgiveness.

The doors close on me.

"Shit."

I tap the call button, hoping to stop the car from falling but the mechanical whirl starts up and the elevator starts downward.

I hit the stairwell and charge down the twenty flights to the ground floor. I'm tired and sick and out of breath but I can't let her leave. I can't let Nora Payne walk away from me for good.

I reach the lobby and bolt toward the elevator. It dings in front of me and the doors open.

"Nora—"

It's empty.

My eyes fall to the floor and my pounding heart breaks all over again.

The black leather choker with the small, white pearl.

I step on and pick it up. She tossed it away and took off. She tossed us away.

I'm not her Dom anymore.

I scan the lobby for her but she's gone.

THIRTY-FIVE

NORA

I t hurts.

I thought ditching him in another city would be satisfying. But it's not.

I thought pressing charges against the prick who invaded my home would feel like justice. But it doesn't.

I thought letting my guard down with someone for one goddamn hour a day would take the stress out of my life but it sure as shit didn't work.

This just fucking hurts.

There's a knock on my door. I don't move from my chair.

"Nora? Nora, honey. It's us."

"Our keys don't work anymore."

Trix and Melanie. I wasn't very specific in my text message.

Fuck Clive.

I roll off the armchair and used tissues tumble off me. I wrap my blanket around my shoulders as I drag my feet to the door to open it.

Trix holds two bottles of wine and Melanie carries pizza boxes.

Melanie's face twists with sympathy the moment she sees me. "Oh, honey…"

"I don't wanna talk about it."

I turn away and march back to my chair.

"Okay," Trix says. "We won't talk about it. We'll just hang out. Okay? No talk necessary…"

"Right," Melanie adds. She sets the boxes down on the coffee table while Trix retreats to the kitchen for glasses. "Talking is for losers."

I yank out a fresh tissue and rest my head on the chair's arm. "Thank you. 'Cuz I don't wanna talk."

Melanie sits on the loveseat across from me. "What do you wanna do, Nor?" she asks, her voice quiet and soothing.

"Cry," I answer.

"Okay." She looks down. "Looks like you've been doing a lot of that already."

"You are correct."

"Are you hungry?"

"No."

She raises her hands. "Okay. We have pizza for when you are." Her eyes flick to the wall beside me. "Nora…"

"What?" I murmur.

"Is that a shotgun?"

I don't look. "Yes."

"Why do you have a shotgun?"

"Because this is my house." I sniff. "I have to defend it."

"Good lord…" she whispers.

Trix returns with three wineglasses and my corkscrew. She sits down next to Melanie, who promptly nudges her leg and points at the wall.

Trix stands right back up. "Hey, Nora, honey... how about we put this someplace safer, okay?"

I roll my eyes. "I wasn't gonna use it, guys. It's not loaded."

Trix picks up the gun and turns it over in her hands, expertly popping the stock open to confirm it's not loaded. "Is this the one my dad gave you?" she asks.

I nod. "For my housewarming party. He didn't like the idea of me living alone on Michigan Avenue." I scoff. "He was right."

She sets it on the mantel above the fireplace and sits down next to Melanie again.

"Nora," Melanie yanks the cork out of one of the bottles. "Wouldn't you be more comfortable upstairs? Instead of all curled up on the chair?"

"No." I sniff. "I can't even look at the bed. It still smells like him..."

"Clive?"

"I don't wanna talk about it."

"Okay. Okay." She picks up a glass. "No talking. Do you wanna maybe come over here with us?"

I eye the couch. "No. He touched that, too. He touched everything except this chair so I'm going to sit in this chair because he never touched it."

Trix looks from me to the mantel. "He didn't *touch you*, did he?"

I sit up, kicking a few more tissues to the floor. "No," I answer. They visibly sigh with relief. "No. He just tricked me into trusting him *but I don't wanna talk about it.*"

"Is that why you had your locks changed?" Melanie asks.

"No, I had my locks changed because he broke them

busting through my damn door while he and I were away last night."

"In New York?"

I blow my nose. "He got arrested while he was telling me he loved me."

"Clive got arrested?"

"No. *He* did."

Trix tilts her head. "Honey, you're using a lot of pronouns here."

I point at them. "I know what you guys are doing. You came here with the booze and the food and the quiet, motherly voices to get me to talk but I don't wanna."

"We just want to make sure you're okay, Nor," Melanie says. "That's all."

"Well, I'm *fine*," I say, my nose stuffed up. "Don't I look *fine*?"

"No," Trix answers bluntly. "You don't look fine. You look like something very bad happened to you and I wanna know what it was because Papa 'Gento got more where that came from." She points at the gun on the mantel.

I bite my lip, tasting tears on it. "He was my Dom and I trusted him," I say. "He made me feel so good and then…" A sob rises from my chest but I force it back down. "Clive got the job at Black Book to steal my client list."

Melanie's eyes widen. "Did he?"

I shake my head. "He said he couldn't. He said he fell for me and he couldn't go through with it but I can't shake this awful *sick* feeling that he lied about that, too, but I *want* to trust him. My body *wants him* so badly. I want to forgive and forget because I love him." The sob takes over. "And I know how stupid that sounds. I hear the thoughts in my head but it doesn't sound like me. It doesn't feel like me. It feels *bruised* and *broken* and the only thing that can make me feel whole again is the one person I can't trust anymore."

They stand up quickly and move to either side of my chair.

I crumble even more, dropping my head into my hands as their arms wrap around me. "And I…"

"Shh," Melanie says. "You don't have to talk."

"Just cry," Trix adds. "Crying is good."

"Well, I don't wanna cry! I want…" I sniff loudly. "I want him, but…"

Melanie pushes my hair back. "But what, honey?"

I bite my lip. "I left him in New York."

They silently stare at each other for a moment. Melanie breaks first with a soft snort that quickly grows into a hard laugh. Trix cracks as well, slapping a hand over her mouth until her face turns red.

I look at them and their hyena smiles, slowly letting the contagious laugh take me, too.

THIRTY-SIX

CLIVE

I f I ever find myself in a situation where I'm allowed to choose the fate of my worst enemy, spending twenty hours on a bus might be somewhere near the top of my list of punishments.

Nora abandoned me in New York and I had to get back home to Chicago somehow. I don't blame her, obviously. The punishment matches the crime.

It gave me a chance to think. To plan what the hell I'll do next. My life-saving, salaried position at Black Book isn't an option anymore. I'm lucky if I still have my job at the gym after no-showing my shift yesterday. If word of this gets back to Judy, I might lose my job at Red Brick, too. There's certainly an argument to be made for me mistreating my sub. Instant blacklist.

So, it's back to square one. Whatever that is.

At least I still have my car.

And a few extra dollars in my pocket so I can get a cup of coffee.

The barista eyes me with suspicion. Either that or the

scent of coffee beans doesn't quite mask the stench of bus on my suit. I don't really care, in the end.

I sit down in a booth and watch the city rush by through the window for who knows how long.

"Wow. You look like shit."

I look up to find a man standing over me in thick, black sunglasses and a leather jacket. He slides the glasses off with his non-bandaged hand and I recognize him as Nora's friend's ex-husband.

"Thanks," I mutter.

"Robbie," he reminds me.

I nod, not really caring.

He raises his drink — a large frappe with a hot pink straw sticking out the top — and takes a long sip. He swallows it down and stares at me for another awkward moment before nodding.

"Sure, thanks. I'd love to sit down," he says.

He lowers onto the bench across from me.

"No," I say. "I'd like to be alone right now, if you don't mind."

"I do mind, actually. I mind very much."

I exhale. "Why?"

Robbie pockets his sunglasses and sits back, easing into a more comfortable position. "You've stumbled into a very interesting family here, Clyde."

"Clive," I correct.

"Yeah, whatever," he says, shrugging. "I really don't care. I care about Nora and when it comes to Nora, Trix, and Melanie, *Clive*, you are vastly unprepared for what you've signed up for."

I glance around. "Well, I don't mean to interrupt this speech you're clearly proud of, but Nora and I are over."

"No, you're not. And here's why." He sits up and takes a quick sip from his pink straw. "What you're experiencing right now is a phenomenon I like to call The Gray Zone."

I raise a brow. "The what?"

"You woke up this morning, looked around, and the bright, colorful world you went to sleep in was gone," he says. "The grass isn't green. The sky isn't blue. Everything is just drab and shitty. You have a job but — *screw it* — you called in sick. They'll manage without you for one damn day. You're in need of a shower but — *fuck that*. Why bother? You're hungry but — *whatever* — you're gonna die eventually anyway. Why not speed it along? Are you with me so far?"

"… Yeah, sure." I nod.

He smiles. "The Gray Zone. Guys like you and me spend a lot of time here, so we learn really quickly the various ways to inject a little color into our lives; Drugs, sex, alcohol." He raises his coffee. "Caffeine, or as I like to call it: All of the above." He takes another long sip from his pink straw and admires the cup. "Damn, that's good caramel."

"Look, Robbie, I don't know what you've heard, but I'm no stranger to drab and shitty. All right? My life has had its fair share of ups and downs."

"You misunderstand," he says, staring at me. "The Gray Zone isn't for people who have fucked-up shit happen to them. That's just The Real World. No, The Gray Zone is for people *like us* who bring it on themselves. You're here because *you* fucked up and lost the girl. There is no one to blame but yourself. Now, luckily for you, you've got Big Brother Robbie here to tell you exactly what to do to win her back."

I laugh. "And what's the catch?"

"The catch?" His face screws up. "The catch is a lifetime of bliss. Take it or leave it, buddy."

"A lifetime of bliss?" I point at him. "I'm sorry, but aren't you still hung up on your ex-wife who left your sorry ass?"

"Hey…" He gestures at his face and grins. "Do I look sad to you?"

I don't answer. It's rhetorical anyway.

He relaxes his cheeks. "But yeah. To answer the question, plainly. I am. Melanie's a work-in-progress. Do you have a slow-cooker, Clive?" he asks.

I blink, caught off-guard. "No."

"She's like that," he says. "Mel's standing in the middle of the pot. Heat's turned on, slowly rising, just a little at a time so she won't notice. Every once in a while, I drop in a new ingredient, mix it up, and walk away. Eventually, she'll be ready. In the meantime, I'll set the table."

"Is that what I have to do?" I ask. "Set the table?"

"For *Nora?*" He laughs. "Oh, hell no. She's not a slow-cooker. Nora Payne is the head table at a five-star restaurant with no prices on the menu and a celebrity chef. She's got a reservation for two and you better show up on-time, dressed to the nines, with an empty stomach and a can-do attitude — or not at all."

"Sounds like more trouble than it's worth," I say.

Robbie tilts his head in disbelief. "If that's how you really feel, then that's cool. I'll just take my wisdom elsewhere…"

He moves to stand up.

"Wait." I sigh at his smug expression. "Sit down."

His lips curl to one side and he lowers into the chair again. "Melanie needs to be coddled. And swooned. And surprised. But *Nora*…" He shakes his head. "Nora needs a challenge. She's easily bored and more than a little paranoid. If things go too well for too long, she gets suspicious and starts to doubt. So, what *you* have to do is eliminate her need to doubt."

"How do I do that?" I ask.

Robbie squints. "You show up to the damn restaurant, Clive."

I exhale in frustration. "Can we drop the cute food metaphors, please?"

"Okay, then." He leans forward. "Nora Payne needs someone she can depend on. Not for money, mind you. She already has more than enough means to survive but there's a big difference between being alive and having a life."

"I get that, but..." I pause. "She trusted me. I betrayed her."

He smiles. "Sounds exactly like the kind of challenge she needs. If you do nothing, you'll only prove every horrible thing she's thought about you and you'll become nothing but a footnote in her black book she'll joke about with her friends at brunch. But if you do *something* and prove her *just a little bit wrong*, well..." He raises his brow. "You just have to be the guy who actually showed up."

"If I just *showed up*, she wouldn't talk to me anyway," I argue.

"Only one way to know for sure." He pulls his sunglasses from his jacket with his good hand. "What the hell else are you gonna do today? Other than sitting around and moping beneath a gray cloud of drabby shit?"

I stare straight ahead as he stands up, feeling the slow mix of adrenaline brewing in my gut. "Yeah, I'll think about it," I say.

"No." Robbie shakes his head. "You have not been paying attention at all. Don't think. Just go do."

"I don't even know where Nora is right now," I say.

"It's *Sunday*. There's only one place she'd be." He slides the sunglasses on and grabs his coffee. *"Go do."*

This fucking guy. Slow-cookers and can-do attitudes? Clearly, he has no idea what he's talking about. None of this will work on Nora Payne.

The Perfect Nora Payne.

I look up at the table across the coffee shop. The one we sat in during our "first date." She told me all about Robbie and his drinking problem and how he...

Never gave up. He's never given up on the love of his life.

"Hey, Rob."

He pauses and turns back to me.

"Thanks," I say. "You're kind of a cool guy."

He smiles. "Yeah, that's me."

Robbie exits the shop and zips up his jacket as he starts walking down the street, happily sucking on his hot pink straw.

If I was that much in love, I don't think I'd give up so easily.

I told her that. Nora thinks I'm a liar now.

I'm going to prove her wrong.

THIRTY-SEVEN

NORA

Tradition is tradition.

Would I rather be curled up in my chair with yoga pants and pints of ice cream? Yes. Yes, I would.

But it's Sunday. And Sunday is brunch day.

It was designed exactly for times like this. Leave your troubles at the door and enjoy a round of drinks with friends. Forget about that problem in your life for an hour.

Forget about Clive Snow for an hour. I can do that. I can forget about his hands on my body and his voice in my ear and every little touch and caress of his lips. I can forget about the way my heart skipped when I saw him and how just one look into his blue eyes gave me butterflies for days and—

Yeah, it's not working. I can't do this.

Melanie snaps her fingers at me. *"Stop that."*

I blink out of it. "Stop what?"

"You know damn well what."

"I'm sorry." I tear another corner off my toast but I don't eat it. "I'm still feeling pretty raw, okay? My head hurts, my nose is sore, and I'm afraid if I drink anything my body will just send it right to my tear ducts."

Trix nods. "You're really rocking that sweater, though…"

I smile. "Thanks."

"You're gonna make it through this, Nora," Melanie says. "I mean, if you really think about it, things could be *a lot* worse right now."

"I know. You're right. I could be fending off reporters over a huge data dump scandal. I could lose my company, my reputation." I sigh. "You're right. I just can't get past something Clive said."

"What'd he say?" Trix asks.

I stab the crust of my toast with my nail. "He said that night in New York was real."

"Do you believe him?"

"I do," I say, exhaling hard. "Was I too harsh?"

"No," Melanie says. "He lied to you and tried to steal your stuff. That's instant not-okay."

Trix tilts her head. "Well…"

I raise a brow. *"You* disagree? Whatever happened to poor equals thief?"

"Okay, you know I'm not one to play the *I told you so* card, but I did tell you so about that one."

"Acknowledged and accepted," I say.

"But… I think I do disagree a little. I mean… Yeah, sure, he started out with some pretty cruddy intentions, but in the end, he did the right thing." She shrugs. "That earns him some points in my book."

Melanie shakes her head at her. "Your moral compass is all over the place lately."

"It's more like a pendulum, truth be told."

"Okay…" Melanie sighs. "I'll concur — *reluctantly* — that

he's not all bad. He did make you very happy for a while… or his penis did, anyway."

"Yeah." I chuckle. "He did."

"Do you think you'll go back to the club?" Trix asks. "Find a new Dom?"

"Hadn't really thought about it."

I try and picture it. Me strapped to a St. Andrew's cross with some other man standing behind me. Bent over and submitting to him instead. His hands on my body and his voice in my ear. His lips…

It's not the same.

How in the world could anyone ever compare to Mr. Snow?

A lump forms in my throat.

I pull my napkin off my lap. "I'm going to the bathroom. I'll be right back."

I stand up and walk away, slowly zigzagging around the tables toward the ladies' room. It's empty, thankfully, and I retreat into the first stall I see before my eyes spill over.

No. No, Nora. You can't do this to yourself.

I swallow them back down and dab my eyelids with my sleeve.

Clive lied to you. It's complicated, but simple. It's hard to fathom now, but someday, you'll find love again. You see it all the time. You built a living based on that very fact. There's always another open space in your little, black book for the next guy. No harm done. World not over.

And you're not alone. You have Trix and Melanie. And Robbie. Maybe even Lenny the massage therapist if you promise not to make insane house calls.

You are Nora Payne.

Fucking act like it.

I stand up tall and check myself in the mirror before heading back. Our usual server stands near a table just outside the restrooms, gathering a round of empty glasses and setting them on his tray.

"Excuse me," I say, prompting him to turn toward me. "Could we have a few waters delivered to our table, please?"

"Yeah. I'll bring them right out, Ms. Payne," he says with a nod.

"Thank you..." I pause. "I'm sorry, I've been winking at you for like a year and I don't even know your name."

His lips curl. "It's Roger."

My jaw drops as I place his voice. He hits me with a sinister wink and spins away, epically balancing his tray of empties as he rushes off toward the back.

I close my mouth. "Well, that's a twist," I mutter to myself.

"Nora!"

I stop in my tracks a foot away from our table. "Clive?"

I spin around as he rushes toward me through the restaurant. People turn in the chairs, muttering among themselves and recoiling as he runs by.

"Clive, what are you doing here?" I ask as he stops in front of me. "And what is that smell?"

"I had to see you," he says. "And... bus."

"Bus?"

"The horrible, awful bus I took to get back here from New York."

My lips twitch. "You just now got back here?"

He nods. "I spent all day and all night thinking about what I could possibly say to you to make you forgive me."

I cross my arms, cursing my curiosity. "And what did you come up with?"

He shakes his head. "A bunch of sentimental crap, mostly. And excuses for my judgment. But it's all meaningless bullshit because even if it worked and everything went back to the way it was, we'd still be living with the fact that I took advantage of your trust and I don't know how to fix that. No amount of trust falls could ever make up for what I did."

I look down, biting my cheek to force the tears away. "You might be right," I say.

"So, I don't blame you," he says. "If you tell me to turn around right now and get out of your life, I'll do it." He takes a deep breath. "But until you do, I'm gonna beg."

He drops to his knees, bringing a few swoons from the crowd.

"Ms. Nora Payne, I'm begging you to take me back."

My cheeks burn red. "You're *begging?*"

"Yes." He holds his hands in prayer. "I'm begging you. Forgive me, please."

"Clive—"

I take a step back but he follows me on his knees.

"Clive, get up—"

"I'll do anything to be with you again," he says. "Just say the word and I'll do it."

My brow piques. "Anything?"

"Anything."

I hold my breath and look around. All eyes are on me. Trix and Melanie. Clive and the staff. Complete strangers have abandoned their meals to see how this plays out. My skin tingles with embarrassment. My heart bleeds for him all over again.

Clive doesn't even blink. He adores me with those

sinfully sweet blue eyes, patiently waiting. And he'll keep waiting. He'll beg and plead to me like…

Like a sub.

"Stand up," I tell him.

He pushes off the floor and stands up tall in front of me.

"Take off your belt."

His brow furrows in confusion. "My belt?"

"Take off your belt."

I extend my hand for it.

Clive studies the hard lines on my face before exhaling and doing as I say. He reaches down and tugs it free, quickly sliding it out of his belt loops and laying it in my open palm.

I fold it in half, gripping it tightly. "Lay your palms on the table," I tell him.

He blinks. "What?"

"Lay your palms on the table, Mr. Snow."

His expression shifts, losing every bit of confusion and replacing it with subtle shock. He glances around as if to silently remind me of where we are but I know exactly where the fuck we are.

He clears his throat and turns to place his palms on our table. "Ladies," he says, nodding at Trix and Melanie.

"Don't talk to them," I snap. "You're talking to me right now."

He turns his head around. "Nora—"

I touch the belt to his back and he shuts up. "Did I say you could turn around?" I ask.

Melanie and Trix take out their phones.

Clive looks forward again. "Nora—"

"You will call me *Ms. Payne.*"

"Ms. Payne," he corrects, "don't you think this discussion could happen somewhere a bit more private?"

I shrug. "Nah."

I snap the belt along his back and he tenses. An audible gasp lingers behind me but I don't bother turning around. Let them watch.

"Tell me, Mr. Snow," I say, pausing to tap him again, "if your submissive lied to your face... what would their punishment be?"

Clive hesitates. I hear him inhale but no words come out.

I hit him again, this time a little harder. "When I ask you a question, I expect an immediate response."

"I..." He breathes out. "I don't know."

"Would you tie them up for a public flogging?" I ask. "How many lashes would make up for lying?"

"Depends on the lie," he answers.

I whack his shoulder. "Conspiracy to commit theft. How many lashes for that?"

He sighs. "Nora..."

"Saying I love you." I hit him as hard as I can and he grunts. "How many lashes for that?"

"I didn't lie about that."

"Bullshit."

I raise the belt as Clive spins around. He catches my wrist in mid-air and forces me to stop.

"I didn't lie about that," he says again, his eyes locked with mine. "If you walk away from this believing anything, make it that."

I look away from him but he nudges my chin right back up.

"Nora, I love you." His fingers slide to my cheek. "I might be your chocolate or your strawberry or your rocky road, but you... you're my vanilla."

Melanie frowns. "The fuck?"

I ignore her as Clive leans in a little closer.

"You're the…" He smiles and he lowers my arm. "You're the silky-smooth, under-appreciated staple that I should have embraced a long time ago. You make everything sweeter. And I can't imagine a life without you."

He takes a step back and lets go of my wrist. His hand falls from my face as he puts a little space between us. My heart aches. I've lost my anchor again.

"But if this is what you want, Ms. Payne, then… you should do it right."

Clive loosens his tie and pulls it up and over his head.

I blink with confusion, my eyes widening as he takes off his jacket and starts flicking the buttons open on his shirt. "Clive…"

"Ten," he says.

He tosses his clothes back at the table and Trix snatches them in mid-air.

"Ten?" I ask.

Murmurs and chuckles rise behind me. He stands tall in nothing but his pants and shoes, his epic arms and chest on full display. My jaw drops along with everyone else's but no one seems to do a thing to stop this.

"Conspiracy to commit theft," he says. "Ten lashes."

He turns around and places his palms on the table again.

Trix gasps at his shirtless chest. "Oh, Daddy…"

"It's happening," Melanie whispers, tilting her phone for a better angle.

This went a lot further than I thought it would…

Uh-oh…

"Ms. Payne," he says, "I'm ready for my punishment."

I glance at the belt in my hand.

Oh, my god…

I bite my cheek, my eyes locked on his muscular back. It feels strange to be on this side but utterly exhilarating, too. My pulse quickens and my sex begins to throb.

I raise my arm and snap it down. The belt hits his right shoulder blade and he cringes.

"One," I count.

I hit his shoulder again, leaving a light pink spot on his skin.

"Two."

A smile creeps across my lips.

I slap his left shoulder, two quick taps just a little bit faster.

"Three. Four."

Clive lets out a light groan but his hands don't leave the table. An intense spike of curiosity trembles me. I wonder what it would take to make him move… make him cry out for me.

I whip him three times in a row, slapping as hard as I can.

"Five. Six. Seven."

His back stiffens, the tight muscles quivering beneath his skin. Heat fires through my core. Just three to go.

I raise the belt but I don't hit him. I let it dangle along his spine, gently tapping until a laugh exhales from his throat. I toy with him the same way he toys with me. He'll make me regret it later, I'm sure.

And I can't wait.

I smack him again. "Eight."

And again. "Nine."

I pause, letting the final suspense last.

Finally, I jerk my arm and whip him on the ass.

"Ten," I say.

Clive spins around to face me. His bright eyes lock on me and I can barely take another breath before he grabs my arm and yanks me closer.

He kisses me hard. I fall into his arms, accepting the embrace as our tongues come together and his body heat blends with mine.

Trix and Melanie erupt into hollers and applause, prompting several other tables behind us to do the same.

"Okay," I say, taking a breath. "I forgive you now."

Clive pulls away but he's not done with me yet. Not by a long shot. He takes his belt from my hand and turns to retrieve his shirt and jacket from Trix and Melanie.

"So, what do normal couples usually do after a public flogging?" he asks me.

I smile, my chest heaving. "Well, according to my expertise… a fuck-ton of sex. Immediately."

He looks over my shoulder. "You ladies got the check?"

Trix grins. "Yeah, we got it."

He grabs me and tosses me over his shoulder. I yelp in surprise, laughing hard as excitement and passion rip through me.

He takes a few steps but turns back and points at Melanie. "Was that video?" he asks her.

"I got every second," she answers with a laugh.

"Send it to her phone, will ya?"

She swipes her screen. "Way ahead of you, Daddy."

"Thanks."

Clive carries me around the clapping tables toward the exit. My skin tingles as every eye in the place watches us go. I don't even try to hide my face. I wear my smile proudly.

He is my Dom. I am his sub.

And I've been a bad girl.

We pass the hostess station and Roger rushes forward to hold the door open for us.

"Have a good day, folks," he says with a wink.

He reaches down and low-fives me as we leave.

THIRTY-EIGHT

NORA

Judy lays the card on the counter between us. "And there you are, Ms. Payne," she says.

I pick up the card. It's still a little warm from her laminating machine. I admire the scarlet-branded logo and smile at the one word glistening in its corner.

Member.

"Thanks, Judy," I say as I slide it into my clutch along with my debit card.

She smirks at me with a hand on her hip. "I knew I had a good feeling about you."

I hide my clutch in the pocket of my trench coat. "Well, when you're right…"

Her hand falls beneath the counter and she unlocks the door. "Enjoy your stay," she says.

I walk in. My eyes adjust quickly to the darker lighting and I stop by the bar for a bottle of water before heading right to the stairs.

A dark form passes me halfway up.

I flash a quick wink at him. "Hey, Roger."

He gestures at me with his black latex hand. "Ms. Payne," he greets.

I continue on without stopping. It's what I was told to do.

The second floor is crowded, making goosebumps raise on my skin. It'll be all right, though. He'll make me feel safe. He always does.

I head toward the St. Andrew's cross in the corner and stand in front of it. My reflection stares back at me and I smile into it as I open my trench coat.

The blood red corset hugs me so tightly I can barely breathe. I suppose that's the point but I have a bit of a history with not breathing on crosses. I would like to not repeat it.

But I have my instructions.

I slide the coat off and let it fall to the floor. I step up to the X-shaped cross, my feet feeling twice as heavy in these thigh-high leather boots.

"Oh—"

I step down and bend over to fish into my coat pocket for my blindfold. Wouldn't want to forget that.

I return to the cross, take one last look at myself in the mirror, and place the blindfold over my eyes. It blocks out every sliver of light around me, plunging me into an epic darkness that sets my nerves on fire.

I place my palms on the cross and wait.

My hearing piques and I listen to the sound of feet and voices behind me. I focus on my breathing, counting each inhale and exhale until I lose count. I feel eyes on me but I can't tell whether or not they're *his*. Is he here already? Standing behind me and staring this whole time... just to see if I'll break?

Finally, a flogger tickles my bare shoulders.

I smile. "Mr. Snow?"

"Hello, Ms. Payne," he says, his voice so close. He moves in behind me and kisses the back of my neck. "You look beautiful."

I roll my head back and his lips graze my ear. "Thank you."

Clive reaches around me and pinches my chin. He draws me toward him for a kiss but I don't dare move my hands from the arms of the cross. I feel his skin on my back and his body heat blends with mine. He's not wearing a shirt.

His fingers move down my shoulder, traveling up my arm to my wrist. "Are you ready?" he asks.

I tremble, unsure. "I think so."

"Tell me when it's a yes."

I take a deep breath, holding it in as it nourishes me, but it's his capable hands on my body that brings me home.

"Yes," I say. "I'm ready."

He steps back but his presence never leaves my side. He takes my hand and wraps a thin rope around my wrist before binding me to the fasteners on the cross. I smile, enjoying the thought of submission. I'm in no danger. He'll take care of me.

Clive ties up my other hand and fixes the rope to the cross. "How does that feel?" he asks.

"Good," I answer.

He presses in behind me again, unable to resist a few nibbles on my neck. I sure as hell don't mind. I let out a quiet moan as he feels up my curves.

"We shouldn't stay too late," I remind him. "You have an early meeting tomorrow."

He laughs and drops his hands. "Don't you ever clock off?"

"It's important for the new app! I *am* your boss..." I tease.

"Only from nine-to-five." He curls his arm around my waist and draws me closer to him. "In here, *I'm* the boss," he says into my ear. "Say it."

"I'm the boss."

"No..." He scoffs. "Say that *I'm—*"

I giggle. *"You're* the boss, Mr. Snow."

His fingers twist my hair. "Bad girls don't get rewarded, Ms. Payne," he growls. "Bad girls get *punished.* Do you understand?"

I quiver in his grip. "Yes," I sigh.

"Do you remember your safe word?"

"Yes."

He runs his mouth between my shoulder blades. "Do you want me... to make you use it?"

I shudder as I squeeze the ropes above me. "Yes, Mr. Snow."

He kisses my back. "Good girl." I feel his lips curl into a smile. "I have something for you."

His hands move out in front of me and he lays something around my neck and fastens it. He pinches my blindfold and pulls it over my head to show me.

I look at our reflection in the mirrored wall. It's a thin, black choker just like the one he gave me before. Simple and classy with that shiny, dangling—

My jaw drops. "Wait, is that *real?*"

He smiles. "Yes, it is. Figured I'd put my first good paycheck to decent use."

"Wow…" I admire it for another second before my gaze finds its way to his bright, blue eyes. "Thank you."

"I want you all to myself, Ms. Payne," he says. "If you'll let me. Again."

I turn my head to kiss him and he wraps his loving arms around me.

"Yes, Mr. Snow."

BOOKS BY TABATHA KISS

THE HEARTTHROB HOTEL SERIES
Just a Touch
Just a Kiss
Just a Fling
Just a Crush
Just a King

THE OLD HABITS SERIES
The Mechanic
The Milkman

THE RICH BITCHES SERIES
Pretty Little Thing
Pretty Dirty Trick
Pretty Ever After

THE SWEET CRAVINGS SERIES
Muffin Top
A Muffin Top Christmas
Hot Sauce
A Hot Sauce Halloween

THE BAD BALLER BOOKS
Bump and Run
Go Deep

Home Run Baby

THE LUMBERJACK DUET
Lumberjack BOSS
Lumberjack BRIDE

THE PINK SERIES
In the Pink
Pink Christmas

For more, go to tabathakiss.com

ABOUT THE AUTHOR

Tabatha Kiss lives in Chicago, Illinois. You can probably catch her huddled up in a hoodie, reading a good romance beneath a tree in Jackson Park with her trusty husky by her side. She enjoys roller derby, sushi, and is always searching for her forever bad boy.

In the meantime, she writes.

Discover more at
tabathakiss.com

Stay up-to-date with new releases,
exclusive giveaways, and more!
tabathakiss.com/newsletter

Contact Tabatha at
authortabathakiss@gmail.com

Made in the USA
Middletown, DE
10 July 2019